MW00527992

Published by Scrivenings Press LLC
15 Lucky Lane
Morrilton, Arkansas 72110
https://ScriveningsPress.com

Printed in the United States of America

Paperback ISBN 978-1-64917-106-1

eBook ISBN 978-1-64917-107-8

Library of Congress Control Number: 2021937670

Cover by Linda Fulkerson, www.bookmarketinggraphics.com

All characters are fictional, and any resemblance to real people, either factional or historical, is purely coincidental.

Many Blessings!
Pam Meyers

Rose Harbor

Newport of the West Series
BOOK FOUR

Pamela S. Meyers

Scrivenings PRESS
Quench your thirst for story.
www.ScriveningsPress.com

Dedicated to the Memory of the
Women Airforce Service Pilots (WASP)
Of World War II. These brave women served their
country by ferrying new bombers to military bases,
testing aircraft, and training pilots. Most have passed away
by now, and only a few were still alive when they began to receive long
overdue recognition for their efforts from the U.S. Government.

The LORD is merciful and gracious, slow to anger, and plenteous in mercy.

He will not always chide: neither will he keep his anger for ever.

[1]*He hath not dealt with us after our sins; nor rewarded us according to our iniquities.*

For as the heaven is high above the earth, so great is his mercy toward them that fear him.

As far as the east is from the west, so far hath he removed our transgressions from us.

Like as a father pitieth his children, so the LORD pitieth them that fear him.

For he knoweth our frame; he remembereth that we are dust.

Psalm 103 8-14 (KJV)

1

August 1943
Somewhere in the air near Sweetwater, Texas

Grace Bauer's stomach roiled. She winced. Not now. Not at five thousand feet and climbing. Pressure built in her throat and she swallowed against it. It was a good two more hours before they'd reach New York. She had to get this B-17 to ten thousand feet. Then her copilot could take over.

Her stomach lurched. "Take over the controls, now."

"Roger." Betty Newport gripped the lever between them, and Grace let go as the B-17 continued its climb to cruising altitude.

She grabbed her discarded paper coffee cup and let her churning stomach have its way, then she sat back and took a deep breath. "I have no idea where that came from."

"Maybe it was the bad barbeque you ate last night."

"No Texas barbeque is bad, especially from Slim's Roundup. Probably the coffee I drank. Whoever made it last must have used the coffee rations from last year."

"I agree about this morning's coffee, but you northerners don't know good barbeque from bad. You okay, or should I stay at the controls?"

"Give me a minute. I'd give anything for a toothbrush about now." Grace closed her eyes. Served her right for ignoring the sore throat that had plagued her the past couple of days. She needed the hours this flight would give her. The more under her belt on the B-17, the better chance she'd have of being trained on the B-29.

As intimidating as the larger bird was, she loved the idea of being the first woman to pilot the monster. And her experience on the 29 should enhance her resumé when she applied with a commercial airline after the war. Airlines may think they only wanted male pilots, but that was a small obstacle.

Twenty minutes later, assured her stomach was going to behave, she glanced at Betty. "I'm good now. Taking back the controls. I can hang on for another two and a half hours." She glanced out the window. "Looks like autumn has taken over the Ozarks. I've always wanted to go there. Frank and I talked about our honeymoon ... "

She blinked away the moisture in her eyes. Would she ever be able to think about the past without tearing up? Eight months wasn't enough time for the ache to go away.

"Don't say it, Grace. Think about other things, like what we'll do tonight on our layover. It's been ages since I've been to New York. Think you'll be up for a night on the town?"

"I hope so. He's married to someone else now, and I need something to shake off this melancholy."

Within half an hour they approached Kentucky, and the flight promised to be smooth all the way to Long Island.

The radio squawked. "Bowman Field to Flight SWWB1726 headed for LaGuardia. Please adjust flight plan as follows." Betty jotted down the coordinates then read them off to Grace.

She began correcting the course. "It's not that much different from the previous plan. We'll still make it on ... " A sharp pain radiated through her wrist and down her forearm. Her breath hitched, but she completed the adjustment as nausea pushed into her throat and chills coursed through her body. "Betty, take controls. Now. See if we can put down at Wright."

"Roger." She handed an empty paper cup to Grace. "Use mine."

A minute later, as Betty asked for permission to land at the Ohio air base, Grace wrapped her arms around her torso as best she could, given her harness, and closed her eyes, grateful turbulence was light today. A bumpy ride would not be good.

After another fifteen minutes, they approached Wright Field near Dayton, and soon they were on the ground and taxiing toward a spot near the tower. Betty brought the plane to a halt, and a couple of airmen approached the plane.

Grace released her safety harness then moved to step through the narrow space between the seats, and her knees buckled.

"Whatever this is, it's bad." She grabbed the back of her seat and let herself slide to the floor of the bomb bay. Pulling her knees up to her chest, she closed her eyes.

The sound of the door being opened on the side of the fuselage told her Betty had climbed down into the well, next to the door.

"We need help. We have a sick pilot here."

At Betty's shout, Grace drew in a breath and willed her churning stomach to behave. Only a few more minutes and she could do what she had to do in something other than a paper cup. At the thought, she remembered the pair of cups next to her seat. She moved to stand but sat again. No way was she able to clean up behind herself. *Pity the person who has to toss them.*

Someone took hold of her arm. "Let's get you out of here."

She opened her mouth to say thank you, but everything went black.

SOMETHING hard and cold pressed against her chest. Grace's eyes popped open, and she stared into a pair of pale blue eyes, hooded by bushy gray brows. The rest of his face was covered by a medical mask. "Where am I?"

He lifted the stethoscope and leaned back. "You're in the office of Wright Field in Ohio. You don't remember coming here on a B-17?"

Snatches of recollections swirled in her head. Taking off for LaGuardia and losing her cookies in a paper cup, pain in her wrist, putting down at Wright. She pushed up on her elbows then fell back. "I need to return to the plane. It's due at LaGuardia this afternoon."

"Your copilot is taking it the rest of the way. You're in no shape to be piloting any plane right now."

She propped herself up on a shaking elbow. "Betty can't ferry alone ... regulations."

"We received special permission for one of our airmen to copilot. He's experienced with the 17."

Tension drained out of her, and she fell back on what she presumed was someone's desk that had been cleared. "I'm sure it's the flu. Are you even a doctor?"

"Name's Dr. Henry Austin in peacetime. I'm Captian Austin at the moment. We're going to move you to isolation over in sick bay until we can be sure you're not contagious. Hopefully it is the flu, but we'll know more later. Here's the gurney now to take you."

"I can walk." She tried to sit up, but surprised at how difficult it was, she fell back on the hard surface. "I hope the bed over there is better than whatever it is I'm on now."

"I SAW HER EYELIDS FLUTTER. I think she's waking up. Grace, honey, come on. Open your eyes."

Mom? Was she home?

"Pop, why won't she wake up?"

"She will, Hannie. She had a very high fever."

Granddad? She must be home.

"Her lids are fluttering. Come on, sweet girl, open those eyes for your mama."

One eyelid opened and then the other. She blinked at the blurriness and forced herself to focus. Mom's face came into view. The dark circles ringing her green eyes belied her smile.

Mom swiped at a tear. "Oh, Grace, we were so worried. Pop, her eyes are open."

Granddad came into view. A medical jacket, as white as his mustache, covered his ever present dark gray vest and knotted tie. He offered a grin as wide as his wizened face and pressed his palm to her forehead. "Grace, you had us worried."

"Where am I?"

"At a hospital in Dayton, Ohio. You became ill while ferrying a plane to New York, and they brought you to Wright Field. You were too feverish to move and have been hospitalized for a couple of days."

Her gaze flicked from him to Mom and back to him again. "How long have you two been here?"

"Since day before yesterday." Granddad held up a tongue depressor. "We drove down as soon as we got the call. They allowed me special privileges here. Now, let me check your throat. Open your mouth."

She did as he ordered, and after he laid the wooden utensil on her tongue, she said, "Ah."

He tossed the depressor in a wastebasket. "Your throat looks better than it did yesterday."

"You and Mom went to a lot of trouble for a bout of the flu."

His lips flattened. "I'm afraid it's likely more than the flu. Now that you're awake, we need to have tests run, although I'm fairly certain you have rheumatic fever."

She frowned. "Never heard of it. How soon can I get back to Texas and start flying again?"

Mom gripped her hand. “I’m afraid your flying days are over, Gracie. We’re making arrangements to have your belongings sent home to Lake Geneva.”

The fever must have affected her hearing. Telling her she couldn’t fly again was worse than Frank’s break-up-letter. Flying kept her sane when her heart was ripped to shreds. “What’s a little fever? I’ll be good as new in a few days, won’t I?”

The jowls in her grandfather’s face slackened. “Over time you should be stronger, but not strong enough to resume transporting aircraft. Especially if the heart muscle is weakened.”

First her fiancé jilted her, and now this. How could she go back home after the attention she received from being a woman pilot and showing Frank off to her friends when she brought him home to meet her family? It was a joy to take up the gauntlet in her dad’s place after he’d been shot down in the Great War.

Tears pricked at her eyes. No chance to fly the 29 or be one of the first women to pilot a commercial aircraft—the one dream that kept her going. Why was God being so unfair?

2

Twelve Days Later

"Well, I got your grandfather off to Lake Geneva. Now it's just you and me until your dad comes when you're released, which your doctor told me should be any day." Mom moved from the doorway to the chair next to Grace's bed. "You'll be pleased to know we've kept your room the way you had it, so it will seem like home when you get there. Reenie and Lenny have orders to not go in there without checking with me first."

"Thanks, Mom, but it's okay if my sister and brother want to use the room. Well, maybe just Reenie. Lenny seems to create a mess wherever he goes. You didn't have—"

"I have no idea who of your friends are still in town. You really haven't been home except for a few days at a time since you left for college. Maybe when you're well enough and get a job, you'll meet people your age."

Grace held up a hand. "Mom, stop. You're rambling like you do when you're anxious about something. I'm fine. I'm getting stronger, and I'm sure I'll soon be back in Sweetwater ferrying planes in a few more months. I sent a note to the commander a few days ago telling him I should be back on duty by the first of the year."

Mom gave her a blank stare. "Did you say what I think I heard? I thought you were told you were discharged from WASP because of your heart condition."

"That was when I first took sick and my rate of recovery was unknown. But I'm walking the hall a couple of times a day now and doing crunches here in my room."

"You have weights in here?" Mom glanced around the room.

"No, but I figured out that my gear bag from the plane weighs about ten pounds. I've been using that. When I started walking last week, I could barely make it around the nurses' station once. Now I'm managing it at least four times. I figure when I'm home I can walk outside and increase my distance. Hiking the lakeshore would be good too. I used to love taking the shore path out to Safe Refuge when it was still in the family."

"That sounds like a good plan, but please don't do anything until you get the go-ahead from your granddad. You don't want to overdo until your heart muscle is strong enough."

Grace waved a hand. "You're forgetting I'm in better shape than most people, from flying those big planes and working out in the base gym. Granddad said that much himself."

"I know, but he didn't say you were ready to fly B-17s again, or should in the future." Her mother stood and walked to the wheelchair in the corner of the room and rolled it over to Grace's bed. "Let's go to the conservatory for a change of scenery."

"Sounds good, but I don't need that chair. I can walk there."

"You'll do no such thing. It's a floor below us, and you need to take the elevator and then walk another long hall."

Grace knew better than to argue. Mom was as stubborn as she was. "What about if you bring the chair, and I'll at least walk to the elevator on this floor and then sit in the chair the rest of the way."

"Deal."

THE NEXT AFTERNOON, the phone next to Grace's bed rang just as she returned from five laps around the nurse's station.

She picked up the receiver as she sat on the side of the bed. "Hello, this is Grace."

"Grace, Commander Benson here. How are you doing?"

Taken aback he called her by her first name without the usual Pilot Bauer, she gathered her wits and answered him. "Commander, so good to hear your voice. I'm doing fine, sir. Getting stronger every day and probably will be released in a few days. I sure miss everyone down there, though. Can't wait to get back."

Silence filled the connection.

"Commander, are you still there?"

"I received your note this morning."

"Wow, that was fast. Does the first of the year sound good for my return? I can't wait to sit in the 17's cockpit again."

"I'm sorry, Grace. I thought you understood when we last talked that you've been permanently discharged from your duties. WASP can't take a chance that the stress of flying bombers on a weak heart like yours could cause a heart attack or a stroke. That's why we had Miss Newport pack your things and ship them to your home in Wisconsin."

Tears welled in her eyes. Not finding a box of tissues, she wiped her eyes with the sheet. *Don't let him hear you crying, whatever you do.* "But, sir, I'm sure by January I'll be good as new."

"That may be true for someone in as good physical shape as you were, but regulations are regulations. If you had a heart attack while airborne and you didn't have a copilot as capable as Miss Newport is ... I shudder to think about it. I'm sorry, Grace. You were one of WASP's best, and we appreciate all you've done for our men. I'm sure you'll find a new way to use your flying skills. Please keep in touch."

Her stomach clenched and she swallowed hard. "I'm sorry

too. I understand it's not your decision. Thank you, Commander."

They said their goodbyes, and she grabbed the bedpan from her bedside table and threw up. The first time to upchuck since that day in the cockpit. Falling face down on the bed, she sobbed into the pillow.

"Grace, what's wrong?"

She raised her head and stared at Mom. "You were right. I'm no longer a WASP. They don't want me back. I really thought in my delirium I heard differently about my prognosis. My commander ... " She used her sheet to blot her tears. " ... called and told me how much WASP appreciates my service to the war effort, but they had to discharge me. I'm ready to go home."

"Oh, Grace, I'm so sorry. We thought you understood all that. I guess we should have clarified to make sure you did. You'll be happy to know I was just told you're to be released tomorrow. Your dad is on his way down here right now and will arrive by dinnertime. We can head back to Lake Geneva tomorrow."

3

Lake Geneva, Wisconsin
Two Days Later

Grace opened her eyes and glanced at the same alarm clock that had kept her on time for the first twenty-odd years of her life. Seven a.m. Back at Avenger Field in Texas, as part of WASP, she'd already have been up for two hours.

The hospital hadn't released her yesterday until almost four in the afternoon. The late start meant they hadn't arrived in Lake Geneva until almost midnight. Wound up from all that had happened and the travel, she didn't fall asleep until after two a.m., and yet now she felt wide awake.

She threw back her covers and padded over the hardwood floor to the open window. Across Main Street, a woman walked her dog through Library Park. A short distance to the east sat the wood-frame home that now served as the town's public library, where Mom worked as its director. A few steps to the south, Geneva Lake glistened in the late summer sun.

Although pleasing, the vista was nothing like the lake view they used to have at Safe Refuge, the family estate they'd had to sell in the crash of '29.

She pushed the unhappy thoughts from her mind and returned to her bed. It wouldn't be easy to fall back to sleep though. She had orders to rest, but all she'd done for days was rest.

She glanced around the room. As the oldest of the siblings, she'd been given first choice of a bedroom when they moved here just before Reenie was born. It really should have been offered to Reenie when Grace was accepted by WASP. But as Mom mentioned the other day, the room looked exactly the way it had the day she left for college. At least the posters of Ronald Colman were gone. She still enjoyed his movies, but she'd stopped idolizing him when her interests turned more to flying.

Grace heaved a sigh. Unlike the schoolgirl who lived here in the past, she was a college graduate and a pilot—though right now she had no airplanes to fly. Piloting was all she wanted to do and had trained for. She'd loved doing her part to help win the war as a WASP, but now she felt like an old dust rag that had been tossed aside.

She stared up at the ceiling. "God, You took Frank out of my life, and now flying. Is this my punishment? I repented, said I was sorry. Wasn't that enough?" A familiar ache filled her chest, and she rolled over. If she could sleep, it would go away.

A soft knock came at the door.

"Who is it?"

"Dad. Can I come in?"

She groaned. Dad coming with his encouragement for the day, as he'd done all her life whenever she was home. Would it be so bad to pretend to be sleeping? He knocked again.

"I'm awake. Come in."

He stepped in, wearing a crisp white shirt and navy-blue trousers. With his red-and-blue striped tie knotted perfectly, and carrying his suit coat over his arm, he was likely the most dapper attorney in Walworth County. And with his graying temples and thick, wavy hair, the most handsome. He crossed the room with only a slight limp, evidence of the prosthetic limb that replaced the left leg amputated upon his return from the Great War.

The limp only appeared when he was weary. Two days of long drives to bring her and Mom home must have been tiring.

"I thought you might be awake."

"I've done nothing but sleep since I was grounded, but can't you at least go into the office later? I wish Granddad could have stayed the whole time to spare you having to drive down to get us."

"He needed to get home to his medical practice and your grandmother. I didn't mind at all coming to get you."

"I still think you could at least take the morning off and go in after lunch."

He chuckled. "Tell that to the judge. I have to be in court at nine and need to stop by the office first." The box spring squeaked under his weight as he sat on the edge of her bed. "How are you feeling, now that you've slept in your own bed?"

"It hasn't been my own bed for a long while. It feels soft compared to the one I had in Texas, or the one at the hospital." She blinked at the wetness in her eyes and turned away. "I'm sorry, Dad."

"Sorry for what?"

"Not being able to make you proud."

A deep V formed between his eyes. "Why wouldn't I be proud of you?"

"I wasn't able to complete my mission. Carry on in your stead as a pilot during wartime."

He heaved a sigh. "Gracie, look at me."

"I can't." She shook her head. "Not only have I disappointed you, I'm blubbering like a baby."

"I don't know where you got the idea you've disappointed me. I'm very pleased that you love flying as much as me, and proud you became a WASP and accomplished so much in the time you served. But, my dear daughter, I'd be proud of you even if you hadn't done all that and were doing something totally different."

The look on his face whenever she told him about flying the B-17 or a difficult landing she had to make in bad weather said otherwise. She turned over and looked him in the eye. "Really?"

"Yes, really. I think I know what's actually bothering you. You've poured yourself into ferrying those planes and looked forward to working as a pilot after the war. Suddenly, you have no identity. When I crashed and had to have my left leg amputated, I thought my life was just about over. But thanks to your mother, I was able to snap out of it and return to law school. I assure you, your life isn't over. It's only the beginning."

He leaned down and kissed her on the cheek. "I spent a lot of time when I was MIA, lying on a cot in that farmhouse cellar in Belgium, feeling sorry for myself. Don't fall into the same trap." He stood. "I have to go. We can talk more about this tonight. Try to get a bit more sleep. Your sister and brother are going to be pestering you with all kinds of questions once you're up."

After he let himself out, she faced the wall and let the bottled-up tears loose. She and Dad had a lot in common, but the pain clawing at her heart was nothing like what he'd experienced. And she had no one to talk to about it.

4

Grace settled into the passenger side of Dad's Buick Roadmaster. It was only a three-block walk to Granddad's office, but until she was given a medical release to add more exercise to her daily routine, Granddad considered three blocks too far.

What her grandfather didn't know was that while she was the only person in the house during the day, she'd been walking the upstairs hallway several times daily for the past month. When she first began, she only lasted about three minutes each time, but now she had it up to ten.

She stepped into the waiting room, and Peggy Adams, the receptionist, stood and came around the desk, wearing a seersucker shirtwaist with decorative buttons that fit her perfectly. She greeted Grace with her dimpled smile then hugged her. "It's so good to see you. I was worried about you, but Dr. Murphy's updates assured me you were on the mend."

"Thanks, Peggy. It's been a rough few weeks, but I've turned the corner." Silence fell between them. They were enough years apart, Peggy being older, that they'd never run around together socially and now had little in common other than that the woman worked for Granddad.

Grace scanned the empty room. "Am I the first appointment?"

"Yes. I had to cancel the first two when a baby who wasn't due for two more weeks decided to make his appearance."

"Anyone I know?"

Peggy frowned and absently patted her auburn waves. "Theoretically, I shouldn't divulge names, but you'll hear anyway, since the family attends your church. Tom and Jean Anderson's baby boy weighed in at six and a half pounds. No name as of yet."

Ignoring the wave of regret filling her chest, Grace forced a smile. "That's wonderful news."

"Isn't it?" A pair of tiny lines formed between Peggy's eyebrows. "Change of subject. I'm glad we have a few minutes to chat. I'm on a bowling team with several other women, and one of our members had to drop out. We launch the new season this Thursday night. If Dr. Murphy gives you clearance to get more exercise, would you be interested in joining us?"

Bowling, of all things. Grace had forgotten bowling was one of the main social activities during Lake Geneva's long, cold winters. "That sounds like fun, but I haven't bowled since high school. And I was worse than any of my girlfriends. If you want your team to win, you don't want me on it."

"That doesn't mean you're a terrible bowler now. We don't care as much about winning as having an opportunity to be with other gals. A couple of hours every week to forget about rationing and shortages and all the bad news coming from the war front is good for our spirits. Come on, Grace, give it a shot."

Peggy couldn't have said it better. The only people Grace had seen the whole month she'd been home convalescing were her family members. And she missed the camaraderie she enjoyed with her girlfriends at college and later in WASP. Even if all she did was bowl gutter balls, it was exercise. Better than walking a circle in the second floor hall.

"Grace? What do you say? I have a feeling your grandfather

will okay it. I'm sure the how-to-bowl part will come back, and bowling might be the right kind of activity for you. You only have to take a few steps, and it will build up your arm muscles."

"There's only one obstacle. Granddad has been pretty strict about my exercising. He'll probably say no."

The door to Granddad's office opened and he stepped into the room.

Seeing Grace, he grinned, causing the creases around his eyes to deepen. "Well, there's my beautiful granddaughter. I guess you're here hoping to get some of your freedom back."

"Yes, and Peggy wants to know if you'll clear the way for me to join her bowling team. I told her that I probably wasn't—"

"That's a splendid idea. Let's get you examined, and then I'll let you know."

After the appointment, Grace used Peggy's phone to call Mom and tell her she was approved to walk outside, and she was walking home. She'd tell her about the bowling team when she got there. Of course, Mom raised an objection, saying it looked like rain, but after a glimpse out the window at clouds that posed no threat, Grace brushed it off.

When she stepped outside, however, the sky to the west had turned leaden. But what was a little rain? She wasn't going to melt, and her grandfather didn't say anything about not walking in the rain.

Grace picked up her pace and started south to Main Street. At the corner she gazed down the street past the stoplight. Home was only three blocks west, farther than she'd walked at home, but doable.

At the town's main intersection, she glanced across the street at the Clair Hotel. A man carrying a bowling bag emerged from the outside stairs alongside the hotel that led to the lower level bowling lanes. Her old bowling ball was probably stored away in the basement at home. If the lanes were open on weekdays, perhaps she could try a few practice rounds before Thursday.

The light changed to green, and she set off, pumping her

arms in sync with her stride. As both her doctor at the hospital and Granddad said, thanks to her good physical condition, she was healing fast. And she supposed those walks in the upstairs hall he didn't know about helped too.

Large drops splattered against her face, followed by a loud thunderclap. Storms didn't scare her, but the possibility of lightning hitting one of the tall trees that lined the sidewalk for the next two blocks did. She sped up to a fast walk, trying hard not to start running. Her chest tightened and she slowed down. One more house to pass, and then she'd be home.

Turning up her walk with thunder booming overhead, Grace stepped onto the front porch and yanked the front door open. Heading to the nearest chair, she dropped into it and put her head back, willing her heart rate to slow. After a minute, she pressed two fingers to her carotid artery. Her pulse was finally slowing.

"My goodness, Grace, I wouldn't think Pop would tell you to run home in the rain, but it appears he must have."

She waved Mom's supposition away and shook her head. "On the contrary. He said walk at an even, measured pace. I did exactly as he said."

Her mother tsked and shook her head. "At what speed? And look at you. You're dripping wet. Now you've probably made yourself worse."

"I kept an even pace until the storm started about two blocks down. I did go faster than I intended, but my heart rate is almost back to normal now." She turned and inspected the chair's slipcover. "I got the chair wet. I'm sorry."

"The cover will dry. I'll start a bath to cool you down, and then you'd better take a nap."

She groaned. "What I don't need is coddling, and I suspect when you were my age you would've done the same thing. In your day, what did women do to exercise and challenge themselves?"

"When we could get away with it, we'd swim and ride

bicycles." Mom harrumphed. "But if you wore one of those ghastly swim dresses, forget about doing more than floating."

"I remember now. You broke the mold by wearing a regular swimsuit."

"Yes, I did. In fact, I met your father at a swimming party at his house the first time I wore that suit." A joyous expression appeared on her face. "We had so much fun that day, racing through the water. But working as a farmette during the war was where I really built up my strength. However, I wasn't sick when I did those things."

"And neither am I. I'm over the fever, and Granddad says my heart sounds healthy, despite the muscle being damaged. Peggy asked me to join her bowling team, and Granddad approves." She pushed to her feet. "I'm going to look for my old bowling ball in the basement. Swinging the ball will help build my strength." She grimaced. "I doubt I could handle a B-17's controls in my current condition."

Mom rested her fists on her hips. "You're not planning to go back to piloting those bombers, are you? I thought you were told—"

"I was told my flying days are over as far as WASP is concerned. Frankly, I have no desire to fly any kind of plane, not even Dad's little Cessna." If only she could believe it.

5

Despite Grace's protests that the Hotel Clair bowling alley was only a two-block walk, Dad insisted on giving her a ride and parked near the bowling alley stairs. She climbed out of his green Roadmaster, careful to not mar the finish with her purse clasp. He'd become very fussy about the car, since it was the last model Buick would produce until after the war.

She reached in the back seat and grabbed her bowling bag by its handles.

"Hi, Grace. I'm so glad you agreed to join our team. It's good you came early. A lot of us do, to visit and catch up with each other." Peggy Adams stood a few feet away, holding her blue-and-white bowling bag. Her colorful head scarf perfectly matched her red V-neck sweater and red-and-navy plaid skirt.

Grace glanced down at her plain gray A-line skirt and short-sleeved white blouse. No one told her she was supposed to look like a fashion plate to bowl. At least she, too, had a scarf to keep her curls away from her face. Albeit not a matching one. "I've been practicing most afternoons this week. But even with practice, I still make a lot of gutter balls. I thought I'd come early to get a few more practice shots in. Cute outfit."

"Thanks. I splurged at the Smart Shop with money I've been

putting aside. Since my oldest is on the high school football team this year, I thought a red-and-white outfit to wear to the games would encourage him. You might remember, I was a cheerleader my junior and senior years."

Grace laughed. "How could I forget? You were the most energetic cheerleader Lake Geneva High has ever had. No one got a crowd cheering better than you. I could use a couple of your cheers tonight."

"Hey, don't worry about your bowling skills."

How could Peggy say that when she hadn't seen how terrible a bowler Grace was? "You'll want to take back your words when I cause the team to rank low in the standings."

Peggy gave a rueful laugh. "The woman you're replacing was the high scorer. We knew our glory days were over when she and her husband moved to San Diego. Let's get downstairs so I can introduce you to the other gals."

They went down the stairs and stepped into the hotel's lower level, which stretched beyond the boundaries of the hotel and took up space beneath Schultz's Dime Store next door. Grace surveyed the large room, already filled with chattering women. The only one she recognized was Helen Rutherford, her mom's hairdresser—not a surprise since most of her childhood friends had scattered, either because of marriage or volunteering in the war effort.

"You weren't kidding about everyone arriving early. I'll be able to throw some practice shots, won't I?"

"Oh sure. There's Helen over on lane 6. Let's go."

Grace waved at the hairdresser and then looked at Peggy. "I have to rent shoes. I'll meet you at the lane."

"Good idea. Some of the sizes run out, especially size sixes. That's why I bought my own shoes."

"Hopefully, the size eights are still there. Until I'm able to work again, my budget is pretty thin. Maybe the larger sizes are more plentiful." She headed toward the shoe rentals.

The afternoons she'd come to the bowling alley for practice, a young man worked the shoe counter, but tonight a teenage girl was handing a pair of green-and-red shoes to a woman. "There you go, Mrs. Davidson. The last of the size eights."

Grace's heart sank.

"Hi. May I help you?" The redheaded teen smiled at her.

"Not unless you can make another size-eight pair appear. I sometimes can wear an eight and a half."

The girl scrunched her nose and faced the wall of cubbyholes behind her, some still containing shoes. She pulled open a large drawer beneath the cubbies. "Sometimes there are extras in here."

Grace leaned over the counter for a better view.

The girl pushed shoes aside with both hands then lifted a pair to check the size. "Size nine." She tossed them back in the drawer.

"Have a problem, Becky? Can I help?"

Grace startled and turned. How long had he been standing there? The tall man offered Grace a slight smile and faced Becky.

"We need more size eights, Mac. I've mentioned shortages of eights and sevens before, but none get ordered." She slammed the drawer shut. "Maybe if you asked, and not me."

He ran his hand over his neatly trimmed graying hair. "I'll check the storeroom." He settled his gaze on Grace, and the smile returned. "Sorry for the delay. I'll be right back."

Her gaze lingered on him until he rounded a corner and dropped out of sight. Never had she seen such blue eyes, since Frank left for a life that didn't include her. She faced Becky, who stood at the counter. "It's a good thing your boss showed up."

The teen pulled a face that caused her freckled nose to wrinkle. "Mac isn't my boss. He used to work here years ago and sometimes helps out on league nights, when we get busy. You're new to the league, aren't you?"

"Yes. I haven't been around Lake Geneva much since I graduated from college and moved to Texas."

"Then you're from here originally?"

"Yes." Grace shifted her weight from one foot to the other. "You might know my parents, Ted and Hannah Bauer."

"The Mrs. Bauer who works at the library?"

"That's my mom." Grace couldn't help but smile.

"She's very nice. She helped me find a book I needed for my term paper. By any chance, is Reenie your sister?"

"Yes. Are you both in the same class?"

"No. I'm a senior, and she's a junior. We're both in the girls' choral group, though. Now that I think about it, you two resemble each other."

"We're in luck." Mac dashed up, a grin filling his handsome face. He held out a pair of green-and-red shoes. "I could do my best imitation of the prince and have you slip your foot into the shoe to see if it fits."

Grace gaped at him.

He grimaced. "I can tell by your expression you have no idea what I'm talking about. "Sorry. Bad joke. My daughter is fascinated with the Cinderella story she found in an old book of fairy tales. Maybe you're not familiar?"

She hadn't thought about that story in years. "That was one of my favorite fairy tales when I was little." She pushed out a smile. "Now I get the joke. Thanks for finding these."

"You're more than welcome. I'm here to serve."

She grasped the shoes, her fingertips brushing against his. Goosebumps trailed up her arm. She quickly dropped the shoes in her bowling bag. "I'd better get to my team. Thanks again."

She dashed away, weaving between the small clusters of chatting women. That was the same goosebump sensation she'd felt the first time she and Frank held hands. If ever there was a warning to stay away from this man, this was it. Besides, he was a lot older than she was, and obviously married. He couldn't have felt what she did, but what if he had? She hoped he was a man of integrity and not one to react to such sensations.

At lane 6, after placing her ball next to the others on the ball return, Grace plopped onto the bench next to Peggy and pulled the shoes out of her bag. "It appears I'd better search for a pair of size eights to buy before next week. The last pair was being handed out as I arrived at the counter."

"I see you got some shoes, though. Did you have to take a different size?"

"No. A nice man found this pair somewhere in the storeroom."

Her friend's lips turned up. "Was he tall?"

"Yes. Becky called him Mac."

"Mac McAlister." Peggy grinned. "I was hoping he'd be here tonight and you'd meet him." She elbowed Grace. "He's the nicest guy, and he's single."

A sinking feeling washed over her. "He mentioned a daughter, so I presumed he was married. But even if he is single, you can get that gleam out of your eyes. I'm not interested in dating him."

"How can you say that? You only just met. Why? Because he has a daughter? In case you're wondering, he was widowed a few years ago."

"How awful for him." Grace stopped tying the lace on her left shoe and stared at Peggy. "How old is the daughter?"

"I'm not sure." Her friend shrugged. "Maybe ten or eleven."

She couldn't imagine losing Mom at that age. But pity on a man or his child didn't mean she should change her mind. "He's very nice and good-looking, but I'm still not interested."

"Oh, Grace, whatever happened to make you say that?" Peggy's expression softened. "You're young and attractive, and the war has taken away most of our eligible men. A date or two doesn't mean you have to marry him."

"Burned once, shame on him. Burned twice, shame on me."

"Not all men are the same. Who burned you?"

"Another pilot." She stopped tugging at her shoelace and stared off. She'd forgotten Peggy's penchant for wanting to know details. "We weren't eye-to-eye on some things, and when he got his orders to head over to Europe, that was the end of us."

"I'm so sorry."

"Me too. I've written off seeing any man for a while. Maybe forever."

"I think you should give Robert a chance, if he's interested. Nothing like a new romance to ease the hurt of a past one."

"I think that's called on the rebound. Who's Robert?"

Peggy giggled. "Mac. I like to tease him and call him by his given name. He's been called Mac as long as I can remember. Grace McAlister has a nice ring to it."

"Will you hush. Grace Bauer also has a nice ring. Like I said, older men aren't my preference."

"He isn't *that* old."

"He has gray hair, Peg. He's got to be going on forty if not forty already."

"I think it's referred to as salt and pepper. There's a lot of brown still there. Some people gray prematurely. I find gray hair on a man attractive. My dad is ten years older than my mother. What would Mac be to you? Maybe ten or twelve years?"

"My fiancé was four years older. That's as big a gap as I like." She stood. "I need to take some practice shots before we start."

Grace stepped over to the return, then carried her ball to the line marked on the polished wood and raised it level with her waist. She settled her gaze on the triangular arrangement of pins at the end of the alley. Holding the ball at waist level, she took several steps and then threw the ball. As always, it began its trip down the middle of the lane, then, as always, it veered right and into the gutter.

Whatever made her think she could do this? She walked to the return to wait for her ball. When it popped up onto the top rack, she took it and went through the paces again. Exactly like last time. A gutter ball. She threw up her hands and shook her head.

"Would you like to learn how to throw a hook?"

"I'm fine." She turned and stared into Mac's blue eyes. "Thanks for the offer."

"No, she's not fine, Mac. She needs help. Our team needs your help."

Grace shot Peggy a look she hoped said, *butt out*. But the only response was a grin and a thumbs-up. Did she put Mac up to this?

"Okay. Yes, I do need help. If I can't at least knock a few pins down, I'll be fired from the team before I even start."

Her ball popped up on the return and rolled to a stop.

"I'll show you how to throw a hook." Mac grabbed her ball and handed it to her and then picked up an unused ball sitting on the return's lower rack. "It may feel strange at first because of the angle, but it's the best way to make the ball do what you want. Let's step back to your starting point."

They moved to the line and he faced her. "Show me how you hold the ball when you start out."

After she showed him, using his ball, Mac slid two fingers into the holes, then pointed at his thumb. "The way you're holding the ball now, with your thumb pointing straight up at the ceiling, is wrong. The thumb needs to be pointed off to the side, not straight up."

She copied him. "I can't get as far over as you can. Does that matter?"

Mac set his ball down then reached over and gently placed his right hand over hers and turned the ball until her thumb was in the correct position. "That's where it should be. How does that feel?"

"It feels strange, like you said." What he didn't know was that the strange feeling was from the shivers caused by his touch. If he didn't take his hand away soon, she'd likely drop the ball on his foot.

"I know, but stay with me. You'll soon get used to it. He removed his hand and glanced at her feet. "When you take your first step, lead with your left foot, keeping your hand position. Try approaching the foul line. I'll walk with you."

They approached the line, then he took her back to the

starting position and had her go through the motions again. "We don't have time for you to practice the approach more than that. Hopefully two times will be the charm."

She nodded. *If you say so.*

"Next, when you get to the foul line, you'll instinctively want to look at the pins. Don't. Keep your focus on the arrow in the floor closest to the right edge. You want to aim the ball at that arrow."

She moved her focus from the pins to the arrow. "I never noticed those arrows before."

"A lot of people don't at first. Now go back to the starting point and step toward the line. When you get to the line, swing your arm back and extend it as though you're going to shake hands with someone. And don't take your eyes off the arrow. I'll wait over there." He indicated a spot out of her line of sight.

At the starting point, she offered a tentative smile to Peggy and Helen and another woman she didn't know, all grinning like a trio of jack-o'-lanterns.

She faced the pins and made sure her thumb was angled the way it should be. Then, doing everything he'd taught her, she threw the ball toward the arrow.

It rolled slow and steady until it reached the edge of the gutter. She glanced at Mac. "See, it's going in the gutter again."

"No, it's not. Look at it."

The ball rolled along the edge of the gutter. As it approached the pins, it hooked left, slammed into the center pin, and they all scattered. Every one of them.

Applause broke out from the bench and Mac let out a whoop.

"I did it, Mac." She faced him, loving the wide grin on his face. "I can't believe it. How can I ever thank you?"

"You already have." He lifted his arms as if he was going to hug her, then let them drop. "The best part of teaching is seeing success in the student. Now you'll be able to enjoy yourself tonight and won't get fired from the team."

"Are you a teacher?"

"Yes, I teach high school English in Elkhorn. I need to get back to the counter. If you need any more help, Grace, let me know."

"How do you know my name? I don't think I told it to you earlier."

"I asked Becky." He sauntered off.

She returned to the bench and sat next to Peggy.

"That was fun to watch," Peggy said.

"I've never understood how to make the ball hook. The way he explained it was so clear."

"What did I tell you?" Peggy leaned over and hugged her. "Do you still think he's too old?"

"For me? Yes. And as I said before, I'm not interested. Do I have time for one more practice shot?"

"Yes. We don't start for five more minutes."

She walked to the return for her ball. Mac was a nice man and easy on the eyes, but she'd be crazy to begin dating again. Especially an older man.

6

Thanksgiving Day, 1942

Grace carried a basket of warm yeast rolls to the dining room, their fragrance setting her mouth to watering. She set them beside the sliced ham in the center of the tabletop then slipped into the seat to the left of Dad, who sat at the head of the table. She glanced across at Mom then at Oma, Dad's mother, her snow-white hair piled into a crown of curls on top of her head.

The rest of the seats included her kid brother, Lenny, and sister, Reenie. Granny and Granddad sat at the other end of the table. Almost everyone was there except for Rory, four years her junior, who was off somewhere in the Pacific, fighting the Japanese. She wasn't home for Thanksgiving herself last year because of WASP, but at least she'd been able to call home.

Not so with Rory this year. She said a silent prayer that her brother would return home safely and wasn't onboard the *Houston* when it was sunk by enemy fire.

"Shall we pray?" Dad held out his left hand to her and his other hand to Mom.

Grace took his hand, and to her left, Reenie gripped hers.

She bowed her head determined to focus on the prayer, but as soon as Dad listed all the reasons to be thankful despite Rory being in harm's way, her mind drifted. Maybe for Dad and the others, God would respond to his petitions, but the Almighty had made it clear, He'd stopped listening to hers.

As usual, Dad's prayer droned on while the food cooled. A vision of Frank's dimpled grin filled her thoughts. He may have betrayed her, but that didn't mean she wanted him to come home injured or, worse yet, dead at the hands of the Germans. *Please, Lord, protect Frank, not for my good but for his.*

Dad finally said amen, and the next few minutes were consumed with the platter of ham being passed, along with serving bowls of mashed potatoes and green beans canned from last summer's victory garden.

"I wish we could have turkey today."

"Lenny, you know all available turkeys have been shipped to bases to feed the troops." Dad forked a piece of ham. "Ham is just as good as turkey, and you should be grateful we have that, thanks to your mother saving ration stamps for the past month. Hopefully, by next year we'll eat turkey again."

"I can still wish for it." The boy shrugged and forked a bite of ham.

Mom sighed. "I want all my children home by next year, and I'm praying this whole thing will be over soon, and it will be the war to end all wars."

"That's what we said about the Great War, Hannah." Dad cut into his slice of ham and lifted a bite-sized piece to his mouth.

"How well I remember." Mom stabbed at her green beans. "I've been remembering the Thanksgivings at Safe Refuge. Plenty of food, family, and celebration."

Granddad nodded. "It would be wonderful if we could have those days back again. I wish I'd known better than to sink most of the family funds into the stock market. Then we'd be sitting around that large dining room table and, Grace, you'd be able to live in the cottage like your mother did until she was married, same as your granny did before her."

Her mother and Granny exchanged smiles across the table.

"One of my favorite memories of the cottage was delivering you, Grace, right there in the downstairs bedroom," Granddad said. "I wanted to get your mother to the hospital, but you'd have none of that. Good thing your granny and I lived in the big house next door. You came so fast I barely had time to prepare. You're still the go-get-em kind of gal. You decide what you want to do, and you do it."

She offered a slight smile. "I think those days are over."

"How can you say that, Grace?" Mom gaped at her. "Yes, your flying bombers is over, but you have your whole life ahead of you. God will show you what He has for you to do next."

"I don't think He cares anymore what I do." She shrugged and focused on her grandfather. "Granddad, it must have been hard to move away from that big house and live here with us."

"It wasn't easy—all of us under this roof." Granny laughed. "When Lenny came along, it became even more crowded."

"I was a tiny baby." Lenny groaned. "It couldn't have been that crowded."

"It didn't seem crowded." Granny smiled at him. "I loved having the grandchildren right here with us. Just like your sister, Lenny, you decided to come early in the middle of the night, and there was no time for the hospital. And since your grandfather was involved with an emergency, I was the one to deliver you. Thankfully, God woke up my nursing skills. But you pretty much delivered yourself into my hands."

Granny looked at sixteen-year-old Reenie. "One of the best days of my life, Reenie, was when you were born and were named after me. Although I'm glad they decided to call you Reenie and not Maureen. Having two Maureens in the same family would have been confusing."

"What if I decide to use Maureen for my daughter someday?" Reenie laughed. "Reenie sounds so juvenile."

"I'd be honored." Granny focused next on Grace. "I'm sorry your time in WASP was cut short. God is faithful, and He'll reveal His plan for you in His due time."

Her hopes of getting through the day without having to talk about her future plans dashed, Grace cast about for an answer. "I'm getting tired of waiting for His revelation. I'm not good with words like Reenie, who I imagine will one day be a famous author. I can type okay, and I know office workers are needed, but I can't imagine being chained to a desk all day." She let go of a sigh. "All I've ever wanted was to be a pilot."

Time for a change of topic. She hadn't missed the look of admiration in Granny's eyes back when she announced she was joining WASP to pilot bombers around the country. Although her grandmother never said it, she had to be disappointed in her. When no one spoke up, she focused on cutting her ham.

"Grace, where is the young man you married?" Oma asked. "I've not heard you speak of him since you arrived home."

Feeling like the center circle at target practice, she drew in a deep breath. Mom had warned her Oma was easily confused these days because of dementia.

Dad's eyes filled with sadness, and he looked at Oma. "Mom, Grace isn't married."

Grace shot a look of thanks to Dad then faced her grandmother. "We broke off the engagement, Oma. He's stationed overseas now."

"Oh. I thought you were married." Oma stared at Grace, confusion on her face. "Did you call it off or did he?"

Mom placed a hand on Oma's forearm. "Louise, perhaps you and Grace can talk about it later."

Grace blinked at the moisture in her eyes. The poor woman was declining. "It was a mutual decision." Not exactly the truth, but what else could she say?

"Oh dear. Well, a pretty young woman like you will have no trouble finding a husband."

Awkward silence filled the room as everyone focused on

eating. Appetite gone, Grace used her fork to push her food around her plate. What would Oma think if she knew the secret Grace was hiding? Pressure built at the back of her eyes, and she pushed away from the table and picked up her dish. "Reenie, can you help me with cutting the pie?"

Mom moved to stand. "You girls don't need—"

"Sit, Mom." Grace picked up her empty water glass. "You worked most of the morning. It's our turn to help."

In the kitchen, Reenie began scraping the scraps from the dishes she'd gathered into a can they used for the compost pile out back. "Can you believe what Oma said? She never used to be so direct."

"Didn't Mom and Dad tell you?" Grace asked. "She has dementia. Sometimes she doesn't have a clue what she's saying."

"I know, but it's worse than it was a month or two ago. I thought it was something that would go away after a while—like a bad cold."

"Unfortunately, no. Dementia sometimes happens as people age. There's no cure."

Reenie dropped dirty dishes into the sink's sudsy water. "Is there any way the family can take back Safe Refuge?"

Grace stopped cutting the pie and gaped at her sister. "Have you been reading my mind? As far as I can tell, not unless the current owners want to sell and we pay them the asking price."

"It just doesn't seem right that Granddad and Granny have to live out their days in that little house on Dodge Street." Reenie let go of a sigh. "I think it's terrible that Oma didn't want to live with Uncle Peter in Chicago, and now she's moved in with them."

"The Dodge Street house isn't that small. It has three bedrooms."

"We have an extra room here now. Since Oma is Dad's mother, why isn't she living here?"

"Because Mom wants to keep Rory's room as he left it," Grace said, "She thinks when he comes home, he'll be able to see he's really home. After he moves out, which he's bound to do, Oma could move over here."

"It was the same with your room. We weren't supposed to go in there and move things around."

"I know. She told me and I tried to convince her to let you use my room, but she would hear none of it. I'll make sure to insist we switch rooms when I move out again."

A wide grin filled her sister's face. "I'd love that. Back to Safe Refuge. Granny especially talks about the rosebushes her father planted on the Safe Refuge property, and Mom mentions the spring house a lot. Did you know that's where Dad proposed to her before he left for the war?"

"Of course. We only hear the story every year on their anniversary. Believe me, if there were some way to get the property back, I'd do it. Help me get the slices of pie on plates and bring them to the table. While you're doing that, I'll get the coffee poured."

Grace moved to the stove, where the percolator sat. Reenie's idea wasn't so crazy. If she could find a way to return Safe Refuge to the family, maybe it would make up for the wrongs she'd done and put her back in good graces with God. She heaved a sigh. It sounded more daunting than learning to fly the B-29. But at least she could try.

7

Three Weeks Later

Grace tightened the scarf around her neck and pulled her knit cap over her ears as she and Lenny trudged along. She'd worked so hard to get the victory rolls in her hair just so that morning, and now the hat would flatten them. But she wasn't about to walk from home to the tree lot in fifteen-degree weather without the hat. With that sharp wind blowing off the lake, she'd feel like an icicle in no time.

It wasn't the best day to shop for a Christmas tree, but tomorrow's forecast didn't sound any better. She hoped the activity would help erase the frustration she'd felt since the week after Thanksgiving.

That Monday, out of curiosity, she'd called a Realtor to inquire about Rose Harbor. He said the property had changed hands recently and was owned now by a man who lived in California. He'd not heard anything as to what the man intended for the estate.

At her question of how the family might be able to regain ownership of the estate, he suggested they do a title search and look for any possible loophole in past transfers of the property.

After the new year, she'd check into doing a search on her own. No use getting the others' hopes up unless there was a loophole.

As they walked down Lake Street, she glanced over at the frozen lake. Less than two weeks ago the bay had been free of ice, but with the frigid temperatures the past few days, the only unfrozen surface was around the docks next to the Riviera building, where machines kept the water stirred to prevent it from freezing. "It looks like it won't be long before people can start ice skating."

"It won't do me any good. My skates are too small." Lenny picked up a handful of snow and made a snowball. "Mom told me with the cutbacks and rationing, I may not be able to get new skates this year. I guess I'll be spending my weekend afternoons reading a book." He swung his arm back and threw the snowball at a tree.

Grace stifled a smile. Mom told her a few days ago where she'd hidden Lenny's new skates. Christmas was only a week away. The boy wouldn't have to wait too long. "Nothing wrong with reading. You can learn new things. You can't do that while you're ice skating."

They crossed Broad Street, and about halfway past Flat Iron Park, Grace glanced over to say something and heaved a sigh. Now where did that kid get to? She pivoted and stared down the sidewalk. Mom was going to shoot him for getting his pants wet kneeling in the snow. Why in the world did she insist the boy come with her? He was going to be as much help as a sloth.

"Leonard Nathan Bauer, we don't have all day." She marched up to him, her mittened fists on her hips. "You'd better hope those trousers are dry by the time we arrive back home or Mom will be furious."

The boy turned and grinned, his dimples deepening, the same as his big brother Rory's. "Sis, come see this nest. It must have fallen from up there." He pointed to a maple tree branch above his head. "It's amazing how birds can make a nest out of leaves and twigs and do it so well it lasts long after the birds are gone. How do they know how to do it?"

Holding tight to his treasure, he stood, his trousers sporting a pair of huge wet spots from the knees to the ankles, and held up the nest. Ice clung to the tiny branches and sticks that had once been home to a feathered family who'd long deserted it for warmer climes.

"Don't they teach you in Sunday school how God made the earth and everything in it, including people and animals? He gave them instinct to know how to build their nests."

"I guess I forgot." He approached her. "I'm gonna take this home. Can you put it in your handbag?"

Gripping the flap on her shoulder bag, she stepped back. "Not on your life is that thing going in my purse. Leave it here. You can come back for it later."

He pulled a face. "Someone might take it."

"I doubt it."

"I'll bury it to be safe." He dug a hole in the snow next to the sidewalk and dropped the nest into it, then smoothed snow over it. "I don't know why I needed to help you pick out a tree. You won't listen to my opinion."

"Because I can't carry a tree home by myself. Now let's go." She hoped by the time they made the return trip with the tree, he would've forgotten about his treasure. She began walking, and he slogged along, the unfastened buckles on his galoshes clacking. "There's a path through the park to the tree lot. We don't need to go all the way to the corner."

"Why didn't you use Dad's car?" he asked. "It's big enough to hold a tree."

"Because we're saving the gas for him. He has to be in court in Elkhorn before we'll have enough ration stamps to fill the car. You know that."

She stepped onto the path while Lenny chose to create his own route a few feet away.

"If Jo is at the tree lot, is it okay for us to play together while you look for a tree?"

"Who?"

"My classmate's dad owns the tree lot. I think Jo might be there since it's Saturday."

"Okay. Just don't go far. Once I pick out a tree and pay for it, I'll need your help."

They arrived at the lot, and Lenny took off to look for his friend. Carolers' voices filled the air singing "Joy to the World," their voices harmonizing perfectly. The familiar melody soothed like nothing else had recently, and Grace stopped to sing along barely above a whisper.

Christmas had always been her favorite season—the music and celebrating the birth of Christ, along with parties, exchanging gifts, and decorating the tree. The song ended, and the sense of Christmas joy did too.

How could she find any joy with her brother overseas somewhere in the Pacific and her dream job ripped out of her life, leaving her back in her hometown with no purpose? She tamped down the sadness and wandered over to a row of trees propped up against a makeshift fence.

A short distance away, a man lifted a tree away from the fence. With an expectant expression on his face, he looked at the woman with him, presumably his wife, and gave it a shake. Clumps of snow dropped to the ground. After a moment, she shook her head. He grimaced and leaned the rejected tree against the fence.

Grace had to agree with the wife. The tree wasn't very full. None of the others in the grouping were to her liking, so she turned into the next row, examining the trees as she walked. She bumped into something solid and stepped back to see what got in her way. At least it was the back of a man, and not a child she might have knocked over.

"Excuse me."

"That's okay, I'm well-padded in this cold." The man spun

around. The same blue eyes that nearly discombobulated her at the bowling alley stared at her. "Well, hello, Grace."

With a Santa beard over half his face, she barely recognized him, except for his eyes.

"Mac, I didn't realize it was you at first."

"What gave me away?" He laughed and pulled the beard away from his face.

"Your blue eyes. They're quite distinctive. But why are you here wearing the Santa beard?"

It helps to entertain the children while their parents shop. It also keeps my face warm a lot longer than a scarf would."

She frowned. "Don't tell me in addition to helping at the bowling alley, you also assist the lot owner with selling his trees."

"I only work for free at the bowling alley." His hearty laugh filled the chilled air. "I own this lot."

"You sell Christmas trees?" She gaped at him.

"I guess I didn't mention it to you the times we've talked, and I've not been to the bowling alley for a few weeks, with it being the busy time of year for the tree business."

"I wondered where you were."

"You missed me?" He pulled his sheepskin collar tighter to his neck. "That's nice. Were you needing another bowling lesson?"

Her face heated. She hoped he'd think her blush was because of the cold. "My game has much improved, thanks to you, but I can always use another lesson. You were a fixture there the first weeks I bowled." Anxious to change the subject, she glanced around the lot. "My brother is here somewhere playing with ... " She frowned. "He said his classmate's dad owned the tree lot, and his name was Joe. Don't you only have a daughter?"

"Jo is my daughter, Jo—short for Joanna." He grinned. "She's here, but I haven't seen her in a while. Is Lenny your brother?"

"I'm glad I got straightened out about that." Grace laughed. "Yes, he's in the same class as Jo."

"I don't think I ever heard your last name, so I never

connected Lenny to you. My family has used your dad for some litigation. For such a small town, I sure missed making the connection."

"There are several families in town who seem to be related to everyone else, but we're not one of them."

He quirked his head. "Didn't your family used to own one of the estates on the lake?"

"Yes. Safe Refuge. The family lost it when the stock market crashed. The new owners changed the name to Rose Harbor."

"From the sound of your voice, it appears you're still mourning the loss."

"I am, but not as much as my granny. She speaks of the property as though it was a living being who passed away." She needed to change the subject before she became a blubbering idiot. "So, in addition to teaching, you own a Christmas tree lot. That's an interesting combination."

"I kind of fell into both. I was raised on a large farm off Hospital Road, north of town. I'm now part owner of the farm. We raise corn, soybeans, and have a coop of chickens. We used to have a small herd of cows, but my dad sold them all just before Pearl Harbor. My brothers run the farm, and I run the Christmas tree farm, which is on the same property. I should say the brothers *did* run the farm. They're both serving in the Pacific."

"If your brothers aren't home, who's helping with the farm?"

"We have a couple of hands, and I pitch in when I can."

How did she not know this family? "Did you attend school in Lake Geneva?"

"I did, but I expect I was a few years ahead of you. Graduated high school in 1926 and went to teacher's college at Whitewater." He tilted his head. "When did you graduate?"

Exactly ten years older, as she'd guessed. "In 1936. Went to the university in Madison, then started piloting planes to the military bases."

"You did tell me that, last we talked. I know your dad is a pilot too. Did he teach you how to fly?"

"He started teaching me on my sixteenth birthday, and I was hooked. Of course, I needed more training before I could fly the bombers." She grinned at the feeling of euphoria she experienced whenever she spoke about flying. "I love flying. There's nothing like it."

"I can see that by your smile. Why did you stop? The war isn't over yet."

"I became ill and had to quit. Were you deferred from the draft because of the farm?"

"That and my age put me toward the bottom of the most eligible list, and ..." He looked off then back to her. "My wife died in a drowning accident, trying to save our daughter. I'm Jo's only living parent."

What a chump she was for feeling sorry for herself. She knew he was widowed, of course, but not how his wife died. "I'm so sorry, Mac. What a terrible thing to go through."

"It's been rough, especially for Jo." He exhaled, his breath creating a cloud. "Let's find you a Christmas tree before we both freeze to death out here."

She followed as he led her across the lot to a row of trees. Peggy's words popped into her thoughts. *He's such a nice guy, Grace. Spend some time with him and see what develops.* She would possibly let down her guard, but she hadn't given up on her dream to be a pilot, some way, somehow. And after what she'd been through she doubted she'd meet Mac's qualifications for a girlfriend, let alone a wife.

"What kind of tree do you have in mind, and what height?" he called over his shoulder.

Grace snapped out of her reverie. "We've always had short needle. I'd better stick with that. We have high ceilings, so we want one that's ..." She walked up to him and raised her right arm to the top of Mac's head. "Maybe your height or a bit taller."

"What was that for?"

The impish grin on his face delighted her. "I know how much I've had to stretch to put the tree topper on our trees in the past. It worked."

"In all my years selling trees, I never had someone do that before. Sounds like you want one about six feet tall."

It felt good to hear him chuckle at her reasoning. Not in a mocking sort of way. More like being amused at the way she thought.

He showed her several trees until he found one she liked and the price equaled the amount of money Mom had given her.

"Now to find my brother to help me carry it home." She glanced around.

"I'll be happy to deliver the tree to your house. No need to carry it." He made a face. "Maybe I should have asked where you live before offering my services."

"That's very kind. Thanks. We're at the corner of Madison and Main, across from the library." She pulled a ten-dollar bill from her purse. "I believe the price is five dollars."

"Put your money away." He grinned. "This one is on the house, to celebrate your return to good health and coming home to Lake Geneva."

"I don't know if I consider being back here something to celebrate." Her breath caught. "I'm not doing anything toward the war effort now. Just sitting at home reading and working jigsaw puzzles."

"I understand. I like keeping busy too. Helps me to not think too much."

"Exactly."

His eyes twinkled. "Come with me, and I'll show you where Lenny and Jo are. You can wait there until I close the lot in about half an hour. Then I'll give you and Lenny a ride home along with the tree."

"A ride sounds great. I think it's gotten colder since we arrived." She followed him to the back of the lot, and they came to a small cabin that didn't look much larger than the ice fishing shanties out on the frozen lake.

"Ladies first." He opened the door.

Inside, the warmth of the small room wrapped around her like a cozy blanket.

Lenny sat at a small table with a girl who bore a strong resemblance to Mac. Same blue eyes and same smile.

"Aw, is it time to leave already?" Lenny held up a cup. "We've been drinking cocoa. This is my friend, Jo."

"Hello, Jo." Grace smiled at the girl. "It's nice to meet you."

"Nice to meet you too, Miss Bauer."

"Do you know Mr. McAlister?" Lenny asked, his eyes wide.

"Yes. We met at the bowling alley, but I didn't know he sold Christmas trees. He's offered to take our tree and us home in his truck after the lot closes. It'll be a little crowded on the seat but it's only for a few blocks."

"I can ride in the back with the tree." Lenny looked from Mac to Grace for approval.

Grace shook her head. "I don't know—"

"It's only for a few blocks."

"I'll go slow," Mac put in. "He and Jo can sit under a blanket."

She nodded slowly. "Mr. McAlister is okay with it, so I am too."

Lenny let out a whoop. "Jo, you can see my room and my toy soldiers I've been telling you about."

"Hold on, little brother. The McAlisters probably need to get straight home. Jo can come another time." She glanced at a book and papers on the table. "What have you two been doing?"

"I've been helping Jo with her arithmetic."

"I'm afraid my daughter takes after me in the arithmetic department." Mac moved toward a hotplate on the stove and lifted a kettle. "I can offer you tea or cocoa. That is, if these kids didn't drink my whole supply."

Never had a hot drink sounded so good. "Tea sounds perfect."

Mac prepared her tea and handed her the steaming cup. "Time for me to get back out there. The end of the day is usually busy, and my elves are probably wondering where the boss went." He buttoned his jacket, replaced the Santa beard, and pulled the stocking cap down over his ears. "Be back soon. Make yourself at home. Ho, ho, ho."

The door shut behind him, and Grace dropped onto the only other chair in the cabin and sipped the tea. She had to agree with the girls on the bowling team. Mac was very nice. But she wasn't looking. Especially not for a man whose daughter was the same age as her kid brother.

8

It wasn't long before Mac returned to the cabin and shooed Grace and the children outside. "Let's get the Bauers' tree loaded on my truck. Jo, grab that blanket to wrap around you and Lenny. You'll be in the back with the tree."

By the joy on the girl's face, it was apparent she didn't usually get to ride in the truck's bed.

Within a short time, Grace settled onto the passenger side of the truck's cushioned bench seat, and Mac slid in behind the wheel. "Tell me again where you live. I remember it's on Main Street, but I was so busy playing Santa and selling trees the details slipped my mind."

Afraid he'd take it wrong since he didn't know her well, she bottled a joke that forgetfulness comes with age. "We're at the northeast corner of Main and Madison Streets, across from Library Park."

"Right. Let's get the tree and you delivered." He pulled out on Center Street and turned north, then at the next corner headed the truck west on Main. "It's too bad the town has to forgo Christmas lights and the big tree in the middle of the main intersection. I think we're all weary of this blackout business and the war in general. Is it really possible the Axis could fly this far inland and bomb us?"

"Yes, it's possible, especially with German aircraft that keep increasing their range. We're pretty far inland, but they could reach our eastern shore. The planes that bombed Pearl Harbor came from aircraft carriers, and there's no reason that they couldn't position carriers closer to our west coast and do the same thing. Same goes for the Axis, but we've been more aware of the danger from that direction. That's why our boys are keeping eyes to radar and other means of tracking them so it doesn't happen again, but it could."

"Okay. I'm duly chastened for my ignorance. It sounds like I'm going to have to step up my prayers for God's protection. My family is always praying for protection of my brothers and all the fighting men. Are you a praying woman, Grace?"

The question threw her off guard. Despite feeling God had deserted her as far as her personal life went, she still believed in Him and had never stopped praying for her brother and the others at war. "Yes, I pray every day."

"Good to hear."

Why did it seem he wanted her to say more? "Here's my house, you can turn on Madison and pull up to the curb at the side of the house."

After he parked, they climbed out of the truck.

"That was dynamite!" Lenny jumped down from the back. "Only it was too short."

"I'm glad you liked it, Lenny." Mac laughed and helped Jo to the ground.

"I sure did. Can we do it again soon?"

"We'll see," Mac said. "Come on and help me with the tree. Assuming you want it in the living room like most families, it might be better to carry it around to the front door." He glanced at Grace as if to make sure he made the right assumption, and she nodded.

Lenny moved to the back of the truck without a word.

Grace shook her head. If she or their parents asked him to help with something like that, he'd have a million excuses why he couldn't. She and Jo followed Mac and Lenny as they carried the tree toward the front door.

She dashed around them and shouted into the foyer, "Our tree is here and coming through the door now!"

"I wondered where you two got off to." Mom hurried in from the kitchen, drying her hands on her apron. She stopped and stared at Mac. "Oh, I didn't realize you had someone with you."

"Mom, this is Mac McAlister. He owns the tree lot and offered to deliver the tree." She reached for Jo and tugged her to her side. "This is his daughter, Jo. She's in Lenny's room at school."

Mac nodded at Mom. "Pleased to meet you, Mrs. Bauer. Where do you want this?"

"Thank you so much for delivering the tree. I have the stand set up in the corner of the living room. I'll show you." She stepped through the wide opening into the room and pointed.

"What's all the commotion?" Dad came down the hall. "I go to my study to get some work done, and bedlam breaks loose." He laughed. "Don't all look so serious. I'm only joking. That looks like a fine tree you picked out, Grace."

"Thanks, Dad, but Mac here did the choosing."

"Pleased to meet you, Mr. Bauer." Mac held the tree trunk with one hand and stuck out his other hand.

The men briefly shook hands. "McAlister, Dad said. "You have farmland out on Hospital Road. Haven't I done some work for your family?"

"Yes, that's us. This tree was grown on the plot of land you helped us incorporate as a separate entity from the rest of the farm."

The men, along with Lenny, got the tree settled into the stand and made sure it was straight.

After some discussion about which side was its best, Mac

looked at Jo. "Honey, we need to get going and let these people get on with their evening."

"Oh, please don't leave yet, unless you have to. I have bean soup on the stove and cornbread in the oven. Join us, and we can all decorate the tree after we eat." Mom glanced at Grace, likely seeking her approval.

Grace shrugged. Part of her wanted them to stay, but part of her didn't.

"Please say yes, Daddy." Jo grinned at Lenny then at her dad. "I haven't had this much fun in ages."

"She knows when she calls me Daddy, I have a hard time saying no." Mac laughed. "May I use your phone to call my parents and tell them not to expect us for dinner? We usually eat there on the nights I work the tree lot."

As she followed her mother into the kitchen to help get the meal on, Grace mentally lectured herself. She had to keep a guard on her heart. As much as she didn't want to like Mac, she found that she liked him a lot.

THURSDAY NIGHT, Mac parked his truck on Main Street, a few doors down from the Clair Bowling Lanes. He hadn't planned on showing up at the bowling alley on the day before Christmas Eve, but when he realized that quite a few of the high-school-aged workers wouldn't be coming because of the holiday, he'd changed his mind.

Would Grace be there? The way her family had talked on Saturday night when he delivered their tree, they had a lot of family activities planned around Christmas. He sensed they were trying to make things as festive as possible, despite the war and their oldest son being somewhere in the Pacific. The same as his family.

He raced down the stairs, hoping Grace hadn't already been to the shoe counter. In recent weeks, she'd been arriving early to snag one of the size eights. Little did she know that ever since that first night, whenever he was there he'd set aside shoes for her. She never stayed for conversation when getting her shoes, but maybe after his spending the evening last weekend decorating the tree with her family, he'd be able to chat with her a little.

Grace was already at the counter when he approached.

Before he could speak, she beat him to it. "Hi, Mac. Am I glad to see you. I was helping Mom decorate gingerbread men and wasn't able to leave early. It appears Becky isn't working tonight. I was about to help myself, but I see the other size eights are already taken."

"Good to see you, Grace." He slipped behind the counter. "Most of the younger employees aren't working because of the holiday. I wouldn't be surprised if I end up being a pinsetter later. I'll check in the storeroom for the extra shoes. Maybe I'll have the same luck I did last time."

"I prefer to say it was a blessing, not luck." Her full lips lifted into a hint of a smile.

His breath stilled. His wife used to say the same thing. Because of her, he'd stopped calling himself lucky. That all stopped one horrible winter day. He managed a tight smile as the familiar darkness settled over him. "I'll be right back."

In the storeroom, he shut the door then slammed his left fist into his right palm. He needed to push those dark thoughts away. Grace's comment had nothing to do with Emily. Once in a while, he'd even heard his mother say the same thing. He opened a file drawer and pulled out the size eights he'd set aside for Grace.

By the time he returned to the counter his spirits had lifted, the same way they had last week when Grace came to the tree lot, and later, when her mom asked him and Jo to stay for soup and decorating the tree. He wasn't the only one whose spirits lifted that evening—he hadn't seen Jo that happy in months.

"You're definitely blessed tonight, Grace. I found this pair in the back." He handed the shoes to her, making sure not to touch her fingertips like he had that first night. He couldn't deal with the shivery sensation that had trailed up his arm that time. But the smile on her face had almost the same effect.

She thanked him and walked away, her skirt swishing against her shapely calves as she walked.

"Mac, I'm glad you're here." Jen Lazzaroni, one of the bowling alley's owners, scurried up. "I hate to ask, but we're shorthanded behind the pins tonight. Would you mind being a pin bo—man? I'll be happy to pay you."

Grateful for the distraction, he nodded. "Let's just say substitute pinsetter. I think I remember how to do the job. No pay necessary. You know I enjoy helping out wherever I'm needed."

The woman's grin was enough pay as far as he was concerned.

"Thank you. Lane 4 is where you're needed. Go on over there and get acclimated. I'll take over here. I told my sister she shouldn't schedule leagues tonight, but you know Alma's soft heart. She thought it would be good for those who are especially lonesome during the holidays."

He grabbed a pair of men's bowling shoes, required footwear when working as a pin setter. Now if only his knees would hold out through all the jumping down from the ledge to reset the pins. The old football knee injury didn't take kindly to that type of abuse.

At lane 4, he stepped between the benches and spotted a head full of reddish-brown curls bent over a pair of green-and-red size eights. His spirits lifted. Being assigned to Grace's lane had to be some kind of sign. But what was the message?

She straightened and their gazes met. "Mac, you're not going to tell me these shoes were already spoken for."

"You're looking at your pinsetter for the night. I hope you ladies go easy on me." He sat next to her and quickly put on his bowling shoes.

"Go easy on you, Mac? Why should we give you special treatment?" Helen spoke from the other side of Grace.

"Well, for one thing, I've got ..." He was about to say he had a few more years on his bones than the kids who usually reset the pins, but why emphasize his age in front of Grace? Ten years difference didn't matter a whit to him, but something she said the other day made him think it might to her.

"I'm out of practice is all. At least go easy at first."

Helen laughed. "Hey, if I can, I will. But don't count on it."

Shoes tied, he stood then gave Helen and Grace a wave and nodded at Peggy and Harriet, the other team members, who were just arriving. "I want to see a lot of strikes, ladies. Don't disappoint me."

The game began, and with so much jumping down to reset the pins, it didn't take long for his knee to start hurting. He'd have to tell Jen he could help in a lot of ways, but after tonight pin setting wasn't one of them.

By the time the third game ended he was limping, the last thing he wanted Grace to see him doing. She looked up as he plopped down beside her and removed his shoes.

"Why were you limping? Did you hurt yourself tonight?"

So much for hiding it. "Not directly. I tore cartilage in my knee playing football in high school. Jumping to the floor so many times aggravated things. I'll take some aspirin when I get home. It'll be okay by tomorrow."

"My grandfather is a doctor. Maybe if you went to him, he could help."

"If the answer is surgery, I'd be laid up for a long time. I can't afford to do that, what with the work on the farm and teaching and ..." He stopped himself from saying if he should decide to move Jo away from the area.

"And what?" She was already wearing her street shoes.

"I lost my train of thought. Do you need a ride home? Maybe we could have coffee somewhere along the way."

She stared at him without speaking.

Maybe this time her answer would be yes.

"Thanks for the offer, but I don't drink coffee at night. It keeps me awake." She set the size eights on the bench next to him. "Can I leave these with you for returning, since you're right here?"

"Um, sure. Maybe another time during the day we can have that coffee." He jammed his foot into the remaining shoe and stood, then picked up her bowling shoes along with his. "Merry Christmas."

As he stepped around the bench, the injured knee slammed into the back of the seat. He forced himself not to react to the pain and bent to re-tie the lace. Not bothering to mask his limp, he headed for the shoe counter.

"Are you crazy, Grace?" Helen's remark reached him as he left. "The only decent single man in town asks you for coffee, and you turn him down."

He doubted he was the only decent man in Lake Geneva, but right then he felt like a has-been.

9

Loud banging jolted Grace awake.

"Grace, wake up! We're waiting!" Lenny's shout through the bedroom door was loud enough to wake the dead. She glanced at her clock. What was he doing up at seven a.m.? The boy usually didn't rouse until at least eight unless it was a school day.

"We'll open presents without you if you don't get up now!"

She threw back the covers and ran her feet over the throw rug to locate her slippers where she'd stepped out of them. How did she forget it was Christmas morning? She'd crawled into bed last night much later than usual, thanks to helping Mom put finishing touches on her meal prep for today. She jammed her feet into her fleece-lined moccasins, a Christmas present from two years ago. "I'm awake, little brother. I'll be down in a few minutes."

"Okay, but hurry."

The family always opened presents in their bathrobes, so no need to dress, but she did have to wash her face and brush her teeth. She hoped Mom had coffee made. She'd been stockpiling the weekly rationed supply for a month so there'd be plenty this morning.

She grabbed her flannel robe and shuffled to the bathroom. Lenny had probably retreated to the living room, where he could ogle the gifts that bore his name. Christmas morning would never be the same when he outgrew the wonder of Christmas. Oh, to be a child again and free from the burden of worry and regret.

Ten minutes later, she entered the living room. Mom, wearing the same dusty-rose chenille robe she'd had as long as Grace could remember, handed her a steaming cup of coffee already doctored the way she liked it, with cream and a pinch of sugar.

"Yay! She's here. Now we can start." Lenny picked up a gaily wrapped box. "I'll go first."

"Hold your horses, young man," Dad held up a hand, palm out. "We need to read the Christmas story in the Bible first."

Lenny grimaced. "But we already did that last night at church."

"It doesn't hurt to hear it again, Leonard," Mom said. "Put the present aside. In fact, why don't you read it to us? You're old enough now."

"Your mother is right." Dad handed the Bible to Lenny. "It's already open to Luke, chapter two. Read through verse twenty."

The boy sighed and began reading, "And it came to pass in those days, that there went out a decree from Caesar Augustus that all the world should be taxed."

Grace turned away to hide her smile.

"Slow down and read it normally," Mom said. "You'll get to open your presents in due time. Start from the beginning."

Despite his loud moan, he did as asked. When he finished reading, he handed the Bible back to Dad. "Now?"

Dad tightened the belt on his navy flannel robe and checked his watch as his lips turned up. "Now."

Lenny grabbed the box he'd set aside and had the paper ripped off in seconds. "I did get what I wanted." He lifted the lid on the box and grinned. Kicking off a slipper, he thrust his bare foot into the boot of one of the skates and pressed against the toe. "Plenty of room. They should last me a while."

"Unless you have a growth spurt." Mom sighed. "They're from Granddad and Granny." She picked up another gift and held it out to Grace. "For you from me."

Grace removed the simple bow and brown wrapping paper and studied the book cover. "Amy Carmichael. I've heard the name before."

"She's a missionary in India who is confined to bed. She has beautiful insights on the Bible and God. I think you'll enjoy her writings."

Since she'd been home, Grace had made sure she went through the motions of reading the Bible first thing in the morning, and until recently, speaking of the Lord at necessary times. So far, she'd not attended church, not even last night's service when she begged off, saying she'd make Mom's planned dessert for Christmas Day and have it done by the time the family returned. Being sick the first month or so she was home, her lack of attendance was understandable, but lately it was getting harder to come up with an excuse.

It would break Mom's heart if she knew that no matter how many times Grace had called out to God, praying for Him to forgive her, God remained silent. She pushed out a smile, hoping it appeared sincere. "Thank you. I'm sure I will."

After a late breakfast, Grace left the other presents she'd received under the tree for all to see, but she took the book Mom gave her to her room when she went there to dress. She put it into her nightstand drawer, next to her Bible and the cross necklace she'd stopped wearing. She shut the drawer, just as she'd closed an imaginary drawer on her life as a devoted follower of Christ.

Tears welled in her eyes. She wasn't mad at God. He wasn't the one who'd done wrong. She only had herself to blame—something she'd have to live with forever.

Later, after everyone enjoyed a long chat remembering past

Christmases and drinking coffee, Grace sat on the couch watching Reenie and Lenny play Supremacy, the new board game the family had received from Oma, who was with Uncle Peter and his family in the city. The game was similar to Monopoly, and it didn't take long for her brother and sister to figure out the rules.

With their chatter in the background, Grace leaned her head back on the couch cushion and closed her eyes. If Frank hadn't dumped her, by now she'd be married. As much as she enjoyed succeeding in the man's world of piloting aircraft, she'd still dreamed of being a wife and mother someday. Now that dream would never come true.

What was Frank doing this Christmas Day? Was he home with his wife, or flying sorties over the battlefields that never took a day off? He'd been married long enough now that he might possibly be a dad. She'd always thought he'd make a splendid father. She blinked at the moisture gathering in her eyes. She had to get her thoughts off what would never be.

"Cheater! I don't want to play with you anymore, Reenie Bauer."

Grace's eyes popped open as Lenny flung the game board in the air, sending tiny replicas of army equipment and soldiers flying.

"I did not cheat, you little brat. That's the last time I'll play a game with you." Reenie jumped to her feet.

Mom flew into the room. "What in the world is going on?"

"She cheated, Mom."

"I did not." Reenie crossed her arms and jutted her chin.

"You two get outside." Mom went to the gifts by the tree and picked up Lenny's new skates and handed them to him. "It's a beautiful day, and skaters are already over there on the ice. Reenie, you know where your skates are. Go get them."

Ready to retreat into her private world of self-pity, Grace leaned against the couch back.

"Grace, I suggest you join them. Just be home by two

o'clock." The front door slammed, and voices drifted into the room. "Sounds like Mama and Pop are here. Don't just sit there, go ice skating with the others."

"That's probably too much exercise for me."

Granddad stepped into the room. "What's too much exercise for you?"

"I suggested she go ice skating with Lenny and Reenie."

"That's a wonderful idea. You're already building strength in your arms and legs from bowling. Skating will be good for you. Doctor's orders. Go ice skating."

Heaving a sigh, she stood. "You're all ganging up on me. I'm going."

MAC TIED the lace on his skate. "Don't go out on the ice, Jo, until I get the other skate on and I can go with you."

"I told you, Dad. I don't want to go out there. Please, let's go home. I want to read the new Nancy Drew book I got for Christmas."

This was exactly why they needed to move south. He'd hoped the new skates she'd received that morning would entice her to try skating again. She'd had a meltdown when she opened the present but calmed after a bit. He hoped that after one turn on the ice, she'd remember how much she enjoyed the sport and forget about that horrible day.

He jammed his foot into his other skate and ran the laces around the hooks of the boot so fast he missed one. It could wait till later. He stood and skated over the ice and sat on a bench next to his weeping daughter. He slipped his arm around her and pressed her head to his shoulder. "Jo-Jo, this isn't like the ice you fell through four years ago. I checked yesterday, and even this close to shore, it's at least ten inches thick."

Jo took ragged breaths through her sobs and swiped at her wet cheeks with the back of her mitten-covered hand. "I-I-I can't get it out of my mind. Mom isn't here because of me. She's probably so mad at me."

He gave her shoulder a squeeze. "Sweetheart, remember what we talked about before." He swallowed against the large lump in his throat. "She'd never be mad at you for what happened. She's with the Lord now, and very happy being with Him. She wouldn't want you to not love skating like you used to."

Her sobs quieted and he leaned down and checked her skates to be sure they were secure. Assured they were fine, he stood and gently gripped her arm. "Come on. Let's give your new skates a try. Get out there and see if you remember how to skate backward."

"Of course I remember." Her laugh sounded forced.

"Prove it. I need to see for myself." Mac crossed his arms and winked.

With a how-can-you-not-believe-me sigh, she stood and skated backward onto the ice, picking up speed as her confidence grew. "See? I remember!"

"Look where you're going!"

She smacked into an older man's legs and landed on her bottom while the man did a little dance to regain his balance.

"Little girl, you need to watch where you're going," The elderly man moved toward Jo with small steps, rather than skating, and placed his fists on his hips. "I could have fallen and broken my leg. Where are your parents?"

She pointed at Mac, who was skating toward them as fast as he could.

"I'm so sorry. My daughter was excited to try out her new skates and forgot to look where she was going."

The man harrumphed. "That's no excuse. I told my daughter I'm too old for skating now, but she insisted."

A young woman skated up. "Dad, there you are. We've been looking for you."

"That little hooligan nearly ran me over." The man pointed at Jo, who remained seated on the ice.

"I'm sure it was an accident." The woman offered Jo a sympathetic smile. "Are you okay, little girl?"

Jo scrambled to her feet and tucked under Mac's arm. "I'm sorry I ran into you."

"I bet you are." The man grimaced.

"No one was hurt." Mac gripped Jo's shoulder and squeezed it. "Let's let bygones be bygones."

The woman stared at Mac. "Aren't you the man who sells Christmas trees?"

"That would be me. I'm Mac McAlister, and this is my daughter, Joanna."

"Ginny Simpson. My husband and son are over there. I'm sorry for my dad's surliness. We thought getting him out to skate with us would lift his spirits." She skated a bit closer to Mac, her eyes twinkling. "We buy our tree from you every year. They stay fresh longer than those we've had in the past. Come on, Dad. Let's join the others." She took her father's arm, and they skated off, her father definitely not too steady on his skates.

Jo looked up at Mac, and he nearly melted at the tears in her eyes.

"No worries," he said. "It was only an accident. Some people are just grouchy. We don't know what kind of day he's had so far, or what else is going on in his life. Let's forget about it and skate, but don't try going backward until you learn how to make sure you're not going to run into someone."

"I don't want to stay here, Dad." Jo wiped the moisture from her cheek with her mittened hand. She looked off, and a grin took over her face. "There's Lenny and his sisters. He did get new skates."

Grace? Mac's breath caught. She may have been out of his sight since the other night at the bowling alley, but she hadn't been out of his thoughts. Working to keep his excitement in check, he skated after Jo, who was already yards ahead of him, shouting out Lenny's name. He skidded to a stop a short distance away from Grace as a man skated up to her and wrapped her in a hug.

The smile on her face was probably there for the same reason she turned him down for coffee. Well, he had no choice but to join them since Jo and Lenny were already skating circles around the pair. He shouldn't have expected a pretty woman like Grace to be without a man in her life. Another sign he should put plans in motion to move to Florida.

10

Grace leaned back to look at the tall man, a mature facsimile of the high school senior she fell in love with at the age of fifteen. Dark eyes as mesmerizing now as they were nine years ago. "Richard Garrett, is that really you after all this time? You're a doctor now, right? Last I saw in the paper, you were stationed in London."

They ended the embrace, and the same deep dimples she remembered appeared.

"I was stationed near London, at a hospital that serves the airmen from both England and the U.S., and before that, as a flight surgeon at field hospitals in France and Italy. Earlier this month I transferred to Walter Reed Hospital in D.C. Since the transfer coincided with Christmas, I was able to take leave until January second."

"Good for you. Those field hospitals must have been dangerous, so close to the action."

"They were far enough back from the front that we were relatively safe, but once in a while things got a little uncertain. There was a lot of work for us, putting our boys back together as best we could before they could be sent home to the States."

Grace listened with rapt attention, keeping one eye on Lenny.

"In England, we were located away from the city and not in much danger of being bombed, but we received a lot of casualties from the London bombings. This year has been brutal on our pilots." He smiled at her. "Hey, my parents caught me up on your being with WASP. The Luftwaffe has taken down a lot of B-17s, some you probably ferried to their assigned bases."

She pushed away the dark cloud that never failed to come over her when she focused on such thoughts. "I try never to think about that part of the war, but whenever I flew, I always said a prayer that whoever took the plane into battle would be safe from harm."

"I like that. I always prayed for the men whose injuries I repaired in the field. Once I was in London, most all those I doctored were eventually sent back to the States."

The question that had popped into her mind since their conversation began poised itself on the tip of her tongue. She assumed Frank was still alive, but who would tell her if he was one of the casualties she'd been hearing about? "I wonder if you know an Army pilot who's stationed somewhere in England. His name is Frank—"

"Jo, it's time for us to get home."

Grace whirled and saw Mac approaching on skates.

"But, Dad, I'm teaching Lenny how to skate backward," Jo wailed. "He got new skates for Christmas too."

How did she miss his being nearby? She grinned. "Hi, Mac. Merry Christmas."

"Merry Christmas. Sorry to interrupt. Just trying to round up my daughter."

"You're not interrupting. Have you been here long?"

"No. We arrived a short while ago."

"Good. I'd hate to think the kids could have been skating together for a while if we'd seen you." She glanced at Richard and back to Mac. "Mac McAlister, meet Richard Garrett, who is home on leave from the army. We were friends in high school."

"I'd say we were more than friends." Richard skated closer and dropped his arm over her shoulders. "Or are you forgetting we went out exclusively my senior year, despite your dad's not liking the idea of his sophomore daughter seeing an older senior?" He removed his arm from Grace's shoulders and held out his hand. "I go by Rich these days. Good to meet you."

Mac gripped his hand.

"What Rich didn't tell you is that it's Dr. Garrett, and he'll be stationed at Walter Reed Hospital in D.C. after the holidays." Grace faced Rich. "My parents were married at Walter Reed after my dad came home from the Great War. He was there being treated as an amputee. There's more to the story, but that will have to wait for another time."

Rich's eyes widened. "I'd like to hear the rest of that tale, and about your experiences piloting bombers." He tugged her closer. "Here we were a couple of crazy kids thinking we were in love, and look how differently our lives turned out."

Grace hesitated, not appreciating the possessive way he was acting with her.

"Are you free tomorrow night for dinner?" he asked. "We can catch up on old times, like the prom at the Riv my senior year and how we danced almost every dance." He glanced over at the Riviera at the east end of the beach. "I see they've enclosed the terrace where we snuck out to steal a few kisses. Too bad."

How could she forget the dreamy way he held her tight while they danced and the softness of his kisses on the terrace? He was her first love and the first boy she'd ever kissed.

Though she didn't recall any mention of being in love, it may have seemed that way to her fifteen-year-old mind. Maybe the nostalgia he was feeling was rubbing off on her. It would be best to decline his invitation—but what could it hurt? Just old friends getting together. "That sounds like fun. Where should I meet you?"

"No need to meet. I'll pick you up at six o'clock. Do you still live at the corner of Madison and Main?"

"Yes, we're still there. Six o'clock sounds good."

She turned to say something to Mac. "Where did Mac go?"

"Isn't that him with the girl Lenny was playing with?"

Grace followed the direction Rich pointed and spotted Mac and Jo skating away holding hands. A sinking feeling came over her. She hadn't meant to ignore him. An apology was in order when she next saw him at the bowling alley. She checked her watch. Mom wasn't going to be happy. It was nearly two-fifteen.

"Lenny, find Reenie. She might be over there with those high school girls." She pointed in the direction of a group of teenagers. "Mom's going to come out here to find us if we don't get home soon."

The boy rolled his eyes and skated off.

"I love my siblings, but sometimes they drive me crazy." Grace faced Rich. "Is your family having Christmas dinner soon too?"

The corners of his lips turned down. "Yes, we're expecting my great-aunt and uncle over from near Walworth. I love the old couple dearly, but I'm afraid I'm in for a long rest of the day. With my brother stationed in the Pacific with the navy, it's been a quiet sort of holiday."

"I'm sorry. It's not the same for us either, with Rory not here. He's in the Pacific too. We've not had any contact from him in months. I'm trying not to worry, but some in my family are speculating he was on the *Houston* when it was taken down. Since my dad was shot down over Belgium in the Great War, he's probably more concerned than any of us, because he knows what could have happened to my brother."

"I'll pray Rory is alive and safe. I can't remember—was your dad a POW?"

"No. A Belgian farmer and his wife hid him in their cellar." She sighed. "Let's hope by next Christmas the war will be done and all our men will be home. I'm looking forward to tomorrow night. See you then."

She spun around and spotted Lenny a short distance away, honing his skills at skating backward while Rennie watched. "Come on kids, we need to get home."

11

When the side doorbell buzzed at six o'clock the next evening, Grace checked herself in the full-length mirror on the back of her bedroom door. Satisfied the two-year-old, green corduroy dress with its square neckline still looked fresh and stylish, she headed for the back stairs.

At the side door, careful to not draw attention to her movement, she peered out one of the narrow windows that framed the door on either side to be sure it was Rich. He stood waiting in a thick, heavy topcoat, his back straight and erect.

Grace flicked the entry hall light on and swung the door open, and he offered her his killer dimpled grin.

"There you are, beautiful as always."

"You haven't seen me since I was fifteen and had pimples on my nose." She stepped back to allow him to enter.

"I saw you yesterday."

"That doesn't count, because I had on a wool hat and a scarf around my neck." She waved toward the dining room. "Before we leave, my parents want to say hello. They're about to have dinner. Don't bother to remove your coat. We'll only be a minute or two."

Dad stood from the table as they entered the dining room. "Richard, it's good to see you again." He held out his hand. "It's been a long time. Grace says you go by Rich now, and that you're a doctor at Walter Reed."

Rich shook Dad's hand. "Yes, I'm not officially working there yet, but I did visit for a day last week, and I'm excited to get started."

"Did Grace tell you her father and I were married in Walter Reed's chapel?" Mom rose and approached. "The hospital staff was wonderful that crazy day."

"She did tell me, but I'd love to hear the details sometime."

"Why don't you join us for dinner here, and we can tell you all about it?" Dad indicated an empty chair next to Lenny.

"Yeah," Lenny put in. "I want to hear all about the war."

Rich looked at Grace with a questioning expression.

Already sensing her old feelings for the man emerging, she'd much prefer being with others. "I think that's a good—"

"Thanks for the invitation," Rich said quickly, "but Grace and I have a lot of catching up to do. What if we bring dessert back here after dinner, and we can talk then? I'd really love to hear the wedding story." He winked at Lenny, "And share some of my war stories."

"Of course." Dad waved a dismissive hand. "You two go on and get reacquainted. No need to bring dessert. We'll look forward to the visit later."

Grace led the way to the front door foyer and went to the hall tree for her wrap. Rich took it from her and held the fleece coat as she slipped it on.

"Rather than walk through the house again, let's use this door and walk around to your car," she said.

The cold night air felt good, and she liked walking in silence as though they hadn't been apart more than a few days and not years.

He glanced at her as they approached the car. "How does the Gargoyle sound?"

"It sounds good. I haven't eaten there in a long while."

"I haven't either. I was thinking of eating in their Rathskeller, or would you prefer their fancier dining room upstairs?"

"The Rathskeller sounds wonderful."

"Good. I plan on shooting for the moon with a steak if it's on the menu. He opened the passenger door and made a slight bow. "Please be seated, madam."

"Thank you, sir." She slid onto the seat and ran her hand over the plush cushion.

The driver's door opened, and Rich settled behind the wheel. "You look nice, Grace. Green looks good on you."

The man hadn't lost his charm. "Thank you. This is a nice car. It's hard to see the color in the dark. Is it blue?"

"Yes, a dark blue. Dad bought it new before GM retrofitted their production line to manufacture plane engines and tanks. He doesn't drive it much, and mom never did learn how to drive. They live close to town and walk to the grocery, the bank, and church. He said I could take the car to D.C. if I wanted to, but I declined. I'll be living in army housing near the hospital, and public transportation is available if I want to go anywhere else in the city."

They parked on Broad Street a few steps from the restaurant, which was situated in a large, two-story home. The owner had converted the first floor and basement into a restaurant and lived on the second floor. They approached the arched entry to the grounds and walked around the fountain, which was turned off for the winter, then toward the outside steps leading down to the Rathskeller, the restaurant's more casual dining room.

"Do they still have a fishpond in the garden out back?" Rich asked.

"Yes. I enjoyed strolling through there this past fall, once I was able to get out for exercise."

As they descended the steps, Rich took hold of Grace's elbow. Surprised at how familiar his gesture felt, as though the past eight years had dissolved into one, she slipped her arm out of his hold.

Inside the wood-paneled dining room, the host led them to a table in front of a large stone fireplace, its flames low enough to add atmosphere without overheating the room, then offered to take their coats and hang them in a cloakroom nearby.

She offered Rich a smile and held his gaze, expecting him to say something, but he didn't. She'd seen Dad do the same thing, and he explained that sometimes, out of nowhere, a memory from the war would take over his thoughts, and he couldn't say or do anything but wait for it to pass.

"I love the smell of a fire in winter, don't you, Rich?" She glanced at the crackling fire and inhaled the pleasant aroma.

He blinked. "What did you say?"

"I love the smell of a wood fire."

"Oh yes, especially at Christmas." He blinked again.

The brunette waitress approached. "Good evening. Can I get you something from the bar?"

Rich startled. "I'd like a ginger ale." He turned toward Grace, "What about you, Earhart?"

Hearing his pet name for her caught her off guard, but she didn't miss the pointed stare the waitress shot at Rich. She gathered herself and nodded. "I'll have the same."

The woman jotted the orders on her pad, then offered Grace a weak smile. "I've seen you at the bowling alley on league night, but I don't know your name. Are you related to Amelia Earhart? I'm Lillian Cameron."

Embarrassed she didn't remember seeing Lillian before, she managed a smile. "Grace Bauer. Earhart is just a nickname. No relation to Amelia. How long have you been involved with the bowling teams?"

"This is my second year. What about you?"

"My first."

Lillian left a pair of menus on the table, saying she'd return shortly with the soft drinks, and moved to another table.

"I don't think our waitress liked me calling you my nickname for you," Rich said. "Did you see how she frowned at me?"

"I have to admit I was surprised to hear you call me Earhart. I know you made it up because I love to fly. But to someone else it might sound strange."

"I suppose so. It seemed so natural to use the name, especially now that you're living your dream."

"Maybe you should just call me Grace. We're not in high school now, and I've not piloted a plane since I became ill a few months ago. The only activity I'm involved in right now is bowling in a league like the waitress said. Funny how I can pilot a big bomber plane but haven't yet been high scorer on my bowling team."

"I can't believe you're that bad of a bowler." His brows rose into a pair of perfect arches. "And I saw your skating skills yesterday. You're good at that too."

"I've had more practice skating than bowling." She chuckled. "I haven't bowled since ninth grade. A nice man at the alley has been giving me pointers, and I'm improving."

"And in no time, you'll no doubt be the top scorer on your team." Rich picked up a menu and glanced at it. "Steak is on the menu. I'm choosing the monster sirloin. I remember it from the last time I was here. Are you game?"

She grinned and nodded. "Yes, please, but a smaller cut for me."

Lillian returned with their soft drinks then pulled out her pad. "Are you ready to order?"

"We both want steak." Rich pointed to the menu. "I'll take the monster Gargoyle sirloin. Does that come with potatoes and a vegetable?"

"Yes. Tonight, it's roasted potatoes and green beans."

"Sounds fine. I'll take mine medium rare." The lady prefers a smaller cut. Bring her the filet." He glanced at Grace. "Is your preference still well done?'

"Absolutely not. After living in Texas, I've learned the way to eat a good steak is medium rare."

"That's the girl. I knew there was a reason you got ahold of my heart all those years ago."

The waitress's left eyebrow rose. She gave Rich another piercing stare, then she slapped her order book closed, turned on her heel, and left.

"I wonder what that was about." Rich frowned.

"What do you mean?"

"Didn't you see the dirty look she gave me?"

"Yes, but it's probably best to ignore it. Excuse me, I need to visit the powder room." She picked up her clutch bag and wove her way between the tables to the restrooms.

A few minutes later, Grace stood at the sink washing her hands.

"Finally, a break. I don't think I could hold ..." Lillian stopped short in the restroom doorway and caught Grace's reflection in the mirror. "Well, hi. I'm glad you're in here." She stepped in and let the door close. "I know it's none of my business, but I don't care for people who cheat behind their main squeeze's back. I'm not a tattletale, so I don't plan to tell Mac you're two-timing him. But I'm warning you, you might end up with no man if one fella finds out about the other."

Grace scrambled for the right response, but before she could say anything, Lillian stepped into the stall and slammed the door. The lock clinked as she slid it in place.

Her stomach heated. She gathered herself and spoke to the closed stall door. "What makes you think I'm seeing Mac?"

"It's obvious you two are sweet on each other. He's always hanging around your team, and he doesn't take the time to teach anyone else how to bowl like he's done for you. My team has been speculating how long it will be before he pops the question. A nice man like him doesn't deserve the likes of you."

Heat crawled up Grace's neck. "You're mistaken. Mac and I are friends, is all. He's only coached me a couple of times. As for the man I'm with tonight, we dated in high school. He's with the Army Air Service and is heading to D.C. to continue serving there. I'm not seeing him either." She yanked at the continuous roll of cloth towels feeding from a metal box on the wall and dried her hands on a clean spot.

Behind her, a toilet flushed. She flung the door to the dining room open, wanting to get out of the room before Lillian emerged.

How was she going to get through the meal with that woman as their waitress? She marched across the room toward her table. *Rich can't know what happened in there.*

She and Mac weren't sweethearts. Friends, that's all they were. She sat in her chair and crossed her arms.

Rich turned in his seat from talking to a couple at the next table and stared at her. "Whoa, you look mad enough to spit. Who got you fit to be tied?"

"No one." She relaxed her arms. "Why?"

"You marched over here like you were on your way to war, and you're as tense as a cat in a room full of rocking chairs."

"I haven't heard that expression since I left Texas." Grace couldn't help but chuckle. "Where'd that come from?"

"I heard it a lot while serving with a bunch of southerners. Are you going to tell me who you're so mad at? I hope it's not me."

"It's not you. But I don't want to talk about it." She picked up her ginger ale then set it down, hoping he didn't notice the liquid sloshing in the glass. If she were a drinking woman, she'd ask for a shot of whiskey straight up.

Rich leaned toward her, his dark eyes filled with concern. "Was it something with our waitress? I saw her go in the ladies' room shortly after you."

Lifting her gaze to the ceiling, she let go of a sigh. "There's no hiding it, since she was the only other person in there. I can't talk about it now. She's coming toward us."

"Can I get you two anything else? More ginger ale? Coffee or tea?"

"I'm fine." Grace shook her head, keeping her focus on Rich.

"I'd like another." Rich held up his glass.

"Coming right up, sugar," Lillian purred. She took his empty glass and marched toward the kitchen.

"Sugar?" His brows rose.

Grace shrugged. "A lot of women can't ignore a good-looking man who just returned from the war."

"I've never seen her in my life." A frown creased his brow. "You must have told her about me."

"In so many words. I didn't think you'd mind." Grace sipped her drink and let the cool bubbly liquid soothe her throat. "I'm sorry if I spoke out of turn."

"I really don't mind. I'm sure my homecoming will be in Thursday's edition of the paper anyway."

"Here we are. A medium rare filet for the lady, and a ginger ale and medium rare monster for the gent." Lillian set plates in front of them, then focused on Rich. "You want steak sauce to go with that, handsome?"

"No thanks. I want to taste my steak without any competition."

"A man after my own heart." She winked at him, then turned on her heel and left.

The aroma of steak wafted to Grace's nose, but she had no desire to eat now. "I told her we were just old friends and you were home from the war, so she probably thinks you're fair game. I'll tell you the rest of what was said after we leave. Can we just enjoy our meal?"

Rich's eyes were as wide as quarters. "I can't wait to hear it."

When he didn't offer to say a blessing on the meal, out of habit Grace silently said a word of thanks, then cut a bite of steak. The tender meat all but melted in her mouth and her appetite returned. How the restaurant managed to obtain such high-grade meat during wartime was beyond her, but she was going to enjoy every bite.

After they ate in silence for a few minutes, Rich leaned back in his chair and sipped his drink. "I fully expected to find you married with at least one youngster by now. So many of the guys in my unit got married right away when they received their marching orders. And some found out a few months later their wives were pregnant. Tough news, since they probably wouldn't see their child until he or she was walking and talking."

Heat rose into her face. Soon he'd be asking why she was still unattached. It was none of his business that her love life had gone south. "I could say the same about you. It appears you're also still single."

"I didn't date much as an undergrad because I was premed and on the fast-track to finish in three years instead of four. I had a girlfriend while I was doing my residency, and we planned to marry." His face grew serious. "Then Pearl Harbor came, and I announced I intended to enlist as soon as my residency was over and I received my M.D. She immediately returned the ring because she refused to risk possibly becoming a widow at such a young age." He picked up his drink and sipped.

That seemed a bit harsh to Grace. "Wow, not very nice, Rich. I'm so sorry."

"I'm not. I didn't need to have a girl at home worrying over me. I needed one who supported me and my work." He set his drink on the table. "I enlisted in the Medical Army Air Forces a week after I had my M.D." He threw up his hands surrender fashion. "I've been too occupied since then to date at all." He reached over, took her hand, and squeezed it. "Until tonight. It's like all the years between us have disappeared."

A lump as large as Texas filled her throat. The time had flown, but too much had infiltrated her life during those years. "I'm not the same person I was in high school, Rich. What we had was fun and very innocent. I never dreamed I'd be flying bombers and the U.S. would be in yet another war. I'm enjoying tonight too. But I wouldn't put too much stock in it."

His smile faded and he withdrew his hand. "I'm not the same either. Believe me, no one is unchanged once they've seen the horror of war. I've seen firsthand how bullets and bombs tear up a human body."

"As you know, my dad was shot down over Belgium and was cared for in hiding by a brave Belgian couple. They tried to nurse his injured leg, but when he got back to the states he had to have it amputated at Walter Reed." Moisture filled her eyes as it always did when she thought about Dad and how he was reminded of his loss daily when he attached his prothesis to his stump.

He looked off, his Adam's apple bobbing, then faced her. "So, why are you still single? I would expect by now some Army pilot would have claimed you."

Buying time to put words together, she sipped her drink. "I was engaged to a bomber pilot. We met when he was stationed at the base where I trained in the 17 and quickly fell in love. A few months after we met he received orders to report for overseas duty. There was no time to marry before he shipped out, and we planned to marry as soon as he was back in the States."

His eyes filled with concern. "Is he deceased?"

"I think I could handle it better if he were. He wrote me a couple of months after he left, saying he'd met an English woman and they eloped. I was a mess for a while and poured myself into flying, volunteering for runs whenever one came up."

He nodded, eyeing her steadily.

"Then I came down with rheumatic fever, and WASP dismissed me. I've been in Lake Geneva the past six months. I'm pretty much over the fever and working to build up my strength. Even though Dad asks me weekly to go flying with him in his plane, I haven't gone. I have no interest in flying at the moment."

In an instant his hand was back on top of hers, and she allowed him to weave their fingers together. "Oh, Grace, I'm so sorry. Here I am going on about my troubles, and you've had more than me."

"I don't think we can measure and compare."

"You're right."

"Are you two wanting dessert?" Lillian's voice interrupted.

The waitress had sneaked up without a sound and was staring at their clasped hands, her full lips turned down. Was there a law against holding hands with an old boyfriend? What was wrong with the woman?

"We'd like dessert to take with us." Rich let go of her hand. "Can you pack up a whole apple pie if you have one?"

The woman bobbed her head, her face void of any expression. "I think there's one in the kitchen. I'll add that to your check," she said evenly, then turned and left.

"What put her in a bad mood?"

"Seeing us holding hands. She probably thinks I lied to her about us."

"Holding your hand feels good." He reclaimed her hand and squeezed it. "Here she comes. Let's give her something to really get her going." He leaned in and kissed her on the mouth, letting his soft lips linger a moment. A shiver trailed down her neck, the same sensation she remembered from that prom night years ago.

"My darling Grace." He pulled back and smiled as he brushed a stray curl away from her face. "I have a feeling that's the first of many kisses to come."

Lillian slapped a white square box tied with string on the table. "The dinners and the pie are compliments of the house. The owner said because you're returning from the war, it's his way of saying thanks." She turned on her heel and marched away.

"That was nice of him." Rich reached in his back pocket and pulled out his billfold. "She probably thinks the owner's gesture caused her to lose a tip. Well, she's wrong." He pulled out several dollar bills and left them on the table. “Shall we get out of here, Earhart?”

The man’s presumptuousness was starting to annoy her. Part of her wanted to say, “What if I’m not ready to leave.” But she was ready. With her stomach still fluttering from the kiss, she nodded. If only they hadn’t made plans to have dessert with her parents. Between Lillian’s strange behavior and Rich’s acting like they were going to pick up on a teenage romance that had died a natural death years ago, she’d had better nights.

12

Grace crossed her arms and kept her gaze on the snow-packed road in the car's headlights. Only a few more minutes and they'd arrive at her street.

Halfway down Dodge Street, Rich slowed the car and pulled up to the curb. He cut the motor. "I'd leave the car running, but I don't want to burn gas. We'll be warm enough for a few minutes."

This she didn't plan on. "My parents are expecting us and—"

"I know, but you were going to tell me what happened in the restroom."

Her shoulders relaxed and she let go of the breath she was holding. "It was all a misunderstanding. I'm friends with Mac McAlister, the man you met when we were ice skating yesterday. He helps out at the bowling lanes on league nights and often comes by my team to watch us bowl. He's the one who has been helping me with my bowling techniques."

She was tempted to make their friendship sound like more than it was just to keep Rich at bay. But lying wasn't the way to handle it.

She continued. "Lillian must have seen Mac and me talking and wrongly assumed we were seeing each other. She thought I was two-timing Mac with you and scolded me good in the ladies' room. I set her straight that Mac and I are friends only, and that you and I have known each other since high school and are old friends."

"Just because Mac watches your team bowl, she thinks the two of you are a couple?"

"Well, we do talk often when I'm not taking my turn. That's all. We've never gone on a date." *Not that he hasn't tried.*

"So, after she found out I wasn't taken, she began flirting with me." Rich huffed a laugh. "Then I had to go and kiss you, and now she probably thinks you're a liar."

"That about sums it up."

He circled his arm around her waist and gently nudged her to his side. "You know, if I were staying in Lake Geneva and not heading for D.C., I wouldn't mind dating you again and becoming more than just an old boyfriend." He smoothed her hair away from the side of her face, the sweep of his fingertips causing a shiver to trail down her jaw.

The memory of stolen kisses on that long-ago prom night returned. By then she was sixteen and dreaming of a future with the bright young man who wanted to be a doctor someday, often visualizing herself as a doctor's wife like her granny.

"What do you say, Earhart?" He lowered his head and feathered her lips with a kiss. "It's not too late for us, is it?"

She squirmed away from him. No way was it ever going to be a right time. Not with the secret locked tight in her heart. "Rich, it's been years, and so much has gone on in both of our lives since those days at Lake Geneva High."

"If you aren't dating Mac, there must be someone else."

"There isn't."

"Maybe this can change your mind." His lips found hers, soft and tender at first, but as her resistance began to waver, she felt his lips begin to part. She pushed against his chest, and he sat back and chuckled. "You're as feisty as you were in high school. I thought hanging around all those military pilots would have loosened you up some."

"If that's what you were looking for tonight, you've got the wrong gal, Rich."

"And I respect that. I'm so sorry for presuming you were. I should have known better. Change of subject. "If you don't have plans for New Year's Eve, I want you to be my date. I'm invited to a party at the home of a buddy whose parents live on the lakeshore, and he said I should bring a date. What do you say?"

When she didn't say anything, he resituated himself in his seat and started the car. "You don't have to let me know right this minute. Your parents are waiting. Best we get moving."

As they drove, she mentally prayed for how to let the guy down easy about New Year's Eve. He was scaring her. A mass pushed at her throat, not unlike that time she became sick during the flight to New York. She swallowed against the lump, praying it would stay put until she was home.

He pulled up to the curb. "Can we use the side door, or should we walk around to the front?"

"The side is fine. It's the entry to Dad's home office, but I have a key." She paused a moment. "Rich, I'm sorry. "I'm suddenly feeling ill. You don't need to walk me to the door. I'll explain to my parents why you dropped me off."

Afraid if she waited for his response, she'd upchuck right there in his parents' car, she opened her door and ran across the street toward the side door. At the porch steps, she peered over her shoulder. He was already out of the car and running toward her. "At least take the pie," he shouted.

Bile pushed against her throat, and she scurried down the walk that led around to the back, hoping he wouldn't follow. Her right foot hit something hard, and she flew forward, landing face down on the cement.

Pain shot through her nose, and she cried out.

"Grace, let me help you up."

"I'm okay, Rich. Just go away." She pressed the palms of both hands into the snow on either side of the walkway and pushed. Her arms felt like wet noodles. "I can't ... Please, Rich, just go home."

"I'm not leaving until you're in the house. Do you think if I keep hold of your arms you can manage to get to your knees?"

"Yes. I think so." He gripped her upper right arm, his touch as gentle as his voice.

She leaned into his strength and sat up. Warm liquid drizzled into her mouth. Blood? She glanced down at where her face had just been. In the moonlight dark blotches splayed across the walk. "I'm bleeding."

"Grace, I'm letting go of your arm for a minute. Don't move." He stooped for a moment then held something up. "Is this what you tripped over?"

Even in the dark, the shape of what he held up was unmistakable. "I'm going to shoot my little brother. What in the world was he doing with a baseball bat in the middle of winter?"

"You'll have to ask him. I'm going to fashion a snow-pack out of my handkerchief to put on your nose." A few moments later he pressed a cold compress to her nose. "Lean forward and hold this in place with your left hand. Then if you can, with the other hand pinch your nose just above the nostrils. I'll get behind you and lift you to your feet."

She got into position. "It's hard to hold the snow pack and pinch my nose at the same time."

"Just do the best you can." His hands slid beneath her arms. "On the count of three, I'll lift you. One, two, three."

Suddenly, she was upright and he was at her right side, his arm around her waist.

"That's the girl. Before we begin to walk" —He pulled her clutch from his coat pocket—"I found this on the ground. Is your key to the door still in it?" She liked the doctor version of him better than the presumptuous one trying to score with her.

"Yes. But it would be easier to ring the bell and wait for one of my parents to come."

"Good idea. I'll slip the purse into your coat pocket. Get ready to walk."

They took a few steps. "How are you doing, Earhart?"

"I'm not ready to fly, if that's what you mean."

They arrived at the porch, and she was suddenly lifted into his arms.

"Carrying you is far easier than having you try to make it up the steps on your own." After they reached the top, he set her on her feet and gently moved her hand and the makeshift icepack off her nose.

He ran his fingertips around her nose and beneath it. "Still a little bleeding going on, but not as bad as earlier. Should I ring the bell?"

"Yes. Ring two short buzzes followed by a long one. That signals it's family and not a legal client."

"This time of night clients come calling?"

"If they're in trouble they sometimes do."

A few moments later the porch light went on, and the door swung open.

Mom gaped at Grace. "What in the world happened?"

"It's a long story, Mom. I fell on the sidewalk, and I think I broke my nose."

"Is anything else hurt? Can you walk?"

"Yes, with Rich's help I walked from where I fell. He carried me up the stairs."

Mom stepped back and held the door wider. "Go into the kitchen."

Grace leaned on Rich as she did before, and they started down the hall.

"Ted!" Mom shouted. "Come quickly. Grace is hurt."

In the kitchen, Mom helped her out of her coat and handed it to Rich, then ordered her to keep her head down and led her to the sink. She ran a clean towel under some cold water and used it to wipe the blood from Grace's face. Dad arrived, and Mom had him remove the pair of ice cube trays from the refrigerator and empty their contents into another clean cloth.

"I think the bleeding is nearly stopped. Slowly lift your head so I can see it better," Mom ordered.

Grace did as she was asked.

"You'll probably be black and blue by morning." Mom frowned as she studied Grace's nose.

Grace glanced at Rich and gasped. "Your shirt looks as bad as my coat."

"Not the first time I've had blood on my clothes." He shrugged. "I'm a doctor, remember."

The mass that started her racing from the car pushed against her throat, and she swallowed hard. "I'm going to throw up." She pulled her arm from Rich's grasp and started across the kitchen on wobbly legs.

"Where are you going?" He came up beside her.

"I'll lead the way." Mom scooted across the kitchen toward the small lavatory off the hall.

A moment later, Grace and Mom crowded into the powder room and shut the door. She bent over the commode and found relief.

A rap came at the door and Mom opened it.

"Here's a fresh icepack, Hannah," Dad said. "Should we call your father?"

"I don't think that's necessary. The bleeding has almost stopped, and there's nothing that can be done for a broken nose. Wait, Ted. On second thought, yes, give my parents a call. He may want to try to align the nose so it doesn't heal as crooked as it is now."

Dad's footsteps faded as he headed for the phone.

"Mom," Grace said, "Rich is a doctor, too, don't forget."

"I did forget." She stuck her head out the door and called out, "Don't call Pop. Let Rich look at her first."

"Too late. Nate is on his way." Dad came to the door. "I'm

going upstairs for a clean shirt for Rich. We've got his soaking in cold water."

Mom took hold of Grace's arm. "Let's get you upstairs and into clean clothes while your father takes care of Rich."

With her mother holding on to her, they reached the second floor as Dad was heading down, a clean shirt in his hand. "I could have helped her up here. Are you going to bed, Grace?"

"No, she's not," Mom replied. "Just getting her out of her bloody clothes."

"What's going on?" Lenny came from the direction of his room. "Are we having dessert soon?"

"If I have anything to say about it, you'll be getting no dessert tonight."

"Why are you mad at me, sis? What did I do?"

"Why didn't you put your baseball bat away when you were done with it? I tripped over it and smashed my face into the cement. My nose is broken, thanks to you."

His eyes rounded. "I'm sorry, Grace. I was using the bat to swing at snowballs Jimmy Schneider was pitching to me. I guess I forgot to put it away."

"Shame on you, Lenny." Mom's stern voice signaled what was coming next. "You've been told time and again never to leave your toys strewn around the yard. You're grounded for the week, and that means no skating or having friends over."

"But it's Christmas vacation. Me and my friends were planning on going to the movies tomorrow afternoon, and I'm supposed to go out to Jo's New Year's Eve for a hayride and bonfire with other kids from church. It's going —"

"You'll have to let them know you can't go. In fact, it would be a good idea if you got yourself ready for bed. You'll be having no dessert tonight."

His lower lip trembled as he turned toward his bedroom door. "I'm going, but I said I was sorry."

"Come on, Grace," her mother said. "Let's get you into some

clean clothes. We don't want to keep Rich waiting, after he's been such a good help to you."

After assisting her out of the stained dress, Mom sponge-washed her arms and around her neck and chest. She handed Grace a blouse and skirt, then sat on the edge of the bed while she changed. "Now, are you going to tell me why you were running around the house to the back yard?"

"I cancelled the evening because I felt sick. I'm grateful I got home without him taking advantage of me. He's the perfect gentleman now that he's in doctor mode. I'll tell you the rest later. When I felt I was going to throw up, I ran toward our door to get inside to the commode. I heard him coming after me. I had no idea what he intended to do and hoped he wouldn't follow. I ran to the backyard, thinking I'd get sick back there. But I tripped over Lenny's bat and after I fell I screamed."

"I'm confused now more than ever." Mom pressed her fingertips to both sides of her head and shook it. "Did Rich do this to you or not?"

"No. He got aggressive when we were talking in the car, but nothing I couldn't handle."

Grace explained how Lillian scolded her for two-timing Mac and then, once the waitress thought Rich was available, she began flirting with him.

"He presumed that being with military pilots and all I would be an easy mark. I've been asking myself if I sent any message at all that I was like that. I don't think I did. When I fell, the doctor part of him kicked in. He was at my side in seconds and has been gentle as can be with me. If I was going to hurt myself, at least I did it in the company of a doctor. He made that cold compress with snow and his handkerchief. I'm feeling stronger now. Shall we go back downstairs?"

They stepped into the kitchen and found Rich there, wearing Dad's shirt, which appeared a little tight over his broad shoulders. He caught Grace's eye and grinned. "I'm glad to see you looking better, but I suggest you keep an ice pack on your nose to keep down the swelling."

Dad entered through the back door carrying a pan of snow, and Rich grabbed a clean dishcloth from where it sat on the counter. He made a large snowball then wrapped the cloth around it and brought it to Grace.

"It's swollen up good already." He studied her nose and lightly touched it. "I doubt your grandfather will want to adjust it tonight."

The side entrance doorbell buzzed in the signal Grace had given Rich earlier, followed by Granddad's shout. "I'm here. Where's my patient?"

Grace eased into a chair at the table. "Sounds like we won't have to wait long for a second opinion."

"We're in the kitchen, Pop." Mom called out.

Holding the pie box by its string, Granddad appeared in the kitchen doorway, his usually clean-shaven face covered with gray whiskers. "Found this on the porch. Do you usually keep your desserts out there?" He set the box on the table, then shrugged out of his coat and handed it to Dad. "I got here as fast as I could. Mo opted to stay in our warm bed."

"I could have waited for you to remove your pajamas before you got dressed." Grace fought down a snicker at seeing his pajama top peeking out from beneath his wrinkled shirt.

"Hush, granddaughter." He brought a chair and sat facing her. "Let's take a look at your nose." He studied it and then asked for a knife.

"I hope you're not going to perform surgery here." Mom opened a drawer and handed him a table knife.

"No surgery necessary." He held the utensil up vertically, a small distance from her nose tip. "It's out of alignment, but it's already swollen too much for me to realign it correctly."

"It's nice to know the other doctor who examined me agrees." She looked over Granddad's shoulder at Rich.

"Two?" Granddad quirked a brow. "Who is the other one?"

"Turn around and meet Dr. Richard Garrett."

He pushed to his feet and faced Rich. "The same Richard Garrett who was sweet on my granddaughter when you two were teenagers?"

"One and the same, but I go by Rich now. I'm home on leave for the next week and report to Walter Reed Hospital January second. I was nearby when she fell, and I helped her to the porch."

Grandad scowled. "Not sure I fully understand. What caused you to fall?"

"Lenny left his baseball bat laying across the walkway," Grace said.

"That boy. Did you lose consciousness?" He studied her nose again.

"No."

"Have you taken anything for the pain yet?"

"I was about to give her a couple of aspirin," Mom said.

"Good. I suggest you leave a couple more by her bed with water in case she wakes up later and wants to take them." He glanced around at everyone. "I have no idea why that pie was sitting on the porch, but if you're not going to invite me to help eat some, I'll be on my way."

"We were bringing it here to have with Grace's parents, but our plans changed." Rich said. "I left it on the porch when I went to help her after she fell."

Granddad waved a hand at Rich. "It's getting too complicated for me."

"Of course you can have some pie, Pop." Mom lifted the box and carried it to the counter. "Ted, can you please light the burner under the percolator? We have it set up already. We were to have dessert together and tell Rich about our wedding at Walter Reed. Pop, you can add to the story from your perspective."

While the coffee pot gurgled, Mom and Grace got the pie sliced and onto dessert plates. Granddad vacated his chair and insisted Rich sit next to Grace while he moved to the other side of the table. She would have preferred being next to Granddad to Rich. But he didn't need to know all the details.

Grace had often heard the story about how Dad had been transferred to Walter Reed and had to have his leg amputated. He was very depressed, and Mom surprised him by showing up. She arranged with the hospital chaplain to marry them, and Granddad hopped a train, carrying Granny's wedding dress for Mom to wear. But she'd never heard the story told the way it was tonight, with everyone telling it from a unique perspective.

As the voices droned on, her head bobbed. Rich scooted his chair closer and rested his arm across her shoulders.

The scraping of chairs over the wood floor jarred her out of her half slumber, and she jumped. "Is everyone leaving already?"

They all laughed.

"We've been here an hour. We noticed you'd nodded off but decided it was better to let you sleep." Granddad worked his way into his coat. "We'll decide on what to do about realigning that nose tomorrow."

Grace stood and began gathering the dirty dessert plates.

Rich stepped up to her carrying his coat. "Is it okay to call you tomorrow to see how you're doing?"

"Sure. That's fine." There was much more she wanted to say, but not here, in front of the others. "I'll walk you out."

At the door, she looked up at him. "I think it's better to not see each other again before you head to D.C."

His eyes darkened. "Really? Yesterday you were so thrilled to see me and gave me a hug. Grace, you're a two-faced, cocky pilot just like the male ones. And after I doctored you and made nicey-nice with your family, you can't even spare time be my date for New Year's Eve?" He pulled the door open. "Have a nice life, Grace." He stepped through the door and yanked it shut hard enough that the doorframe rattled.

She leaned her back against the door and slid to the floor.

Mom and Dad were there in seconds. Mom hunched down

beside her and drew her into her embrace. "What did he do, Grace? Did he hurt you?"

"No. Just yelled a lot and slammed the door as hard as he could."

"Get out the way, Hannah. I'm going to give that insolent guy a piece of my mind. No one talks to my daughter that way." Dad tried to open the door, but Mom leaned against it.

"Ted, no. Let him go."

Outside, a car engine roared to life and tires squealed as they struggled to gain traction.

Dad peered out the side window. "He didn't drive like that when you were with him, did he?"

"No."

"I never liked him when you were so looney for him in high school. It wasn't the age difference, it was his cocky attitude."

Mom stood and helped Grace stand. "Let's get you to bed, honey."

In her room a short time later, Mom assisted Grace out of her clothes and into her nightgown. "You've really got a black and blue nose now. I have been thanking God over and over for protecting you."

"I know you have, Mom. Thank you."

Later, Grace crawled under her comforter and stared through the inky darkness at the ceiling. "God, thank you for Your keeping me safe. I didn't deserve it, but thank you."

13

Three Weeks Later

Grace picked up the telephone receiver and asked to be connected to Helen's beauty salon. She'd thought she would get through the day okay, but she was wrong. Through the wait, she mentally rehearsed her words. What she planned to say was not totally the truth, but she'd already been living a lie for weeks, so what was one more? It wasn't like she had many options. Lying meant saving face for herself and her family.

Helen's voice came through the connection. "Powder Puff Salon. How may I help you?"

"This is Grace. I tried to reach Peggy, but I can't find her. I'm sorry to give you short notice, but I'm not feeling well and won't be able to bowl tonight. I hope you can find a sub so late in the day."

"Oh no, Grace, I'm so sorry. I hope it's not something related to the rheumatic fever."

"It's not. I've had bad cramps all night and didn't sleep a wink." Her heart hurt at hearing the lie come from her mouth. But she couldn't tell Helen or anyone the truth.

"Oh, the good old time of the month. No worries. I have

Meg Wallace in my chair right now. I'll see if she can do it. The only problem is her husband, Jack, is serving with the army in D.C. She'll need a babysitter, and a lot of the league gals have already hired the town's supply."

"Maybe my sister, Reenie, can babysit. She owes me for at least a dozen favors. When she comes home for lunch, I'll ask her."

After Meg agreed to sub if Reenie could babysit, they said their goodbyes. Grace hung up the phone and went to the stairs. As she climbed, every step felt heavier than the last. The day would soon be over, and tomorrow would feel different. She wasn't the first woman to do what she did. She could only hope that next year wouldn't be so hard, nor the years following.

She slipped into her bedroom and crawled under the covers. She'd stay awake until she heard Reenie's voice downstairs, then after speaking to her, sleep the day away—the only way to escape the guilt and sadness.

She did sleep, but as evening fell, a knock came at the door and she pulled the covers over her head. A loud rapping came next. "Grace, are you okay?"

"I'm all right, Mom. Come in."

The door opened, and Mom stepped into the darkened room. "Have you been lying in the dark all day?"

"Just since the sun went down. I didn't feel like moving to turn on the light."

"When you told Reenie you wouldn't be down for supper, I couldn't help but be concerned. I didn't realize you're the one Meg Wallace is subbing for at bowling until Reenie just mentioned it. Your father drove her over to the Wallaces' a few minutes ago." She sat on the edge of the bed and pressed her hand to Grace's forehead. "No fever, and I've not heard you coughing. Your nose has healed nicely and the bruising is almost gone. In what way are you sick?"

She rolled over, facing away from her mother. "I can't talk about it."

"What's that supposed to mean? You've seemed down in the dumps the past couple of weeks. If it's because you miss flying, maybe you and your dad could go this weekend."

"I doubt that would help."

"Is it something that happened while you were in WASP?"

"I can't talk about it."

Mom stood. "All right, but if you change your mind, I'm here."

The door shut softly, and finally released from their prison, tears trailed down Grace's cheeks.

WITH A GLANCE toward the bowling alley entrance, Mac handed a bowler a pair of size sevens. Though she always arrived early to be sure to get a pair of the size eights, Grace was late tonight. He should come clean and admit to her that she needn't worry, because he always had a pair tucked aside just for her.

He hated to admit how much he looked forward to their chats on bowling night. Last week, the first time he'd been back to the bowling alley since Christmas, he'd asked her out for coffee after bowling and again she turned him down, this time with such decisiveness he decided he'd never ask again. He hadn't missed the way Grace had hugged that army doctor on Christmas Day when they were ice skating. Maybe that had something to do with her refusal.

What was his name? Richard something. She indicated they hadn't seen each other in years, but if they started dating that week, they could be practically engaged by now. The war had seemed to escalate a lot of relationships. Every week the *Regional News* had at least two or three wedding announcements, with the bride being a local girl and the groom about to be shipped out with the military.

"Hi, Mac. I hope there's a pair of size sixes left."

He snapped out of his thoughts and faced his next customer. "Hi, Mrs. Wallace. Subbing again tonight?"

The wife of the *Regional News's* owner nodded. "Yes, I'm taking Grace Bauer's place. She's a little under the weather tonight."

Though he'd never wish for Grace to be sick, his shoulders relaxed. It was a relief she wasn't with the army doctor.

UNABLE TO SLEEP ANYMORE, Grace flicked on the light and glanced at the clock. Two a.m. She leaned over and pulled an envelope of newspaper clippings from the nightstand drawer. Spreading them out over her comforter, she sorted through them, separating articles about WASP from the ones published in the Lake Geneva paper about her joining the program.

At the bottom of the collection she found what she was looking for—an article snipped from *Aero Digest*, an aviation magazine. She scanned the words she almost knew by heart. Some time ago, in 1934, a seasoned female pilot had been hired as a copilot by Central Airlines, only to be forced out of the job a year later by the all-male airline pilot union. No woman had since been hired as a pilot by any of the airlines.

The WASP pilots often discussed their postwar opportunities to pilot commercial aircraft. After they'd flown the big bombers, how could anyone think they weren't qualified? Well, for her the war was over, and there was no time like the present to start applying for a pilot's job. She may have been grounded from piloting bombers, but nothing was said about other aircraft.

She'd heard Reenie arrive home from babysitting about nine thirty. Did Mac miss her tonight? As time crept past, she'd visualized him smiling at each woman as she returned her shoes and he and Becky placed them back in their proper cubbyholes. What a nice man to help out like that, when he had no vested interest in the bowling alley. She stuffed the clippings back in the envelope and returned it to the drawer, then turned out the light and drifted off, imagining herself piloting a plane full of travelers.

The next morning Dad was at the breakfast table, the Lake Geneva paper open and folded to neatly rest next to his cereal bowl. He looked up and smiled. "There's my girl. Are you feeling better?"

Grace went to the stove and lifted the percolator from where it sat over a low flame. "Yes, but I may as well have stayed in bed. Here I am with another day stretched out before me and nothing to do." She sat to Dad's left and sipped her coffee, the one and only cup she'd have, thanks to rationing, and waited to be scolded for being so negative.

"I picked this up at the Civil Defense meeting last night. Maybe there's something suggested in here that you could do toward the war effort." He pushed a red-and-white booklet across the table.

Grace picked it up and read the title out loud. "What Can I Do? The Citizen's Handbook for War."

"It's broken down by skills acquired in peacetime that can be used in a volunteer position in the war effort."

Flipping the book over, she scanned the index of different occupations and where to find volunteer jobs for those skills. "Accountants, architects, lawyers, librarians. You and Mom are covered, but I don't see pilots on the list." She tossed the booklet on the table.

"Be creative. Think about it. You're organized and good with numbers, and you can make small repairs on aircraft." He picked up the booklet and opened it. His smile dissolved. "It says, 'Stay with your job where mechanics are needed.'"

"See? I don't fit."

He returned to the paper. "Hey, right here it says the Red Cross chapter down the street needs volunteers in the Home Service Department."

"What's that?"

"It says they assist families in locating their loved ones overseas when there's a family emergency. You're familiar with how the military works. It says to contact Mrs. James Senft, who heads up the department." He stood, laying the paper beside her plate. "I need to get to the office. Look at it for yourself. I'll see you tonight."

Grace picked up the paper and skimmed the article. The want ads for jobs were thin, and she wasn't qualified for those listed. On the few interviews she'd had, as soon as the interviewers saw she had an engineering degree, they'd said she was overqualified and not what they were looking for.

After her breakfast, she tore a sheet of paper off Mom's grocery list pad and jotted down the name of the woman at the Red Cross. Time to stop feeling sorry for herself and do something for others. It wouldn't be a paying job, but sometimes in doing volunteer work, the reward was in helping others.

14

Grace climbed the cement steps to the Red Cross chapter located in a small bungalow three blocks north of her home. Affixed to the wall beside the door, was a poster Grace hadn't seen before. It portrayed a soldier with the familiar Red Cross emblem next to him and stated, *Your Red Cross Is at His Side*.

It was all the encouragement she needed. That and the *Open* sign in the door's small window. She entered a room that must have been the living room when the building was a residence.

An older woman looked up from writing in a notebook and stuck her pencil in the graying bun on top of her head. "Hello, how may I help you?"

"I'm looking for Mrs. Senft."

"She's in a meeting at the moment, but it shouldn't be too long. Are you wanting to contact someone in the military?"

Yes, my brother, but that's for another time. "I heard volunteers were needed for the Home Service Department and wanted to offer my help."

A wide smile took over the woman's face. "Mrs. Senft will definitely want to speak with you." She opened a desk drawer and took out a paper. "In the meantime, all people volunteering have to fill out this application form. You can do that while you're waiting." She handed the paper to Grace. "You look vaguely familiar. Have we met before?"

"I don't think so. I bowl in a league on Thursday nights."

"I don't bowl." Tiny lines marred the skin between her eyes. "Let me think. Yes, that's where I saw you. In the *Regional News*. You're a pilot."

A warm feeling washed over Grace, and she hoped her grin wasn't too eager. "You have a good memory. That article was over a year ago."

"I remember because I clipped it out, as I do all articles about our local people serving in the war effort. My folder is quite thick by now. I'm sorry, but my memory isn't as sharp as you think. I don't remember your name."

"Grace Bauer. I'm back now from WASP and looking to help out here."

"Welcome home, Grace. My name is Alice Thornton." She held out her hand and Grace gave it a squeeze. "We're most appreciative of your service. I'm almost certain Mrs. Senft will want you on her team. You can sit over there and use the table to write on." She indicated a folding chair behind a small table.

Grace thanked Mrs. Thornton and crossed to the chair. The form appeared similar to a job application, asking for any past experience that might be of help to the organization. So far as she knew, the Red Cross didn't have a fleet of planes, but she put that down anyway, since her position did give her contacts at various air bases around the country.

Just as she completed the form, a tall woman with graying hair stepped into the room wearing a stylish, belted blue suit. The receptionist whispered to her.

The woman nodded and approached Grace, holding out her hand. "Grace Bauer? I'm Anne Senft. I understand you're interested in being a part of Home Service."

"Yes." Grace stood and shook her hand. "From what I've read about the service, it sounds like something I can do."

"Splendid. Let's go to my office and talk."

Grace followed her down a short hall to a room at the end and sat in the chair Mrs. Senft indicated in front of the desk.

The woman scanned the completed form and looked up. "One doesn't meet a female pilot every day. I knew your name sounded familiar. I remember reading a feature article about you in the *Regional News* when you first joined WASP."

That article again. Grace's cheeks heated.

Deep lines formed a V between Mrs. Senft's eyes. "Why is it you're back home and looking to volunteer at the Red Cross?"

"I came down with rheumatic fever, and that was the end of my WASP career. I feel fine now, but rules are rules."

Mrs. Senft gave her a sympathetic smile. "The military is full of rules, and I presume that holds true for WASP. Are you aware of what Home Service does?"

"I know you assist families of those serving in the war when their loved one needs to be contacted, but that's about all I know."

"Yes, it's that and more. We notify soldiers of deaths in their families, and if a home emergency requires their soldier to be granted a furlough to help out at home, we arrange for that." Her face lit up. "We even ordered flowers for a soldier's sweetheart last Valentine's Day. That's the most unusual request we've fulfilled so far."

"What a wonderful gesture. I didn't intend to bring this up during our interview, but my brother is stationed in the Pacific with the navy, and we've not heard from him in months. We're not sure what ship he's serving on, but some in my family fear he may have been on the *Houston*. His letters stopped coming shortly after the ship went down."

Mrs. Senft nodded.

"Trying to get answers out of the navy has been unsuccessful," Grace went on. "We just want to know if he was on the *Houston,* and if he died in the battle, or if he's one of the survivors in a Japanese POW camp. Is this something this service does?"

"I'm so sorry your family is in that sort of limbo." Mrs. Senft sighed. "It happens way too often. Yes, we do such searches, but unfortunately any information regarding Japanese POW camps is sketchy. We have contact with humanitarian aid workers in Japan and other Asian countries, and sometimes get information on POWs that way."

She pressed her lips together for a few moments then looked Grace in the eye. "Can you start tomorrow? I'll train you myself, and we'll try to locate information on your brother as part of your training. Does that agree with you?"

"Yes. Of course." Grace restrained herself from jumping out of her seat and hugging the woman. "Thank you so much, Mrs. Senft. And I do want to assist others in searching for their loved ones and getting messages to them."

A soft smile emerged on the woman's face. "I thought you'd say yes. Be here at nine tomorrow morning. We usually bring our lunches and eat in the room across the hall, or if it's nice, at a picnic table in the back yard." She turned and opened the drawer of a credenza behind her, gathered materials, and dropped them into a large envelope.

"Here's some light reading for tonight. Welcome aboard, Grace Bauer. And from now on, please call me Anne, except when we're in public, of course. Do you have any questions?"

"Not at the moment." Grace grinned and shook her head. "I'm very grateful, and I know my family will be."

Anne frowned. "Just keep in mind that not every story has a happy ending."

A sinking feeling fell over her, but she pushed out a smile. "I know. We just want to know the truth."

"That's the right attitude." Anne stood, and Grace did the same.

The telephone rang, and Grace indicated Anne should answer it. "I can find my way out. I'll see you in the morning."

Home was only a three-block walk down Madison Street. She was now able to walk at full speed but was tempted to run the whole way. Probably not a good idea.

When she reached the high school's side door, Reenie stepped out. Her eyes widened. "What are you doing here, Grace?"

"I was at the Red Cross office to sign up for volunteering, and I have some exciting news. But why are you leaving school in the middle of the afternoon?"

"I don't feel good. The assistant principal called Mom and told her they were sending me home. Do the monthly cramps get any better by the time I'm your age?"

"I'm not that much older than you." Grace laughed. "I still get them pretty bad. Mom told me that after she started having babies it was better."

"Well, that won't be for a while with me. Aren't you going to tell me your news?"

She linked arms with Reenie as they walked. "I'm going to help families get in touch with their loved ones in the service when there's an emergency. I told Mrs. Senft, the woman I'll report to, about Rory. She's going to train me how to search for information on military members starting tomorrow, and I can search for our brother for my first case."

"Oh, Grace. That's wonderful. I'm scared he's been killed on that ship, and the navy hasn't let us know yet."

A wave of sadness came over Grace. What if they couldn't find him? "I know. Me too. I'm going to think positive thoughts that we'll find him alive. Maybe he's living with an island couple somewhere, like Dad did in Belgium during his war."

They walked in silence past the school yard and the rest of the way home. Before they stepped inside, Grace faced her sister. "I can loan you my electric heating pad. Take a couple of aspirin, then lie down and place the heating pad on your tummy, and you'll probably drop off to sleep."

"Thanks, sis. I'm glad you're my sister, even if I give you a hard time once in a while."

"Only once in a while?" Grace chuckled. "I'm glad we're sisters too."

After Reenie left her bedroom, heating pad in hand, Grace propped herself up on several pillows against her headboard and began reading the pamphlets Anne had given her.

"Grace, wake up." At Mom's voice, Grace opened her eyes. She sat up and glanced around the room.

"Mom, where's Rory?"

"Somewhere in the Pacific. Not here."

Grace gave herself a mental shake and fell back on her pillows. "I was dreaming Rory came home from the war and was here in my room talking to me." She began gathering up the pamphlets. "I must have nodded off."

"Why are you reading these?" Mom picked up one of the leaflets.

"I'm to start volunteering tomorrow at the Red Cross to help with Home Service. They locate military members for their families when there's an emergency the soldier needs to know about. I told Anne Senft, the chairman of Home Service, about Rory, and she's going to train me by helping me look for him."

"Oh, Grace, that's wonderful." Mom pulled her into a hug. "If anyone can find him, Anne can."

Her smile dissolved and her expression turned serious. "I haven't said anything about you not joining us for church on Sunday since you've been home. I didn't expect you to at first, when you were so ill, but now that you're bowling and volunteering at the Red Cross, I strongly suggest you join us next Sunday. You're starting to take the focus off yourself. Make sure you put it first where it belongs—on God. You don't have to respond, just think and pray about it."

Despite Mom's comments, which had kept her awake until the wee hours, Grace was up the next morning at six and decided to walk before getting ready to report to the Red Cross. Soon after she crossed Main Street to the park and turned east, light snow began to fall, the kind of soft snow she loved to walk in. She tipped her head back and let the flakes fall onto her tongue.

Mom was right. She'd thought by staying home from church and only pretending to read her Bible every day she'd be able to live without God in her life, but it had only made her feel worse. What puzzled her was, in spite of what she'd done, good things were happening in her life. The prospect of finding Rory through her new volunteer work had lifted her spirits. The cause of her deep-seated pain hadn't gone away, but at least she had purpose again.

At the back of the library, she paused to look out at the frozen lake, surprised to see a familiar figure on the ice. She'd had no idea Mac was such a good skater.

"Mac!" In the early morning snowfall, her voice didn't seem to carry far. She walked to the fence and called again.

He halted and looked in her direction, then waved and glided over the ice to the shoreline. "Good morning. What brings you out so early in the cold?"

"I start volunteering at the Red Cross today and thought, since I'll be doing a lot of sitting, I should follow doctor's orders and get my exercise now. Do you come here to skate often?"

"No. Actually, this is the first time I've come since Christmas Day. I couldn't sleep for thinking about Jo and how she hates skating now. The only time she's enjoyed it since her mom died was when she and Lenny skated together on Christmas and she forgot about her memories. I love this place, Grace, during all the seasons, and I really don't want to move south. But what else can I do?"

"Maybe get her help to face her fear. I don't see how removing what is causing her fear will help. What if she finds herself on a frozen lake years from now, and the fear comes back?"

"I hadn't thought about that. I wish there was a professional I could speak with."

"My granddad might be able to help. He works a lot with soldiers who've experienced warfare and shell shock. It doesn't always have to be a war experience. If you want me to, I can ask him about it."

"You mentioned that before." His face brightened. "Yes, please ask him. I hate to pull her away from the only home she's known and her friends. And that goes for me as well."

"I'll let you know Thursday at bowling, if you'll be there."

He answered with a grin. "I'm planning on it. See you then." He skated in a circle then drew his arms in and spun like a top.

The spin ended, and she shouted out to him. "You're a good skater. Where did you learn those moves?"

"From my wife. Emily could have gone to the Olympics if we hadn't met and married."

"You can't be married and be in the Olympics?"

"Of course, but the timing was never right, thanks to Jo. She was born in 1931, and Em wasn't skating the whole time she was pregnant. There wasn't time to get in shape for the '32 games in Lake Placid. She tried out but didn't make the team. She said having Jo was far more important than a medal, but I know she was disappointed. When the 1936 games in Germany came around, she was pregnant again."

Mac stepped off the ice and tromped through the snow to the fence. "She lost our son when she was almost six months along. The doctor didn't know why, but he died in utero. They had to force a miscarriage to deliver him." His eyes watered, and he blinked. "Sorry, the emotion is still a bit raw. Then two years later, she drowned over there." He pointed down the beach toward the Riviera.

"Oh, Mac, I'm so sorry." She gulped, wishing she could jump over the fence and hug him.

"Thanks. I'm really fine. I know both of them are in heaven, and Jo and I are doing okay, too. Except for her fear of the ice."

Grace glanced at her watch. "I'd like to talk a bit longer, but I've got to get ready for volunteering. I don't want to be late the first day."

"And I need to head home to get ready for another day of teaching." He turned and waved his gloved hand. "Have a great day."

"You too." Grace headed for home. It was the first time Mac had mentioned his wife by name. Somehow, that and hearing how they lost their baby before he was born made his losses more real. They both needed some joy in their lives. Time was a great healer, and no doubt it helped Mac. That and his faith. She doubted she'd ever have enough time to heal, but attending church again might help.

15

The following Sunday, Grace stepped into Faith Community Church. Having opted to attend the early service rather than the later one with her family, she'd hoped to avoid seeing anyone she knew. At least, anyone she knew well.

Surprised at the number of people already in the back pews, where she wanted to sit to be able to easily slip out, she scanned the sanctuary, hoping at least for an end seat.

"Hi, Miss Grace. Do you want to sit with my dad and me?"

Startled, she looked down at Jo's smiling face. Of course they'd be at the early service. Mac was an early riser. She looked in the direction Jo was pointing. Mac waved, and she waved back. Did he know what a magnet that heart-stopping smile of his was?

"Yes. That would be nice," she whispered and let the girl lead her down the aisle.

Mac stood next to his place at the end of the row. She'd always thought him handsome wearing casual clothes, but now, seeing him in a suit and tie discombobulated her even more than she already was.

"This is a nice surprise. I don't think I've seen you at this service before." He let Jo slide in past him, then stepped in next to her and indicated the empty space between him and the end of the pew. At least Grace got the aisle seat she wanted.

"I don't usually come to the early service," she whispered as she sat, fully aware of his arm brushing against hers. "With me here it's a bit tight," she whispered. "I see an empty spot across the way, perhaps—"

"We're fine." He handed her a bulletin. "I see you didn't get one. I can share Jo's."

She smiled her thanks and glanced up at the hymn board on the wall behind the organ. *Wonderful. "Great Is Thy Faithfulness" wouldn't have been my first choice for the opening hymn.* She wanted to believe God was faithful to her, but if He were, maybe she wouldn't have gotten into the pickle that had changed her life forever.

A lady who looked familiar smiled and waved at her. Probably a friend of Mom's. Grace had attended this church growing up and used to love coming to the worship service, but that was back when she was in good standing with the Lord. Now she felt like an interloper.

She unbuttoned her wool coat and tried to ease her arms out of its sleeves.

"Let me help you." Mac reached behind her and held the coat still until her arms were free, then let it drop over her shoulders. "Is that okay? If you prefer, I can take it to the foyer and hang it up out there."

"I'm okay, thank you." The man was nice, too nice for the likes of her.

The music leader motioned for everyone to stand, and the organist played the melody for the first hymn. Everyone began singing. Next to her, Mac's tenor voice, as good as any soloist she'd heard, surprised her. She sang too, but kept her voice low, trying not to focus on the words because when she did, she wanted to cry.

When Pastor Larsen began his sermon, Mac took a small notebook and pencil from his suitcoat's inside pocket and opened his Bible to the scripture posted next to the hymn board. In the past, she always carried her Bible to church too, but today it stayed home, still tucked in her nightstand drawer.

Despite her efforts to pay attention to the sermon, Pastor Larsen may as well have been speaking Chinese. She gave up trying and read Mac's scribbled notes as he wrote. Finally, the sermon ended and everyone stood for the closing hymn.

Outside, Mac stopped walking and faced her. "Jo and I usually go to my parents' for what my mom likes to call brunch. A new term for me, but she read about it in a magazine. It's like having lunch and breakfast at the same time. But they're in Milwaukee today, visiting my aunt and uncle." He tugged Jo under his arm. "We're going to find a restaurant here in town. I'm not sure if they'll be serving breakfast, lunch or brunch, but would you like to join us?"

A visual of the three of them sitting in a booth and eating together flowed into her mind. A stranger would probably think they were a family. The kind of family she'd always presumed she'd have someday.

"That sounds like fun, but I need to get back home. My grandparents are coming later for Sunday dinner, and I promised to help Mom."

Not a total fib. Granny and Granddad were coming over for dinner, as they did every Sunday, and she almost always helped Mom in the kitchen. But it all happened without it being said out loud.

His smile dissolved. "It was a spur of the moment idea. Maybe next Sunday, if you come to first service you can join us at the farm for Mom's brunch."

"That sounds nice. I'll let you know." She managed a smile. "Have a great day, you two." She turned to walk home.

"Would you like a ride?"

Turning on her heel, she faced him. "Thanks, but it's a beautiful day. I'm going to walk and enjoy this January thaw. Can you believe it's going to be close to forty degrees today?"

He waved her on. "Enjoy. I saw in the paper we're to be in the deep freeze again day after tomorrow."

16

Three weeks later

The middle-aged woman sitting across from Grace offered a tight smile. “Thank you so much, Miss Bauer. You’re an angel.”

Grace held up a hand, palm out. “I’m just the go-between, Mrs. Nolan. It was the personnel at Hickam Field in Hawaii who located Marv for us.”

“Yes, but you began the search. I didn’t expect him to be able to come home for his grandfather’s funeral, but he needed to know about it.”

“Yes, he did, and I’m so glad I was able to help you. I’ll walk you out, unless you have any questions.” Grace stood.

“Not at the moment.” Mrs. Nolan rose and came closer to Grace. “I’m sure you have other men to search for, so I won’t take up any more of your time. But I must give you this first.” Her plump arms wrapped around Grace.

The woman pressed her head against Grace’s chest, her curls tickling her nose. Grace’s arms instinctively embraced her. She used the moment to supress the moisture in her eyes then gently eased the woman out of her arms.

They walked together to the reception room where Grace turned her over to Alice, then quietly returned to her office while Mrs. Nolan blubbered on about how wonderful Grace was. If the woman knew the real Grace, she'd not think she was so wonderful.

Back at her desk in her tiny office that had likely been the home's storage room at one time, she opened Rory's file. Nothing new had come up from Anne's tried and true contacts —all humanitarian aid workers in Asian countries.

Several of the contacts had been able to enter Japanese POW camps in recent weeks and reported not coming in contact with anyone named Rory Bauer. One had said that the given name Rory wasn't a common male name in the U.S., and he would have remembered if he'd met someone with that name.

She leaned her folded arms on her desktop and rested her forehead on top of them. "God, all we want to know is Rory's whereabouts." As long as her prayers weren't for her benefit only, surely for the others' sakes, He'd answer.

"Grace, we heard something."

She snapped her head up and stared at the envelope Anne held out.

"It's from a humanitarian aid worker in Burma. Not firm information, but it's a start."

"Burma? Where that railroad POW camp is?" Grace took the paper-thin envelope that, when unfolded, also served as stationery. Her eyes scanned the tiny writing then handed it back to Anne. "Read it to me, please. I can't make out the writing."

"It was difficult for me too, but the important paragraph is the middle one. It says, 'I think the man you are looking for is part of the U.S. Navy group that survived the *Houston's* sinking. I do not want to say for sure it is him until I return there. I plan to attempt another visit next week. I never know from one visit to the next if they will allow me in. It is known that they do not run their POW camps according to the Geneva Accord. I will be in touch as soon as I have more information.'"

Grace's eyes watered. She took the letter back and slipped it into Rory's file. "A glimmer of hope. Although I don't know what to hope for—him alive and being tortured in a POW camp, or happy with the Lord in heaven."

"I think knowing for sure is the answer." Anne let out a sigh. "It's the not knowing that is so difficult."

"You're right. Should I keep this news to myself or tell my parents? I hate to get their hopes up for nothing."

"Your father was MIA in the first war, and that had a happy ending. He's a veteran himself. I'm sure he'd want to know the status of his son."

"I wish there was a way to take a photo of the letter, but since we don't have that, can you please dictate to me what you just read, and I'll write down the words so I get them right."

IN HIS FAVORITE chair later that evening, Dad faced Grace, who sat on the sofa next to Mom. "Okay, Reenie is home from debate team practice. You've kept us in suspense long enough."

Grace waited for Reenie to sit on her left, then pulled a paper out of her pocket and unfolded it. "We heard from someone who thinks he knows where Rory is."

"Is?" Mom gripped Grace's arm. "Meaning there's a chance he's alive?"

"Yes, but I must warn you that reports say the Burmese POW camps where the railroad workers are assigned are brutal. Much worse than even the Japanese ones." She swiped at the tears filling her eyes. "I can't help but wonder if it would've been better if he'd died in the battle and not been able to swim to shore, if it's true he survived."

"Sounds like it's a bad thing he grew up near Geneva Lake

and learned to swim so well," Lenny piped up from where he sat cross-legged on the floor.

"Lenny, mind your words," Reenie scolded. She elbowed Grace. "Go on, sis. Read us whatever is on that paper."

Grace nodded and read the paragraph aloud, then looked up. "It will probably be at least a month or two before we hear from this person again."

"Reminds me of those days you were missing in action and we had no word of your status or whereabouts." Mom stood and crossed to sit on Dad's chair arm, then draped her arm across his shoulders. "The silence was excruciating. And then being told you were killed in action was heart-breaking. Of course, that was wrong, but we didn't know the truth until you wired me from England."

"I wanted so bad to let you know I was alive and knew the family was thinking the worst." He grasped her hand. "It sounds like our Rory might be in a POW camp that is far worse than what I went through. God, have mercy. I hope when the Lord takes me to heaven, I'll see the people there who helped me, and I can thank them for their bravery and care."

Lenny rose to his knees. "Tell us again how you got shot down, Dad."

"Not now, son. We need to concentrate on Rory. Shall we pray for him?"

Everyone agreed, and Dad bowed his head. "Heavenly Father, we are grateful for the news the aide in Burma shared. At least we have hope that our Rory survived the battle. We know he's likely being horribly mistreated and pray You give him strength to persevere."

17

Grace stepped into the bowling alley and scanned the room, already full of chatting and laughing women, some sipping on drinks and others taking practice shots. She approached the shoe counter and waited while Becky took care of someone.

An arm reached around her from behind, gripping a pair of bowling shoes. "Looking for these?"

She laughed and faced Mac. "Are those for me, by chance?"

"Yes, ma'am." He handed her the shoes. "How have you been? I wasn't here last week because Jo came down with chicken pox and I had to keep her home. Can you believe my dad has never had chicken pox? He said when my brothers and I came down with it, he stayed clear of us."

"Lenny mentioned some of his classmates were out with it, and I wondered if Jo was one of them. Lenny had it as a baby, when my sister brought it home from school. If your father catches chicken pox now, it would be much worse on him than it is on a child."

"Let's hope he doesn't catch it."

"I have some good news," Grace said, drawing him a few steps from the counter. "First, I'm loving my work at the Red

Cross, and second, Anne Senft received some news about my brother through a worker in Burma. No direct sighting of Rory, but a sliver of hope. How are you doing?"

"That's wonderful about your brother. I'll keep praying for him." He shrugged. "As for me, no complaints. I haven't yet turned in my notice to the school board. I'm having second thoughts about moving. It's not really fair to my parents to leave now, what with my brothers both serving in the war. I've been thinking about what you said about your grandfather being able to help Jo. Can we talk about it later, over coffee and dessert?"

"That sounds good. The café upstairs?"

"I'll come by your lane after your last frame. I may be already there watching you bowl." He winked and walked away.

She chuckled as she made her way to her team's assigned lane at the end of the row. How things had changed the past several weeks. Mac was becoming a good friend, and she loved how they could banter back and forth without fear of giving the impression she was romantically interested. She arrived at her team's bench and sat to put on her shoes.

Helen returned from taking a practice shot and sat next to her. "How are things?"

"Good. We received a spark of hope this week from an aid worker in Burma that Rory might be in a POW camp there, where some men from the *Houston* supposedly are imprisoned."

"So, you know for sure Rory was on the *Houston*?"

"Yes, I was able to have that confirmed through Red Cross channels."

"Sounds to me like it was serendipitous you started volunteering at the Red Cross."

"Even if I hadn't, we could have requested the Red Cross find that out." Grace tied her left shoe. "It's wonderful how many people the organization has assisted in that way, not to mention other means of support to the military and their families. I wish they could help me look into the history of the Safe Refuge property during the past few decades, but that's not an area they assist in. That will be more difficult than finding Rory, I fear."

"Don't be so involved you don't have time for a social life." Helen nudged her with her shoulder. "You know that old saying, all work and no play makes—"

"I know. Makes Jack a dull boy. Don't worry about me. I'm keeping busy, and that's the main thing."

Later, as she rolled her last shot down the alley for a spare that pushed her team higher in the current standings, she turned to see Mac standing behind the bench, giving her a thumbs up. She returned the gesture and walked over to him. "Are we still on for coffee?"

"That's why I'm here. If you give me the shoes, I can return them for you and then meet you upstairs at the coffee shop."

"It's a deal." She slipped off her shoes and handed them to him, then pulled her loafers from her bag before sitting.

Helen sat beside her. "I couldn't help but overhear. Sounds like your social life is picking up with a coffee date."

"Why do people always read romance into everything? It's only two good friends catching up over coffee. We've not talked for days."

"Uh-huh." Helen giggled and stood. "If that's what you want to call it, fine with me." She sashayed over to the ball return then called out, "Do you want me to bring your ball over too?"

"Sure. Thanks."

After Helen brought her ball to her, Grace stuffed it into her bag and made her way through the thinning crowd to the stairway leading to the Hotel Clair's first floor. At the top of the stairs, she emerged into the hotel's lounge then turned left and stepped through a door into the Tick Tock Grill.

Several people occupied stools at a long counter on the eatery's right side, but no Mac. She caught sight of him standing next to one of the small tables that lined the wall across from the counter and waved.

At the table, she set her bowling bag on the floor and they

settled in their chairs. "You know by meeting you, I've missed my ride home," she said. "You'll have to drive me."

A mock look of surprise crossed his face. "You need a ride to walk only a couple of blocks?"

"Oh, hush. It's dark out."

He laughed. "A bomber pilot, and you're afraid of the dark."

"When you have a mother who worries about you ..." She waved away the rest of the sentence. "What would you know? You only had brothers and have no idea what mothers of girls worry about."

"I think I know. My mom worries about Jo a lot more than she did about me and my brothers. I was only teasing."

"I know." She smiled and glanced over at the menu board on the wall behind the counter. "I'm hungry for pie, but they don't list which kinds they have."

A waitress approached, pad and pencil in hand, her brown hair in a bun at the back of her head. She looked from Grace to Mac. "Good evening, Mac. Haven't seen you here for a while. How've ya been?"

"Doing well, Flo. I've been busy, eating at home most days." He glanced at Grace. "Have you met Grace Bauer?"

She focused on Grace. "Hi there. Are you related to Mrs. Bauer at the library?"

"I think my mom is the most famous member of my family." Grace laughed. "I get that question a lot."

"Grace should be as famous, Flo. She used to fly—"

"Stop, Mac. She doesn't want to hear about that." Grace's cheeks heated.

"Hear about what?" Flo turned her head. "Oh shucks, my customer at another table is waving at me. You two better tell me what you'd like."

"Two coffees," Mac said, "and what kind of pie do you have?"

"We have cherry, and I think there's a slice of apple left."

"I'll have cherry," Grace said.

"We'll make it easy for you, Mac said. "Make that two cherries."

"Coming right up." Flo scribbled on her note pad. "Two cherry pies and two coffees." She scooted off to a table several spots down.

Mac picked up a saltshaker and studied it, then set it back on the table. "Why don't you want to talk about being a bomber pilot?"

"It feels like I'm boasting." She shrugged. "I don't deserve all that attention."

"I don't know why." He tilted his head and frowned. "You performed an essential and challenging service to our country."

"Here you go, folks." Flo scooted up carrying a tray and set two slices of cherry pie on white plates in front of them. "I'll be right back with the coffee, if there's any left. Boss said the last pot made would be all for tonight. I'll be very glad when this rationing business is over."

Thankful for the interruption, Grace hoped Mac didn't attempt to restart the topic. "If she only has enough coffee for one cup, you take it. I'd probably pay for drinking it so late at night. Doesn't the caffeine bother you that way?"

He shook his head. "I drink a cup of coffee every night while listening to the radio and go right to sleep shortly after that. Do you want something else if there isn't enough coffee for both of us?"

"Water is all I need."

"Have you done anything more about looking into getting your family's estate back?"

She forked a bite of pie and brought it to her mouth. The sweetness of the syrup and tartness of the cherries mingled on her tongue a moment before she swallowed. "Delicious."

He took a bite of his own pie and she waited for his reaction.

"You're right. We need to try growing some cherry trees on the farm. My mom makes a great apple pie and wins awards every year at the county fair. You were about to tell me what you've done with the Safe Refuge project."

She took another bite of pie. "I haven't done much. I'm not at all sure where to turn next. It's very daunting. I need to do a title search on the property. Dad says those records for Walworth County are kept at the courthouse in Elkhorn. I can fly a B-17, but doing something like that sounds overwhelming."

Their waitress approached with two empty cups and a pot of coffee. "Success, we have enough left for two cups' worth if I don't fill them to the brim."

After Flo left, Mac sipped his coffee and set the cup on the table. "Would it help if I assisted you in your research?"

"You don't have time for something that doesn't concern you." She stared at him.

"If it concerns you, then it concerns me."

She quirked her head, and warning bells sounded in the back of her mind. "What do you mean by that?"

"Friends need friends. There is a verse in Ecclesiastes that says two are better than one. When one falls, the other is there to help him up. It sounds like you've taken a stumble."

"Ecclesiastes? I'll have to look that up." He did say friends, not girlfriends. "Yes, I'll accept your help."

18

Grace stared out at the barren landscape through the truck's passenger window. It had been over two weeks since Mac offered to help her with the title search, but it had taken that long before he could arrange to take an afternoon off from teaching.

"I hope this title search will give you some answers," Mac said.

Grace heaved a sigh. "I hope so too. If it doesn't, I have no idea where to look next. I feel bad you took a half day off from teaching to do this."

"I had the time coming, and if I don't use it, I'll lose it."

"There's a lot of days left before the end of the school year. What if you get sick, or Jo does, or other unexpected things happen?"

"I'm only taking half a day. I'll be fine. And why the defeatist attitude? As I tell my students before a test, don't go into it thinking you're going to fail, or you just might."

A few minutes after passing a sign announcing they were entering Elkhorn, Mac parked in an angled parking slot across from a two-story brick building that sat back from the road. The cupola on the roof indicated the imposing structure had been built before the turn of the century.

Grace gazed at the structure. “This is the courthouse? In all the years my dad has gone to court here, I’ve never seen it for myself. It looks like it’s been here since the dawn of time.”

“Not quite. I read it was built in 1875.”

“I hope it has indoor plumbing.”

He threw back his head and laughed. “I doubt it did when it was built, but I imagine they’ve installed it since then. Actually, we’re headed to the building next door, the Registrar of Deeds. Shall we go?” He opened his door and jumped to the ground.

Grace reached for the door handle, and it swung out of reach. She paused and stared at Mac’s outstretched hand.

“Don’t you want assistance getting down from your elevated position? That’s a pretty high seat you’re sitting on.”

“You’re forgetting I’m used to climbing in and out of a B-17. This is nothing.”

The sparkle disappeared from his eyes. “I suppose it’s rather silly, but humor me and take my hand anyway.”

She’d hurt his feelings. Why couldn’t she just go along with his polite gestures? She placed her palm on top of his, and he closed his fingers around her hand, causing a tingling sensation. Ignoring it, she jumped to the ground, and he held his grip a few moments before he released his hold.

Annoyed at herself for missing the feel of her hand tucked inside of his, she put a few more inches between them. As much as Grace liked his touch, holding hands was the next step to an official dating relationship, and that could never happen.

They began walking toward the Registrar of Deeds building. The companionable silence they often shared must have remained in Lake Geneva, because right then the air was thick with a silence that begged to be broken. But she had no words.

“Does the cat have your tongue?”

“Mac, I was wrong for giving you a difficult time about helping me out of the truck. I know you—”

"And I'm sorry for treating you like a china doll. Funny, I admire your strength and courage to pilot those bombers, and yet I tend to be surprised when those traits show up in other ways. I've seen it in your hard work to overcome the effects of your illness and more recently your broken nose. How is Lenny doing with collecting his toys from the yard these days?"

"I haven't paid any attention, but then I haven't gone back there in the dark since then. Back to what you were saying, There are a lot of women like me, Mac. Not only in WASP, but those working as army nurses on the front lines. They have way more courage than me. I could never do that."

"Sure you could, if that's what God called you to do. He doesn't call us to anything that He won't provide the means to accomplish. Here we are at the steps. Shall we sit and talk a few more minutes before we go inside?"

She eyed the uneven concrete steps. "I'd prefer not. This skirt is fairly new, and I'd like to keep it looking that way."

Mac softly chuckled.

"What's so funny?"

"In that regard, you are like most other women. And I like that. Let's go inside."

The middle-aged woman at the receptionist desk reminded her a little of Mom. She smiled as they approached. "Hello. How may I help you?"

Grace opened her mouth, but the words she'd planned didn't come out. She leaned in Mac's direction. "Can you explain what we're looking for?"

His eyebrows rose as he whispered, "Sure thing." He cleared his throat. "We want to do a title search for a property on the Geneva Lake shoreline. It's within the boundaries of the town of Lake Geneva, very close to the Linn Township boundary." He took the paper Grace had fished out of her purse and continued. "Here is the address of the property and a couple other details that would help you."

The receptionist studied the note a moment. "I'll be right

back." She stood and used a key to open a door behind her. She stepped through, and the door shut with a decisive click.

Grace rocked on her heels and studied the floor. What if this search uncovered something worse than losing the property? Something that would affect the family in a bad way? "I'm really nervous all of a sudden. Maybe we should tell her we changed our minds and leave."

"Where did that idea come from?"

"I'm not sure, but I'm feeling uneasy."

"Whatever we find, you'll be fine." He touched her shoulder and gave it a quick squeeze.

The door opened, and a man with white fringe around his bald head emerged carrying a large rectangular book. The receptionist followed behind him. He looked from Mac to Grace. "I'm Gerald Wolff, the manager. If you come with me, I'll show you where you can sit and go through these documents."

The alcove he led them to held a large wooden table. Mr. Wolff pulled out two of the six straight-backed chairs surrounding it. "Take your time. When you're finished, return the file to Mavis, over there at the desk." He started to turn away, then stopped. His forehead creased as he looked from Grace to Mac. "I'm just curious. Are you family to the original owners of the property?"

Grace nodded. "My great-great-grandfather built the house after the Great Chicago Fire. Is there a reason you're asking?"

"Nothing more than curiosity. I've always been fascinated by the lovely homes on the lake and their unique histories. I hope you find what you're looking for." He turned and walked away.

They sat, and Grace opened the book and looked at the first several documents.

"It appears the most recent is on top." She went to the back of the binder and began leafing through the documents, careful to not be too rough with the older papers.

A form bearing the name Leonard Hartwell on the first line

caught her off guard, and she gasped. Eyes watering, she rummaged in her purse for a handkerchief and blew her nose.

"Hey, why the tears?" Mac rested his hand on her arm.

"I don't know why I'm surprised to see my ancestor's name on a form, but I am." She pointed to the form. "This is a quitclaim my great-great-grandfather made to transfer Safe Refuge to my great-grandfather, Rory Quinn, whom my brother is named for. We've not heard anything more from the humanitarian worker. I'm afraid our Rory is ... gone." She sighed. "I can't even say the word 'dead' and his name in the same sentence."

"I think we should do this research another day," he whispered.

"No." She straightened and blew her nose. "I know I was ready to leave before, but I'm fine now. I wonder why Leonard Hartwell felt he needed to transfer the ownership of the property to Rory Quinn, his son-in-law. Wouldn't his daughter, Anna Quinn, be his heir?"

Mac gripped his chin between his thumb and index finger and frowned. "If he made Rory the property's owner, then that would take the property off the list of his belongings to be willed. Do you know of any bad seeds connected to him that would make him not want to have control of the estate?"

"I don't know much about him. I've mostly heard about Rory and Anna. I'll have to ask my mother what she knows."

"We may want to find out if the property was ever put into a trust. If it was, they would have avoided probate when it was passed down to the next generation."

"I'm not familiar with trusts. How do you know so much?"

"My parents and I have talked about putting the farm properties in a trust. We were going to do it before my brothers were drafted, but we never did."

They jotted down the information on the form, then sifted through the other documents.

"Wait." Nearing the end of the binder, Mac pointed to a note bound with the document beneath it. "This is interesting. It's another quitclaim transferring Rose Harbor to a Charles Atwater. The note with it says that Atwater won it from Andrew W. White in a poker game. If there was a trust, that would have nullified it."

Grace's jaw dropped.

"I've heard of property being wagered in card games." He chuckled. "But mostly with stories from the Wild West, not on Geneva Lake."

"Is that legal?" Grace leaned closer to read the note. Was this the loophole she was looking for?

"It would appear so. Why don't you ask your dad? He's the attorney in your family."

Grace leaned back and rubbed her eyes. "I will, but I must have missed the transfer papers from when Safe Refuge was sold by my grandfather after the crash."

Flipping through the documents, she found the ones from 1929, and began turning the pages one at a time. "There are a lot from the fall of 1929. No surprise there." She worked forward into 1930 and found what she was looking for. "Here it is. It all looks in order. The property was purchased by an Andrew W. White of Chicago. And there's Granddad's signature next to Mr. White's. She dictated the information while Mac jotted it down.

He finished writing, and she rubbed her eyes. "I'm getting a headache from trying to read all that fancy handwriting. I'm ready to go."

"It's a beautiful afternoon." Mac stood and stretched. "Why don't we get ice cream in town and eat it by the lake?"

19

Mac waited while Bob, the son of the owners of Frediani's Confectionary, placed a scoop of strawberry ice cream on a cone for Grace. His gaze went to a display case of chocolates, not as plentiful as before the war, but any of Mrs. Frediani's hand-dipped chocolates were loved by almost everyone in town. "Hey, Bob, when you're done with our order, can you put a half dozen chocolate creams in a bag?"

After handing Grace her cone, Bob stepped over to the case. "The chocolate creams are gone but there's some vanilla in the back you can have."

"Vanilla is fine. My mom will eat anything from here."

"We love customers like your mom."

Bob returned to the ice cream freezer and peered inside. "We're almost out of chocolate too. But, you're in luck. There's enough for one more cone. We won't have the ingredients to make more until next week."

"Good to know." He handed Bob a couple of dollars. "I'll pay for the ice cream and the candy right now.

Bob gave Mac his change and then packed the chocolate ice cream onto a cone and handed it to Mac. "I'll let you know when the vanilla creams are ready. Enjoy your cones."

Mac guided Grace between the empty tables to the wall of booths. It was good the afternoon movie hadn't let out yet, or seats would be as scarce as chocolate creams. They settled across from each other.

"That's nice of you to buy candy for your mom." Grace licked her ice cream.

"Well, I'm hoping she'll share with the rest of us." He winked. "Seriously, I often stop in here for a few chocolates to take home to her. These days, with the shortages, it doesn't happen as much as it used to. Like what he said about the ice cream, they don't always have the necessary ingredients to make the candy."

"We always get our Christmas and Valentine candy here. Last Christmas, Dad waited too long, and by the time he came they were sold out of everything."

"Do you have a favorite candy?"

She grinned. "I love the peanut clusters. But I'm afraid I won't taste another one until this war is over."

"Candy is a luxury, for sure, and so is ice cream. I heard the navy is making ice cream by taking the ingredients on their air missions. At the high altitude, the mix freezes, and the vibration churns it into ice cream. By the time the plane is back at base, they have dessert. Ingenious isn't it?"

"Why didn't WASP think of that?" She erupted into a delightful giggle. "There's nothing like ice cream."

"I noticed when we passed the movie theater, a Cary Grant movie is showing tonight." He leaned back and caught her gaze. Did he dare ask? "Shall we extend this enjoyable afternoon into the evening and see it?"

"Together?"

"Of course, together. But, if you've had enough of me for one day, I understand."

She pressed her lips together and stared at her lap.

The answer was going to be no. Same as all her answers when he asked her out.

"Sure, that sounds fun." She raised her head and offered a sweet smile.

"Swell." He felt a grin taking over his face. "But that means I'll have to get home soon to get my chores done."

"Hey, Mac!"

At Bob's shout, Mac turned, and Bob held up a white bag.

"Be right back." At the cash register, Mac leaned in and whispered, "Bob, by any chance, do you have any peanut clusters in the back?"

"Yes and no." Bob's lips twisted into a grimace. "Peanuts are in short supply, and the clusters are made for special orders. We keep them out of the display case."

"It's kind of a special order. My, um, friend over there was recently grounded from serving the military as a WASP. Illness clipped her wings. She just told me those were her favorites of all your mom's candies."

"That's crummy. Let me see what I can do." He stepped through a swinging door.

Mac glanced over at Grace, who appeared puzzled. He waved and mouthed he'd be there in a minute.

The door flew open and Bob stepped through, holding up a small white bag. "There's two clusters in here. Don't tell my parents I did this. I don't want to be fired."

"I think your job is safe. Thank you so much. How much do I owe you for these?"

"Your friend's candy is on the house. Tell her Frediani's appreciates what she's done for the war effort."

"I sure will. Thanks."

He crossed to where Grace sat in the booth. "Are we ready to leave?"

"Not until you tell me what you're hiding behind your back." She leaned and tried to peer around him.

He should have had her bag inserted in his mom's. "Just the bag of candy I got for Mom." He worked to keep her bag still out of her line of sight and held up his mom's bag.

"Right." She cast him a skeptical look but stood, and he allowed her to walk ahead of him. "Why don't we leave the truck here since the lake is so close?"

She gave him a questioning look, but nodded.

They started down the sidewalk for the lake. He'd have to make sure to keep Grace's surprise out of her sight line until the right moment.

When they arrived at the Riviera, he suggested they walk around the building, hoping the bench on the other side was empty.

"Good idea, but don't you have to be home soon if we're going to the movie tonight?"

Did she have any idea how she sometimes made him lose all sense of logic? All he'd wanted was to enjoy her company a bit longer. He'd forgotten the time. "You're right. I'd better get you home."

"I can walk from here. It's only a couple of blocks."

"I'll walk you there."

"Mac, that's ridiculous. Your truck is parked by Frediani's."

"I give up. These are for you." He let out an exaggerated sigh and handed her the smaller of the two bags.

"What did you do?"

"Look inside and you'll see."

She opened the top of the bag and peered inside, and her mouth fell open. "Mac, I'm speechless. Thank you."

Loving her smile, he grinned. "As the saying goes, sweets for the sweet. I intended to pay for them, but Bob didn't charge since they're for you. Their thanks for serving the military."

"Thank you." She stepped closer and hugged him from the side. "Can I eat one now?"

Still warmed by the momentary touch of her arm around him, he had to work to find his voice. "I'm surprised you waited this long to start."

She took a morsel out of the bag and bit off half, then closed her eyes as she chewed and swallowed. "Heaven on my tongue." She held out the bag. "You should eat the other one."

"Oh no. I got them for you. Save it for later if you'd like."

"I'll walk with you to your truck, and you can drop me off." She put the other half in her mouth and they started walking.

Their hands brushed and, without thinking, he took her hand. She squeezed it, and he tightened his grip. The afternoon was full of surprises. What would their movie date tonight bring?

20

Grace let herself in the side door. She'd tried to have Mac drop her off at the curb, but he insisted on walking her to the door. Why did she hold hands with him while they walked to the truck? Nothing like throwing fuel on a spark of attraction she'd so successfully ignored—until today.

"Hi, honey, were you at the Red Cross this afternoon?" Mom stood at the at the kitchen stove, stirring something in a large Dutch oven.

The hopeful expression on Mom's face, one she knew was sparked by hope of news about Rory, was enough to make her wish she'd gone straight to her bedroom. "No. Mac and I went over to the county registrar's office to do a title search on the Safe Refuge property."

Mom stopped stirring and rested the spoon on a nearby saucer. "Oh? Whatever for?"

"Just curious about how the property changed hands with each generation, up to when it was sold after the crash."

"We already know how it came down from Leonard Hartwell to each subsequent generation until the crash. Your granddad felt terrible having to arrange for the sale because the other family members were too distraught to think straight."

Startled to see Mom's tears, Grace, pulled her into a hug. "I know he did."

The embrace lasted for several minutes, until Mom wriggled free of Grace's arms. "Enough of this blubbering. I guess my emotions are still raw. I'd better check on the stew." She stepped to the stove and picked up the spoon. "Dinner will be ready in about an hour, when your dad gets home."

"There is something I want to talk to you about. Can I help with dinner while we talk?"

"You could set out the ingredients for the biscuits. You know what they are, right?"

"Yes." Grace measured out the flour, then the shortening. She'd made biscuits so often growing up, she could do it in her sleep.

"So, what did you want to ask about?"

"I'm not sure if it's really a question, but we noticed that before he died, Leonard Hartwell transferred the property to Rory Quinn. Wouldn't Anna, Rory's wife, as his oldest child automatically receive the property when he passed?"

"There's a lot about Leonard Hartwell that isn't spoken of much." Mom stirred the stew for several moments. "I'm not sure if everything I've heard is true, so I've chosen not to pass it along. I know he died a faith-filled man, but he didn't always live that way. We're all sinners saved by grace. I sometimes have to remind myself of that."

"What did he do?"

"Maybe if you talk to your granny, she'd feel more comfortable sharing. He only had daughters, since their only son died as a youngster, and probably wanted to be sure the property stayed in the hands of a family member with good business sense. Remember, back then women weren't given many privileges. We weren't even allowed to vote until right after the Great War. It probably made sense to him to turn it over to Rory."

Grace gathered baking powder and salt and set them on the table next to the flour and shortening. "That does make sense."

"Good. Was there anything else you wanted to discuss?"

"There's one interesting fact that isn't about our family." She headed for the refrigerator and took out a bottle of milk and set it on the table. "The family who purchased the estate when Granddad sold it lost it in a poker game."

Mom turned from the stove, her eyes wide. "What?"

"You heard correctly. As far as we can tell, the man who won it still owns it today."

"That sounds like a story out of the Wild West."

"Exactly what Mac said. I'd better clean up. Mac and I are going to a movie tonight, and he's coming for me at six-forty-five." She started for the hall. Only two more steps and she'd be out of the room and away from Mom's questions.

"Hold up. Did I hear you right? You and Mac have a date?"

Her face heated and she pivoted. "Not a date. Just two friends going to the show together."

"Then why is your face so red?"

"It's hot in here." She scooted through the hall and scrambled up the stairs. What was wrong with her? Would it be so wrong to date Mac with the understanding it was only for companionship? She never thought of the age difference anymore. When she was with him, it was as if they were the same age.

She reached her room and plopped into the chair by the window. She longed to let go of her fear and let the relationship play out, but if it got to the point of him proposing, she'd have to tell him her secret, wouldn't she? And that would be the end of it. If she were smart, she'd call and cancel tonight. But right then she wasn't feeling very smart.

THE FRONT DOORBELL rang a few minutes past six-thirty. Grace hung up her dishtowel. "Looks like my ride is here early."

Reenie turned from the sink of sudsy water. "Your ride? Mom said you had a date with Mac. Did I hear her wrong?"

"It's not a date." She scurried down the hall, but Mac was already standing in the foyer chatting with Dad. Wearing a camel-colored cardigan, a perfectly knotted brown tie, and gray wool trousers, he looked like he was about to go on a date. She hadn't bothered to change from the skirt and blouse she'd worn all day. Nothing like looking frumpy next to his handsomeness.

"Here's Grace. I'll leave you two to your date." Dad placed his hand on Grace's shoulder. "Have a good time." He headed down the hall toward the kitchen.

She took her jacket from the hall tree, but before she could slip it on, Mac tugged it out of her grip and held it open for her. She slipped her arms into the sleeves. "You're going to spoil me with all this chivalry."

"Just doing the gentlemanly thing. Didn't those military guys do those kinds of things?" He let go of her jacket, and it fell across her shoulders.

"Not when we were working." She faced him. "Why did you come to the front door? Didn't you park on the side street?"

"Yes, but a man should come to the front door when he has a date with his favorite gal."

"I thought we agreed this wasn't a date."

"Since your dad said we're on a date, I thought you—"

"Told him we had a date? He just assumed it."

"What's wrong with calling tonight a date? I like you, and I think you like me."

The last thing she wanted was to hurt his feelings. "Yes, I like you a lot, but dating leads to the next level, and I can't let it go that far. Besides, you're planning to move away next summer. It's best to keep it as friends."

"Then you never should have hugged me or held my hand this afternoon." He pressed his lips together and stared at his feet. "I'll never understand you, Grace."

"It was only a side hug to say thank you."

"And the hand-holding? Brothers and sisters don't normally do that unless they are little." He opened the door. "Let's go. We don't want to be late."

Nothing was said until they were in his truck and heading down Geneva Street toward the theater. Grace wanted to tell him to turn the truck around and take her home, but she'd already hurt him enough.

Her answer to his question about how the guys in the service treated her wasn't exactly correct. In their personal time together, Frank rarely held the door for her or helped her into her coat. She supposed he got so used to not doing it during on-duty times it just carried over to personal time.

Nor did he ever do spontaneous things, like Mac buying her the peanut clusters. It would be easy to fall hard for the man. If she were smart, she'd run the other way as fast as she could, but truth be told, she liked being with him. She just had to figure out a way to stop it from becoming more than friends.

21

As Mac parked across the street from the movie theater, Grace decided she needed to cool her independent woman stance and waited for him to come around and open her door.

But he didn't.

The truck shook a tiny bit, and she turned toward the back window. He leaned against the tailgate, arms crossed.

She let out a chuckle. He was retaliating but good and giving her what she deserved.

After climbing out of the truck, she came up beside him. "Do you think the Tick Tock Grill is serving humble pie tonight?"

"I don't know. We can skip the movie and find out." His even tone broadcast loud and clear that he was going to let her stew. But the twitch in the corner of his mouth betrayed him.

"It can wait, and I don't want to miss the movie."

A couple of cars drove past them heading south. He pushed away from the truck and lightly gripped her elbow as they crossed the street and walked up to the Geneva Theater's ticket booth.

Inside the partially filled theater they found a pair of seats halfway down on the right side. She sat in the inside seat and rested her left arm on the armrest. Mac elbowed her arm into her lap. Stifling a giggle, she pushed his arm away.

The newsreel began with a report about Joseph Goebbels's recent speech to the German people. The man actually admitted Germany had suffered some recent setbacks. Finally, some war news that was encouraging.

Mac's elbow pressed against her arm, and she pushed back, reclaiming the territory.

The movie began, and his elbow returned. She started to move her arm away, but he grabbed her hand and kept hold.

"Truce?" He whispered in her ear.

"Agreed."

"Good." He kept a grip on her hand. And she left it there.

With the distraction of the armrest battle and the fuzzy warm feeling produced by their clasped hands, Grace had missed the movie's opening dialogue. Cary Grant was impersonating a tailor and measuring the female star for her trousseau. He was making a mess of it, and laughter filled the theater. She hated it when everyone else got a joke and she didn't. Why did she think this movie was going to be good? He'd paid for their tickets, so if he liked it, she'd have to endure.

Mac leaned toward her and whispered, "Are you enjoying this?"

"Not really."

"Me either." He gave her hand a squeeze. "Let's go."

Outside, they crossed the street to his truck, and he halted in front of the passenger door. "You still want to find that humble pie at the Tick Tock?"

"Not before I apologize. Mac, I'm so sorry for my stubbornness. I know I hurt your feelings."

He opened the truck's door. "Let's sit in here."

Grace climbed in and fished a handkerchief from her purse and dabbed her eyes.

The driver's door opened, and Mac slid in behind the wheel

then nudged her into the crook of his arm. "I'm not going to pretend my feelings weren't hurt about not wanting to call this a date. They were, but I'm a big boy and understand you have your reasons for not officially dating. If you care to talk about it, I'm a good listener."

The ache in her chest enlarged. "You have to trust me. I can't tell you everything. What I can say is, the man I was engaged to didn't treat me very well. I dismissed his bad behavior, always making excuses for him. I broke up with him, but I missed his company terribly.

"When he received orders to head overseas, I reached out to him, and we went back together for the few days he had left before he shipped out. A couple of months later, he wrote to tell me he'd eloped with an English code breaker. I was warned to not get involved with him because he was a scoundrel, but I was too blinded by love."

"And now you're scared of getting involved with anyone."

"Yes." In some ways, that part was true.

"What if you at least give me a chance to prove I'm not a bad guy?"

"I know you're not like Frank, but I'm just not ready."

"Is it because of Jo?"

She jerked her gaze to him, but in the dark she couldn't see his face. "What do you mean?"

"I'm sure you never dreamed of getting involved with a graying fella with an almost twelve-year-old daughter."

Heat rose to her face. Was he reading her mind? "I admit when I first met you, I did think you were too old for me, even for someone to pal around with. But now I never think about the age difference, and Jo is a darling girl. When you move to Florida this summer, I'll miss both of you a lot."

"I'm not moving."

Her jaw dropped. "What? Why?"

"I planned to tell you after the show tonight. Since we didn't stay for the whole movie, I guess this qualifies for after the show.

When I got home this afternoon, Jo was near tears. It took a bit of coaxing, but I finally got her talking."

Grace shifted in the seat so she could see his face better.

Mac went on, "Today at recess, Lenny told her about the birthday party he'll be having this summer and how he hoped it would be a nice warm day because he wanted all his friends to go to the beach, then back to your house for cake and ice cream. She told Lenny she wouldn't be able to come because we were moving to Florida."

"I wondered why Lenny looked so glum at dinner. Mom asked about it, and he wouldn't say. But why the change of plans?"

"Jo said she'd been all for moving because it was what I wanted and she wanted to please me. But she didn't want to leave her grandparents and her friends. She loves the farm and selling trees at Christmastime. We talked about her fear of the ice, and she promised to work on it. I told her your grandfather might be able to help her, and she's willing to talk to him."

"I'm sure Granddad can help her." It was hard to tamp down the joy mixing with the dark emotion that she'd been living with for weeks. Did she dare admit knowing he wasn't moving was the best news she'd had in a while? She didn't want to get his hopes up. She'd have to choose her words wisely. "I'm happy to hear you won't be moving. Not having you around would make my life pretty dull."

He drew in a breath. "You know, it just occurred to me that you and Jo have a lot in common."

"How so?"

"She's been afraid of skating because of the accident with her mom, and you're afraid of being in a serious relationship because of being hurt by someone. Too bad you can't go to your grandfather for help, like Jo is going to do."

"If only it were that simple. But the objects of our fears are different."

"Maybe not as different as you think. Regardless, I'm willing to stop talking about dating as long as we can be friends and spend time together."

"No strings attached?"

"No strings."

"Okay, I agree."

"Whew." He pulled her into a hug. "You had me worried."

Being in his arms felt right. Too right. "Um, hugging like this isn't what I intended."

"Sorry." He laughed and released her. "Impulsive move." He took her hand. "Is handholding also not allowed?"

"I think it's okay."

"I didn't expect that answer."

"In negotiation, each side has to give a little."

"Agreed." He squeezed her hand. "I hear Bishop's has great desserts. And there's no humble pie on the menu."

22

Three Months Later

"Thanks for suggesting this restaurant." Mac slid into the half-circle booth at Hills Restaurant. "I've never been here before."

"I thought it a perfect place to celebrate the end of the school year for you." Grace returned his smile. "How good it must feel to have a break from the routine."

"What I wouldn't give to be in one of those photos." He studied the enlarged photos of mountain scenes on the eatery's walls. "Especially the one that looks like it was taken in the Grand Tetons. Have you ever been there?"

She shook her head. "No, but I flew over them once while ferrying a plane to a base near Seattle. Even from the air, they're impressive."

He had to bite his tongue not to say the mountains would be a perfect honeymoon destination. He'd been doing well the past several months to not say too much about his deepening feelings for Grace, but he didn't know how much longer he could stick to her *friends only* label on their relationship. At least she was okay with holding hands.

"I'm glad we've been able to stay friends after our agreement." He reached across the table and took her hand. "Do you feel the same?"

"I do." She nodded, causing the victory roll on top of her head to bounce. "You've become a good friend to me, Mac, and I appreciate the support you've given me in trying to find a way to regain Safe Refuge."

"And now I'll have more time to help with that."

"I don't know how much free time you're going to have when you're helping your dad take care of the crops and other farm work, as well as the Christmas trees."

"I'll be busy, but we do have a couple of hired hands. I'll have some time for you too. You know the old saying that the best part of being a teacher is June, July, and August."

She giggled. "I never heard that before. I sometimes wonder if I shouldn't have followed through on getting my teaching certificate as was suggested when I graduated. Dad asks me every week if I'd like to fly his Cessna, and I say no. It's not like I'm afraid to fly, but something stops me. Your friend whose courage you keep saying you admire has become a milquetoast."

"No, you haven't. It's a temporary condition. I've been praying for you to get over whatever it is that's holding you back. One day when your Dad asks, you'll surprise him and say yes."

"He thought maybe I'd say yes last month on my birthday, but that never happened." She picked up the napkin-wrapped silverware and released the utensils from their cocoon. "Don't you have a birthday coming up soon yourself?"

"Yep. July twenty-fifth."

"And then you'll be back to being ten years older than me."

"Does that still bother you?"

"No, but there are times I'm reminded of it. You have different memories of our town than me because you've been around longer. Some things you clearly remember happened when I was a baby, so I don't remember at all."

He just smiled.

"My earliest memory was when I was about three and learning how to tie my shoes," she continued. "It took me most of the morning to acquire the skill. You would have been thirteen and well past learning to tie your shoes. That means I have no recollection of anything you remember before you were thirteen."

"I never thought about that angle of things. But I'm more impressed how, even at the tender age of three, you had tenacity. Most kids would give up after several tries, but not you."

The waitress soon came and took their order, then over club sandwiches they reminisced about all they'd done together since they met at the bowling alley last fall.

Doing research at the courthouse, chaperoning Jo and Lenny's class when they took the train to Chicago to visit the Museum of Science and Industry, and dancing in the Riviera's second-floor ballroom when it opened for the new season. He had no idea Grace could dance the swing so well, but his favorite dances were the slow ones, when he got to hold her close.

After lunch they stepped out onto the sidewalk. Mac looked to the west down Main Street then took her hand. "I could walk you home from here, or would you prefer to walk on the shore path for a while?"

"I like the idea of a walk."

He grinned. "North shore or south?"

"Which do you prefer?" she asked.

"Oh, the north one."

Her eyes widened. "Past Safe Refuge?"

"We don't have to go that far. I want to see Lake Geneva Manor from the lakeshore. I was thinking maybe that area would be a good alternative for your family, if you can pool resources from what old money you have and buy a home there. At least you'd have lake rights and wouldn't have to use the public beach."

She bristled and pulled her hand from his grip. "I thought you understood. My family doesn't have any of what you call old money. We were cleaned out with the crash, remember? The desire to regain the property isn't about lake rights as much as it's about the property being a part of our family history. I know I asked you to help me and you have, but this isn't helping."

He scrubbed his hand over his face and heaved a sigh. "Grace, I'm sorry. You did say all that before. Help me to understand what I haven't been able to grasp.

"Think about how it would be if your family had lost the farm during the crash. I know it has been the primary source of income, but I expect there are a lot of memories attached to it of things that only your family could have experienced in that specific place."

"I hadn't thought about it that way." Mac looked off at the lake, its blue waters as smooth as glass. "I get it now. We can turn around and walk somewhere else."

"No, let's continue. It's perfect summer weather, and I haven't seen the house up close for years. I'd like to see it now."

He'd sure messed up, thinking he understood her family's perspective. He had his own issues to contend with. The summer months stretched before him, and he'd been looking forward to spending time with Grace and hoped that with more time together they could move the relationship to a deeper level. But, truth be told, for all his talk about being content to be only friends and not dating, he didn't know how much more he could play that role. He loved Grace and yearned to have that love returned. He wanted her not only as his girlfriend, but also his wife.

23

Grace's pulse rose as they approached the point on the shoreline where Safe Refuge, now known as Rose Harbor, would come into view. She took Mac's hand, grateful he didn't pull away. They rounded a pine tree, and her breath hitched.

"Grace, If you squeeze my hand any harder, you'll cut off the blood supply."

"It's worse than I thought." She loosened her grip, and they stopped.

Off to the right of the home, the foliage had grown thick making it difficult to see the cottage where she was born. Too bad vegetation didn't hide the main house as well. Who thought painting the sagging veranda a grotesque mustard yellow would improve the appearance? No longer would she find it hard to call it Rose Harbor. Safe Refuge was no more.

"It looks bad, doesn't it?" Mac said.

She scowled. "It's worse than bad. It looks like someone ripped off its elegant ball gown and replaced it with a dress from a discard pile at the secondhand store. That color is disgusting. What they've done to my family's legacy makes me want to do whatever it takes to get it back. But I can't do it without money.

I don't want to continue." Using long strides, she stormed toward town.

"Whoa." He came up beside her. "Where are you going so fast?"

"I don't know, but standing around wishing for money isn't going to make things happen. If the home had been kept up, it wouldn't hurt so much to see it belonging to someone else. Perhaps in a few more years it will fall down, and all that will be left is the property. Then maybe I'll be able to afford it."

"Even without a house on it, the property is worth a lot. It's prime lakeshore land."

She looked up at Mac, her eyes filling with tears. "I still can't shake the sense that the key to reacquiring Safe Refuge lies in the fact the person who owns it now is apparently an absentee owner. If Atwell's not willing to take care of the property, isn't there a way to get him to relinquish it? Even if the transfer to him was legal and binding?"

"If you're thinking about how he won the property in a poker game, we've already been over that. The law allowed for such wagers. The legal transfer of title was there."

Grace blinked at her tears. "I can't imagine how that man's family felt to learn he'd lost the home in a card game. If my family had lost the house that way, I don't think I could stand it."

"I know. But there are other transfers of ownership to consider. When would you like me to go with you to the registrar's office in Elkhorn again?"

"Probably not for another week, I'm scheduled to volunteer every afternoon this week at the Red Cross."

"Okay. On another subject, you haven't mentioned the search for your brother, Rory. Did the humanitarian worker hit a dead end?"

"We've not heard anything in weeks. Anne thinks the worker may have been detained and is in a POW camp himself. I'd feel terrible if his searching for my brother got him in trouble. I feel so guilty living here in the States in relative safety, fussing over how to regain possession of our family property. I sometimes wish I'd trained to be a nurse like my granny. Then I could volunteer over there as an army nurse."

He took her hand and squeezed it. "You miss being in the action, don't you?"

The compassion in his eyes jolted her. He may have misunderstood about Safe Refuge but really did seem to understand her. Would he understand as well if she shared her secret? She couldn't take that chance until she was ready to accept his likely rejection. "Yes. I know I'm helping people with my Red Cross work, but I hate sitting at a desk that long. I barely make it an hour before I want to get up and move."

"I know what you mean. Even in the classroom I'm able to stand while I'm teaching and walk around the room."

"My parents both have desk jobs and are fine with it," she said. "That's not for me. And what's funny is, I long to fly an airplane again, but at the same time I can't make myself fly my dad's plane. I drove to the airfield a couple of weeks ago, planning to surprise Dad when he took the plane up. I got to the road the field was on and turned around."

The lines around his eyes deepened. "You're more than welcome to come work on the tree farm anytime. At least you'll be outside. It's hard work, and you'll be wishing for a desk chair after a couple of hours."

"You don't think I can handle that kind of work? She lifted her chin. "I'll have you know, my mom was a farmette during the first war. If she can do it, I can too."

"A farmette?"

"Yes, that's what they called the women who volunteered for the Women's Land Army. They worked on farms to take the place of the soldiers who had left their farms for the war."

"You're speaking of the same Mrs. Bauer, the library director?"

Grace chuckled. “She learned to plow and milk cows and all those kinds of chores.”

“I’m impressed, but that’s your mother, not you. Maybe getting you out on the farm for a few hours will shake whatever is stopping you from flying out of your system. Are you up for a challenge?”

“You bet I am.” She grinned. “Name the day, and I’ll be there.”

“The week after next. Are you scheduled for the Red Cross at all that week?”

“Yes, but I won’t know the days until the end of this week. Tell me what day to not work that week, and I’ll let the scheduler know I’m not available then.”

“Okay. Don’t make other plans that Tuesday. Unless you want to chicken out.”

She crossed her arms. “I’ve never chickened out of any challenge thrown at me.”

“That’s what I’m afraid of.”

THE FOLLOWING MONDAY AFTERNOON, the receptionist spoke to Grace through the intercom,

“Miss Bauer, a gentleman is here needing your service. I told him you didn’t want to be disturbed and he could see Mrs. Senft instead, but he insists he speak with you.”

“Maybe he’s spoken with me before. Did he give you his name?”

“Yes. Robert McAlister.”

“That name is familiar.” Grace worked to stifle a giggle. “Send him back.” She glanced around the desktop and reached for the papers strewn everywhere.

“I’m glad to see you keep an untidy desk like me.” Mac almost filled the entire doorway with his height. The work dungarees and tee shirt, which he rarely wore when he came to town, indicated he must have left his farm chores in a hurry. A sinking feeling washed over her. Had he changed his mind and was moving to Florida?

Working to mask her concern, she pushed out a smile. "Caught in the act." She let the papers drop onto the desk. "I've been in research all morning, trying to locate someone's son. To what do I owe this surprise visit?"

He nodded at the empty chair in front of her desk. "Okay if I sit?"

"Yes, of course."

His movement in sitting caused a whiff of pine to tickle her nose, reminding her of her upcoming workday on his farm.

"I need to have word sent to my brothers." He sat and looked her in the eye. "As you know, the military doesn't divulge the whereabouts of our men, even to family members."

Thoughts of something happening to his parents or Jo flashed into her mind, and she felt the blood drain from her face. "Oh, no. What's happened?"

"There's no emergency. Last night my parents and I decided not to wait any longer to put the property into a trust as a means to protect Jo should something happen to any one of us. We need to contact my brothers to fill them in on what's being done."

"We can do that." Grace reached for forms they used for family messages.

"My dad is getting in touch with your father now to see how to go about doing this in a legal way," Mac said. "His own attorney has temporarily closed his law office, as he's serving with the army. How long will it take for you to find a way to contact Glenn and Doug?"

Her shoulders relaxed. "I'm glad it's for something like that and not to send a death notice. I get too many of those. I think it's a great idea for Jo's sake. It shouldn't take but a day or two." She handed him two forms. "You'll have to fill these out, one for each man, and provide as much information as possible. The more you know, the less time it will take to reach them."

He scanned one of the forms. "I can do it right here, if there's a place to sit."

"I'm afraid everyone who works here is present today. There's no available office space, and the table in the reception area has been in steady use most of today. I can give you a clipboard, and you can sit right here to fill them out while I go ahead with my work."

"Sounds good." He pulled a folded paper from his pocket and opened it. "I jotted down all the information we have on them."

She got him settled, then returned to her research. After a few minutes, she sneaked a glance at Mac. He sat hunched over, his eyebrows almost forming a straight line as he concentrated.

From the night they first met, she'd always thought him handsome, but today he seemed even more so.

What she found more attractive than his good looks, though, was his heart for his daughter and parents. He'd even planned to relocate to Florida because of Jo's fears. She was glad Jo convinced him she didn't want to leave Lake Geneva and agreed to meet with Granddad. Their chats did seem to be helping, according to Mac. The proof would have to wait until next winter when the lake froze over.

He raised his head and looked at her before she could focus elsewhere. An intoxicating grin filled his features. "Are you watching me?"

"Um. No. I was thinking, and just happened to be looking your direction."

"If that's the case, why is your face red?"

"I don't know." She touched her palm to her cheek and felt the heat.

"Come on, Bauer, admit you were watching me." He gathered the forms together.

"You know I don't like it when you call me by my last name."

"I know. Just trying to get a rise out of you."

"I thought you liked me."

"You know I like you a lot." His softened tone soothed the rough edges of her ire.

"I like you too, Robert."

"If you stop calling me Robert, I'll stop calling you Bauer." He picked up an eraser as if he was going to toss it at her.

"Deal." She held out her hand, but before she could ask for the completed forms, he took it and gave it a shake. Instead of releasing his grip, he wove their fingers together, then opened his mouth as if to speak.

The sharp ring of her phone sliced the air. She answered it with her free hand. "Grace Bauer."

"Grace, I hope I'm not interrupting anything." Dad's voice came through the connection.

"No. You're not."

Mac tickled her palm without letting go, and she worked to stifle a giggle. "Stop it."

"What did you say?"

"Nothing. I mean, I wasn't talking to you."

"Is Mac still there?"

"Yes, Dad, he's here. Please take him off my hands. He's worse than Lenny, trying to keep me from my work."

Mac's eyes widened in mock surprise. She frowned at him and yanked her hand out of his grip.

"I think I can help you out," Dad said. "His father is here with me, and we'd like Mac to come by my office as soon as possible."

"I'll send him over." She hung up the phone. "Our fathers want you to go over to my dad's office as soon as you can." The sharp tone in her voice came out stronger than she intended.

"Hey, I'm sorry for teasing you when you're involved in important work. It was childish of me."

"No harm done, since it was Dad. I'm sorry for taking my frustration out on you. Sometimes when we're under stress and worried about our loved ones, we use levity as a means of dealing with it. I see it often with the people I help."

"I guess I'll be on my way." He stood, and their gazes connected. "It was a pleasure."

If they'd been anywhere but there, she'd be tempted to hug him. "Mac, I meant what I said. I needed a bit of a giggle. It's been a crazy morning."

"Understood. I'll call you later." He winked and stepped through the door.

She didn't move for a few moments. Something happened in the short time he was there. She had a big decision to make before things between them went any deeper.

24

Two days later, Grace picked up her office phone and gave the central office operator Mac's phone number.

After five or six rings, the operator came back on the line. "He's not answering, do you want to keep it ringing?"

"Give it a few more rings, then end the call if he doesn't pick up. I'll have to try back later."

After several more rings Grace hung up and drummed her fingers on the desktop, her fingernails clacking against the polished wood. On summer mornings, he usually stayed in his home office and did paperwork after his time in prayer. If he got an early start and was helping with farm work, it could be a couple more hours before he'd stop for lunch and be near a telephone. She picked up the phone.

The same operator as before came on the line. "Hello, how can I help you?"

"Let's try the McAlister main house at three-four-zero."

Mac's mom picked up on the second ring. "McAlisters'."

"Hi, Mrs. McAlister, this is Grace Bauer. I'm looking for Mac. He didn't answer at home. Is he working in the fields today?"

"Grace. Good to hear your voice. He's here now, in deep

conversation with his father. Shall I get him to come to the phone?"

"No, just tell him my dad has been trying to reach him. He wants Mac to stop by his office this afternoon regarding the trust."

"I will. I'm assuming you've not yet connected with our other two sons."

"No. But I think I might have an answer by the time Mac meets with my dad."

"Oh, I hope so. You are such a dear to help us."

"It's my pleasure, Mrs. McAlister."

"We've known each other a while now. I'm Ella to everyone I know, and I wish you'd call me Ella too. Mrs. McAlister sounds so formal. It's good to talk to you, Grace."

She couldn't help but smile. "Then Ella it will be from now on. It was good to talk to you too."

After hanging up, Grace sat back and stared out the window. Ella's cheery voice would give people pause, thinking no one could be that happy all the time, especially during wartime, with two sons in the military somewhere in the Pacific. Today, she was still as cheerful as ever, but it seemed a bit forced. The delay in tracking down the brothers must have put her on edge.

Later that afternoon, Grace covered her typewriter then rose and took her sweater from a hook on the wall behind her.

"Good. You're still here. This involves your brother."

Heart racing, she took the telegram the receptionist held out. "Thanks, Alice. I'm glad I'm still here too."

She dropped into her chair and stared at the name on the subject line, 'Rory Murphy Bauer,' almost jumped off the paper. She drew in a breath, willing her pulse to slow, and sent a mental prayer that this would be good news.

Captain Rory M. Bauer has been located in a POW camp in Burma. Many rules regarding POWs have been broken, and I negotiated with

THE JAPANESE GOVERNMENT TO RELEASE HIM TO MY CARE OR THEY WOULD SUFFER GREAT CONSEQUENCES.

I WAS ABLE TO BRING CAPTAIN BAUER OUT OF THE CAMP WITH THE ASSISTANCE OF TWO BRITISH NAVAL OFFICERS WHO WERE ALSO RELEASED TO ME AS PART OF THE NEGOTIATIONS. THE THREE MEN WILL BE TRANSPORTED TO A MILITARY BASE IN THAILAND WHERE THE U.S. ARMY HAS ESTABLISHED A PRESENCE. CONFIRMATION OF THEIR ARRIVAL THERE SHOULD COME BY TELEGRAM WITHIN 24 HOURS.

CAPTAIN BAUER IS MALNOURISHED AND WEAK. HE IS ALREADY RECEIVING MEDICAL ATTENTION. HE HAS A GOOD CHANCE OF BEING RESTORED TO GOOD HEALTH.

Tears splashed onto the notice, and Grace quickly blotted at them before they caused the words to blur. Whom should she call first? Dad was likely with the clients he said were due when they talked earlier. She'd call Mom at the library. She picked up the phone, and within a couple of minutes her mother's voice came through the connection.

"M-m-mom. He's ..." She swallowed the wad in her throat and hauled in a breath.

"Reenie is that you?"

"No, Mom. It's ... Grace."

"Are you okay? What's wrong?"

"Rory ... "

"Please, Grace, tell me. Is it bad news?"

"No. The worker found him alive in a Burmese POW camp. Very malnourished. He managed to get freedom for two British naval officers, who helped carry Rory out of the camp. They're on their way to Thailand, where the U.S. Army currently has a base. They'll get them headed back to the U.S. and Great

Britain. I don't know what that worker did to free Rory and the other two men."

A sob came through the connection. "Oh, Grace, our prayers have been answered. We must be prepared. He'll likely not be the same high-spirited young man he was when he left. Does your father know?"

"No. He's meeting with a client. I thought I'd wait until I was sure his meeting is over."

"Well, we need to pray the three men make it to Thailand safely."

"And also, that they can be flown out of there as fast as possible."

"Yes. I'm going to call my prayer circle right now. You'll let me know if you hear anything more, won't you?"

"Of course."

Unable to concentrate on anything else, Grace paced her small office. "Lord, I know You and I haven't been on good terms lately because of my mistakes, but the rest of my family have been faithful to You. The Bible says nothing is impossible with You, and like the man in the Bible who said he believed You, but needed help with his unbelief, I'm asking the same thing."

She continued, not only praying for Rory and the other men's safety, but also that word would soon come that Mac's brothers had been located. For years she'd heard stories about her dad's ordeal after being shot down in Belgium. Now here she was in her generation, dealing with war again.

When she could stand it no more, she called Dad's office. At his secretary's chipper greeting, she blurted out, "Lorraine, this is Grace Bauer. Is my dad still in a meeting?"

"The client just left. Do you have word on Mac's brothers?"

"No, but I need to talk to my father immediately."

A few seconds later, Dad's voice came through the connection. "Grace? Lorraine said it was urgent I talk to you."

"Are you sitting down?"

"I'm almost afraid to answer, but yes."

"Rory is alive and has been released from a Burmese POW camp. He's traveling with two British POWs to a U.S. Army compound in Thailand. He's very undernourished and needs immediate medical attention, but he's alive, Dad."

Silence filled the connection.

"Dad, are you still there?"

"Yes." He coughed and cleared his throat. "Never did I think that some twenty-five years after I lived through being MIA myself, my own son would experience the same, but worse."

Hearing his thick voice, she wanted to run the five blocks to his office and throw herself into his arms, regardless of who else was there. "We should receive word by sometime tomorrow that they made it to the base in Thailand and can be flown safely out of there. I'm guessing he'll go to the military hospital in San Diego."

She hung up, then gathered her purse and the battered leather briefcase Dad had given her when she began working at the Red Cross. She stuffed the telegram in the case, along with the papers she'd been working on regarding locating Mac's brothers. They may not get word on Rory until tomorrow, but she wanted to be home when the word came.

Passing through the reception area, she asked Alice to have the central telephone operator ring her home if any calls came in regarding Rory or the McAlister men.

Outside, she drew in a deep breath and began walking south toward home. Geneva Lake sparkled in the afternoon sun. If only she could carry the telephone over to the park and let the peacefulness of the lake calm her spirits. She chuckled at the vision of everyone carrying around a telephone while they were out of doors. They couldn't make a telephone cord long enough to do that. What a crazy idea.

25

One Month Later

At the sound of a car door closing, Mac looked up from shearing a small pine tree. Grace stood next to her mom's green Ford coupe, where she'd parked next to his truck. Finally, after rescheduling her workweek, she was here. He couldn't help but grin. She filled out her olive-green jumpsuit far better than any male pilot.

As if to detract from the masculine outfit, a colorful scarf around her head tamed her curls. As she came closer, his gaze settled on her ruby-red lips. He'd love to kiss that color away if she'd let him.

Perhaps today he'd muster the courage he lacked last night at Riviera Ballroom's Fourth of July dance when they stepped outside on the pier to cool off. Earlier, the four-day heatwave had broken with a wild morning thunderstorm, and the night air had a chill.

When Grace said she was cold, he was more than happy to hug her close while they looked at the full moon's reflection on the lake. By the time he'd mustered up enough courage to kiss her, others stepped outside including a Red Cross volunteer who recognized Grace.

As Grace came closer, he snapped out of his thoughts and said, "Good morning, I see you dressed appropriately for your farm work. I presume that's a WASP jumpsuit."

"You're very astute. We were told we would have to turn in all our gear and uniforms when we returned home, but one of my friends packed up my things, and she snuck it into the box. I thought it might be good to wear today. Sorry to be late, but my brother called from the hospital in San Diego as I was about to leave. He has to grab the phone the patients are allowed to use when it's available, and early morning is usually the best time."

"Understood. How is he doing?"

Her face brightened. "Getting stronger every day. He's gained twenty pounds since he arrived there."

"That's wonderful news. I hope I get to meet him someday and thank him in person for his service to our country."

"Of course you'll meet him. I expect he'll be home within a month or two." She eyed the tool he was holding. "Is that thing in your hand, what we're using today?"

"It is, if you want to shear the trees, or you can mow down the weeds around them."

She scrunched her nose. "Shear trees? I've heard of pruning trees, but not shearing."

"It's similar but dissimilar at the same time. We have to shear off the recent growth to force newer growth to come over it during the next year, to fill any gaps in the branches and make the tree look fuller. I should have begun the process last week, but the heatwave affected the trees, and I didn't want to further shock them by shearing them. The window of time to shear is closing fast. You didn't think the tree you bought off the lot got that perfect shape all on its own, did you?"

Using the toe of her boot, likely another souvenir from her WASP days, she pushed a stone around on the ground. A cute smile took over her face. "Yeah, I guess I did, but just to remind you, I didn't buy that tree, you gave it to us. But shearing sounds harder than mowing weeds. I'll take the weeds."

"Just what I thought you'd say."

"What do you mean by that?" She placed her fists on her hips and frowned.

"Nothing, really." They began walking toward where he'd been working, and Mac held up the shearing knife. "I have my tool. Yours is over there." He pointed at a mower with a gasoline engine mounted over its blades.

Her eyes rounded. "It's motorized?"

"Yep, when we can get gas, it comes in handy. I figured if you can fly a B-17, you should be able to handle this thing."

"I was hoping you'd show me how to care for the chickens and gather the eggs."

"The coop is over on the farm side." He grinned. "We can do that after we're done here."

Grace stepped over to the mower and hunched down, inspecting the contraption as if she were preparing to fly it. "It makes sense to me. Tall weeds would be harder to push a mower through than a lawn." She stood and grinned. "Show me what needs mowing, and I'll get to work."

"COME ON, YOU RASCAL." Grace pushed at the mower's handle. "I'm in charge here, not you." Her arms ached from fighting with the machine. She had half a mind to ask Mac to trade jobs with her, but doing so would be akin to admitting defeat. And defeat was not a word in her vocabulary.

"Whew." Ella McAlister stepped out from between two rows of trees. "It's not as hot as a few days ago, but hot enough. I thought you two could use a cold drink." She held a pitcher of what appeared to be iced tea in one hand and a pair of nested glasses in the other. "You'd better drink up before the ice in this pitcher melts."

Grace pressed her fingertips to the small of her back and stretched. "Ella, you are a welcome sight." She accepted a glass of the amber liquid and studied the lettering on the glass. *Back the Attack.* "That's the new slogan they're using to support the war effort. Is the DX gas station giving these away?"

"Whenever I gassed up recently, I was given a glass." Mac accepted the drink his mother held out. "The station owner said he got a good deal on the tumblers, and the DX company supplied the decals. You get a glass with each purchase until the supply runs out. He's hoping to keep customers coming to him."

"I'll have to suggest my parents go there."

His gaze went to where she'd been working. "You're doing a good job with the mowing, but I noticed you were stretching as if your back is bothering you. We can trade jobs if you'd like."

"I'm fine, thanks to your mom bringing us these drinks." She drained her glass and handed it to Ella. "I'm ready to finish the job." She had no desire to admit the mower was winning the battle.

"Will you be joining us for lunch, Grace?"

"I love your lunches, Ella, but I have a last-minute appointment at the Red Cross office at two o'clock, and I'll need to clean up before then."

Ella nodded. "Well, I can at least prepare you a sandwich to take with you. And I'll send some fresh eggs with you, too."

Grace grinned. "I'd love that."

Shortly before noon, Mac walked her to her car. He opened the driver's door and smiled. "There's a smudge on your cheek. How did you do that? Let me get that off for you." He took a handkerchief from his pocket, unfolded it and gently slid it over cheek.

A shiver ran down her jawline and she jumped.

"I didn't mean to startle you. I got most of it off. Let's see if I can remove the rest of it." He wetted the handkerchief with his tongue then repeated the process, and this time she stood still, ignoring the delicious sensation that erupted as it had before.

The movement halted and he ran the back of his fingers over the spot. "Your skin is as soft as Jo's when she was a baby. How do you do that?"

She raised her eyes until their gazes met. "I don't do anything special."

"You must do something." He leaned in, bringing his face close enough she could feel his breath. "I so much want to kiss you."

Warning bells sounded in her head. She needed to step away. But a kiss didn't mean she would be beholden to him for life, and she'd been wondering what his kiss would feel like. It was just a kiss. She tilted her head back and rose on her toes.

Soft as a feather, he brushed his lips over hers, paused, then brought them back to her mouth. Butterflies erupted in her stomach. The warnings stopped their clanging as sweet melodies took over. He ended the kiss, and she circled his waist with her arms, then pressed her face against his chest, savoring his manly scent.

"Are you sorry?" He whispered as he drew her against him.

She leaned back and looked up at him. "Sorry for what?"

"For kissing me."

"I quite enjoyed it, actually."

The lines around his eyes deepened. "Me too. Shall we do it again and see if it's as enjoyable the second time around?"

The warning bells were back, but she ignored them. "Okay."

His kiss was soft and gentle as before, but accented by the feel of his stubbled cheek against hers, all holding a promise of more to come, if she wanted it.

She stepped back. "I have to go."

"Just one more." He lowered his lips to hers.

He wasn't the only one who'd been wanting a kiss. Her arms circled his waist. The kiss ended and she pressed her cheek against his chest. His kisses so chaste compared to Rich's. With this man she felt safe.

He drew back and kissed the tip of her nose. "You'd better get going."

After Grace slid behind the wheel, he shut the door, then bent and looked her in the eye. I'll call you later. Have a good afternoon."

"You too." She started the engine, and he stepped back out of her way.

Before shifting to first gear, she glanced in his direction. He waved then turned and walked toward the trees.

Feeling as though she could float home, she drove down the lane. Surely there must be a way they could make it work without his knowing her secret.

Movement off to the right caught her attention, and she spotted Jo sitting behind a bush, grinning from ear to ear. A sinking feeling washed over her. She must have seen them kissing. Now the girl was going to think she had a new mom in her future. *I can't ever be careless like that again.*

She swiped at the tear trailing down her face. After those tender kisses, how could she and Mac return to the easygoing friendship they'd shared? They'd have to try, or she'd be forced to give up the best thing that had happened to her in a very long time.

The Lake Geneva city limits came into view, and she banged the heel of her hand on the steering wheel. She'd been so shaken, she forgot to stop at the house for Ella's sandwich.

26

The following day, Grace gave the operator the phone number of the bowling alley in Burlington. She'd already contacted the ones in Delavan and Elkhorn. This one, although farther away than the other two, was her last hope. If the call was fruitful, she'd have to figure out a way to replace the fuel she'd use in Mom's car to get there.

She was about to hang up, thinking they must be closed, when a youngish sounding male voice came through the connection. "Burlington Lanes. Bowl your cares away. How may I help you?"

"Hello, I hope you can assist me. I'm in need of a pair of women's size eight bowling shoes and wonder if you might have a pair you can sell me."

"I'm not sure. Hold on." A muffled sound, probably caused by his putting his hand over the mouthpiece, interrupted the connection, but his shout was loud enough to hear. "Hey, Ma. Some lady wants to buy a pair of ladies' size eights from us. What size is that pair you set back for Mrs. Lister?"

Muffled conversation followed and then cleared. "Hello, this is Irene James. My son said you're looking for a pair of size eight bowling shoes?"

"Yes. I want to purchase them. Do you have a pair you can sell?"

"We do. Someone had us order the pair for her, and they've been gathering dust on the shelf for several months. We've tried contacting the woman, but there's never an answer. Let me try one more time, and if there's no answer or she says she's changed her mind, they're all yours. How soon could you come?"

"I could be there by two o'clock today. How much are they?"

"Um, the woman paid a five-dollar deposit, and they were twelve dollars and fifty cents. Nice leather. If you were military, I'd let you have them, but since you're not—"

"I'm connected to the military. I was part of WASP, women pilots who ferry new bombers across the country to military bases for use in the war. I was discharged because of illness, and bowling was prescribed to help me regain my strength. But, I'd be happy to pay five dollars."

"A lady pilot. Well, if that don't beat all. Forget paying anything. I'm not even going to make that call. It's obvious the woman changed her mind. Come as soon as you can."

Grace jotted down directions to the bowling alley and let out a sigh of relief. Now, if she could only figure out a way to slip past the shoe counter tomorrow night when the month-long summer league started and not run into Mac. She'd not spoken to him since yesterday, when they'd kissed, and hadn't taken any of his calls.

BY THE TIME Grace left home the next evening to walk to the bowling alley, she felt confident she'd be able to avoid Mac should he be there. She hated how much she missed him, and she owed him an explanation, but she wasn't ready to talk until she figured out how to tell him about her past. Until then, if they couldn't be together as friends only ... . Try as she might, she'd not yet been able to complete that sentence.

The shoes she'd purchased fit perfectly, and because the proprietors were so nice, she ended up giving them five dollars anyway. Now, between that and the cost of gas, she only had enough left to pay to bowl tonight.

In front of the Clair Hotel, she glanced over the vehicles parked on Broad and Main Streets. Mac's truck wasn't there. Maybe he decided to stay away, since she'd not returned any of his calls. She scurried down the steps and entered the bowling alley. Off to her left, Becky stood at the shoe counter, her head bobbing as she conversed with a woman Grace didn't recognize.

Suddenly, Mac popped up next to Becky. He must have been hunched down looking in the drawer for a pair of shoes. He and the woman continued to chat while Becky waited on a new customer. The woman must have said something amusing, because one of his heart-stopping smiles appeared and he let out a laugh, loud enough to be heard above the din of ladies' voices.

Her heart squeezed. She loved those times they'd shared a laugh like that, and now another woman was enjoying one of those special moments that would soon be only a memory for Grace.

Without warning, he shifted his focus to her, and their gazes collided. His lips turned up. Grace jerked her gaze away and scurried past the lanes, grateful to see her teammates at the last alley. As far away from the shoe counter as possible.

Plopping onto the bench next to Helen, she pulled out her new shoes. "Sorry I'm late. It will only take a minute to get changed."

"You're not late. We don't start for another ten minutes. Whoa, those shoes look new. Very nice. Where did you find them?"

"At the bowling alley in Burlington." She pulled on a shoelace and tied a bow. "Someone ordered them then never came in to get them. And now they're mine."

"How did you hear about them? Burlington isn't exactly close."

"Word of mouth."

"Did you see Mac when you came in? He was here looking for you. By the look on his face, you'd think he'd lost his best friend. Did you two have a fight?"

"No, we didn't fight, and yes, I saw him, but I didn't stop to say hi because ... I thought I was late."

"Well, now here's your chance. He's coming our way."

She stiffened.

"Grace, here's your size eights—oh, I see you're already wearing shoes."

Why didn't he just go away? Hoping her smile didn't appear as forced as it felt, she faced him. "I was just telling Helen I came across a deal on a new pair someone was selling. I'd better get some practice shots in and see how they feel on the alley."

She stood and stepped over to the return, then came to a stop. Her ball was still in her bag.

"Looking for this?" Mac held her ball out.

She pivoted and looked up into a pair of sad blue eyes. She averted her gaze to a spot past his shoulder. "Yes. I was. Thank you."

"Grace, I have no idea what's going on, but we need to talk." He handed her the ball. "If it's about what happened the other day ..."

"I can't talk now. I have to warm up. Thanks for bringing me my ball."

"Okay. But we're going to talk before tonight is over." He turned on his heel and walked away.

Her practice shot went straight into the gutter. She returned to the seat and began fussing with her shoelace. "I hate breaking in new shoes."

"Are you going to tell me what's going on, or will I have to drag it out of you?" Helen asked.

"There's nothing going on, and that's how it should be." Grace heaved a sigh and faced Helen. "I got a little too far in over my head and came up for air."

"Now that's a cryptic answer if I ever heard one. Something tells me you don't think he's too old for you anymore."

"No. I got over that a long time ago. Too bad his age stopped bothering me, because I wouldn't have started dating him if it hadn't." She swatted at a tear cascading down her cheek. "And caring for him like I do."

"Come on." Helen grabbed her hand and pulled her to her feet. "We need to powder our noses." She called out to Peggy who was returning from making a practice shot. "We'll be back in a few."

They arrived at the ladies' room.

"Good, it's empty." Helen pulled Grace inside the small room and locked the door, then tugged a cloth handkerchief from her pocket and handed it to Grace. "Now, what gives?"

"We were having a wonderful time just being friends then I started following my heart instead of my head." Grace blew her nose. "On Monday, I went out to his tree farm to help take care of the trees. It was a fun morning. Then, as he walked me to my car, something happened, and we ended up kissing."

"Oh, Grace, that's wonderful." Helen pulled her into a hug.

"No, it's not. The moment was magical, but as I was driving away, I spotted Jo hiding behind some bushes, grinning like a Cheshire cat. I'm sure she thinks her dad and I are ..."

"Falling in love?"

"I wouldn't go that far, but it put hope in her heart that I'm going to be her new mom."

"What's wrong with that?"

"I love Jo to pieces and don't want her hurt. I can never be her stepmom, and I need to stop seeing Mac. I've done it all wrong. He's called about a dozen times since then, but I've had whoever answered the phone say I'm not available. I bought these shoes so I wouldn't have to go to the shoe counter tonight. Now he's telling me he wants to talk after bowling. Is there a back door I can use?"

"I presume the reason you can't marry Mac is related to the conversation you and I had a few months ago."

"Yes. In part, anyway."

"Well, I have no idea why you think you can't be in a relationship with Mac, but I suggest you let him decide. He may surprise you. Now, splash some cold water on your face. We've got some bowling to do."

A loud rap came on the door. "Girls, we're waiting."

"We'll be right out," Helen shouted.

A couple of hours later, Grace made the last shot and managed a spare. She turned to see Mac standing behind the bench, his hands jammed into his trouser pockets. No smile, no thumbs up, and no escaping out the back door, even if she knew where it was.

She methodically dropped her ball in the bag, then sat to take off her new shoes.

"Nice shoes." Mac plopped beside her and took the shoe she'd just removed from her hand. He studied it a moment, turning it over. "When did you get them?"

"Yesterday. A woman ordered them at a bowling alley in Burlington, then never came back for them. I only paid five dollars." She untied the other shoe and loosened the laces.

His eyebrows rose. "How did you manage that?"

"The bowling alley owner said she gives a break to people who are connected to the military. I told her what I did before I got sick, and she wanted to give them to me at no cost. But I insisted I give her something, and she said five was the most she'd take." She removed the other shoe and put it into her bag, and he dropped the one he held in next to it.

They both stood, and he picked up her bag.

Outside at the top of the steps, he pointed down Broad Street toward the lake. "I'm parked in front of the Hotel Geneva. All the spots near here were taken."

After walking in silence, they arrived at his truck. After he opened the driver's door, she climbed in and slid under the steering wheel to the other side of the seat, not stopping in the middle to be closer to him as she'd been doing recently.

He slid behind the wheel and started the motor. "Where can we go to talk?".

"I don't care. You choose."

He backed out, started north on Broad Street, and continued almost to where the road curved right to head out of town. Instead of taking the curve, he drove straight and headed up a hill.

"Where are you going?" she asked.

"To a place we can talk. You've never been up this hill?"

"No. I never realized there was a road back here."

"I guess that means you never came to Senior Hill with Rich." He chuckled.

"Rich? Why would I have come here with him?"

"To neck. I thought all the high school kids in town knew about this place. Like this car we're coming up on." He swerved around a sedan parked on the side of the road.

"He never brought me here, but it sounds like you're quite familiar with it."

"Me? Na. Just what I've been told."

"I bet." She snickered. Did he think she was going to fall into his arms and kiss and make up?

At the top, he made a U-turn and stopped alongside the road. "This is what I wanted you to see. It's a perfect night with a full moon. See how it's glistening on the lake down there?"

Grace faced the windshield and her breath caught. Tiny lights of the town's neighborhoods twinkled here and there. Beyond them, the lights of Main Street appeared strangely dim thanks to nightly black-outs. But moonlight couldn't be switched off and the lake glistened beneath the bright orb.

"Oh, it's lovely, and the cricket song makes a wonderful backdrop." She leaned her head back, mentally praying for the words that would put him at peace with her decision.

"You know, Grace, after we kissed on Monday, I spent the

rest of the day feeling as if I were ten feet off the ground. But something happened between the kisses we shared on Monday and the next morning when I called and Lenny said you weren't home. He's not a good liar. I know you were there. It's been that way ever since. I'm not sure what happened, but I think I deserve an answer."

"I know you do, Mac. I was wrong to have my kid brother lie for me. But I didn't know how to explain. I thought maybe you'd give up and just disappear from my life. Crazy, I know."

"You're not going to get rid of me that easy." He slid his arm over her shoulders and tugged her next to him. "I care about you too much, Grace. Am I that lousy of a kisser?"

"Oh, no. You're a wonderful kisser. Too wonderful. I should have never allowed us to get to that point."

"Why? We're both single, enjoy each other's company, and you said the age difference stopped bothering you long ago." He squeezed her shoulder. "Is it because I have a daughter and you don't want to end up being a mom if we ever got married?"

"I love Jo and don't want her hurt. And I'm afraid she will be."

"If you love her, does that mean her dad has a chance of being included in that love?"

"After we kissed, I realized I was falling for you and needed to get away so I could think."

He looked skeptical, and she hurried on.

"As I was driving away, I passed some bushes, and there was Jo, hunched down behind them looking in the direction of where we stood kissing. She had the biggest grin on her face. I knew right then that seeing us kiss gave her hope she'd have a complete family again." She swallowed against the lump forming in her throat. "We can't continue to see each other, because doing so would hurt your daughter."

"You're not making sense."

"I know, but you just have to trust me that you're better off not knowing my reasons."

He angled in his seat and drew her into his arms. "Grace, honey, nothing you tell me would ever cause me to not love you." He ran the tip of his finger around her mouth. "You said you felt yourself falling for me. Has that feeling changed?"

"No, but I think in time I can redirect my feelings."

"Redirect?" He leaned back. "You mean love another man instead of me?"

"Not another man, but something else I'm passionate about —anything to do with airplanes. I can't pilot the big bombers or commercial airplanes like I've dreamed of doing. But I keep thinking the right job is out there. I just have to find it. And when I do, it will be easier to focus on that and not you."

"Then you should aim to find out what you can do as a pilot," he said. "I love teaching, but loving another person is far more satisfying and enjoyable. It's possible to do both."

The man would make a good debater, but he wasn't going to wear her down. "Why can't we be in each other's lives as we've been all summer?"

"You mean as friends only?"

She opened her mouth to speak, but his lips claimed hers before she could utter a sound. Unable to resist, she slid her arm around his neck. He drew his lips away from hers, then cupped her face with his hands.

He ran his thumb over her right cheek. "You're crying. Who did this to you, so that you can't trust me to accept whatever you're afraid to tell me?"

"I'm sorry, Mac. Maybe you should just take me home and we end this right now."

"You're not getting rid of me that fast, Grace Bauer. I don't understand what your reason might be, but I'm going to pray like crazy that God opens your heart to my love, and you will eventually trust me enough to let me love you." He drew her into a hug and she pressed her face against his chest. Hearing his heart beating, steady and strong, she closed her eyes and silently prayed for God to give her the strength not to give in.

Minutes passed, but neither moved. Nestled in his arms, she felt safe. She didn't deserve this wonderful man. If he knew her past, he wouldn't want her as his wife, let alone a mom for Jo. He may think his love was strong enough to overlook her dark secret, but she knew better. He stirred and brought his lips to hers in a soft kiss. A kiss that could be the last they'd ever share.

The kiss ended and she said, "You're a good man, Mac McAlister."

He started the truck and got the vehicle rolling down the hill. Once it was in gear, he reached over and took her hand, weaving their fingers together. "I love you, Grace, and I'll respect your wishes, but I don't have to like them. If you're not willing to tell me your reason, then I think we need to stop seeing each other."

Her breath hitched, but she kept silent until he pulled up to the curb across from her side door. By then the lump in her throat felt as large as a peach pit.

After cutting the motor he faced her. "Since you haven't said anything, I guess this is goodbye." His voice cracked.

"Goodbye, Mac." Grace pushed her door open, jumped to the ground, slammed the door, then scurried up the walk. Footfalls sounded behind her, and she spun around expecting him to take her in his arms.

"You forgot this." He held out her bowling bag.

"Thanks." She took the bag and let herself into the house, then leaned against the door and let out the sob that had been filling her throat the past five minutes.

Outside, his truck roared to life. She pulled back the curtain from the side window and watched his taillights disappear into the night. "Good bye, Mac."

"Grace, are you okay?"

She jumped and turned.

Mom stood several feet away, wrapped in a bathrobe.

"Yes, I'm fine. Sorry to be so late."

"Was that Mac who brought you home?"

"Yes. We've been talking."

Mom flicked on the overhead light, and her lips turned up. "And communicating in other ways than words I see." She pulled a tissue from her robe pocket and dabbed at the corner of Grace's mouth. "Your lipstick is smeared."

"It's not what you think. We just broke up. I'm going to bed. See you in the morning." She moved to step around Mom.

Her mother's arm blocked her. "What do you mean, broke up?"

"Just what I said. I'm not ready to discuss it."

"Okay, but I'm here to listen whenever you're ready."

"Thanks." She continued to the stairs. She doubted she'd ever be ready, but Mom didn't need to know that.

27

The next morning, Grace dressed in a skirt and blouse, her normal outfit for volunteering, although considering she hadn't slept more than a couple of hours, she didn't know what good she'd do today. She headed for the kitchen and was surprised to find her mother sitting at the table, her Bible open in front of her. She dropped into one of the chairs. "What are you doing still home?"

"I decided to wait for you to get up so that we could talk."

"Oh." Tears pressed at the backs of her eyes. Hadn't she cried out every tear left in her body? The tears had their way, and she dug in her skirt pocket for her handkerchief. As always, Mom anticipated her need and was standing next to her with a tissue box.

She took a couple tissues and blew her nose. "Thanks."

"Now, stand up so we can hug," Mom said.

"That I can use." Grace stood and fell into her mother's arms, and the comfort of being there she'd enjoyed since she could remember wrapped around her.

"Are you ready to tell me why you and Mac broke up?"

Grace ached to tell her the truth, as she always had done in the past. But this wasn't a matter of a skinned knee or being spurned by a sixth-grade crush. It seemed the best course to take was to lie. Another transgression piled on top of all the others. "Please trust me. I can't tell you everything, but what happened with Frank and most recently with Rich has soured me for wanting to date, let alone be married. I think what people see on my face is infatuation.

"Are you sure?" Mom asked. "I see the look of love all over your face whenever you look at Mac or talk about him."

Her heart squeezed. "That's what everyone tells me. But yes, I'm sure."

"He's a nice man. He doesn't deserve to have his heart toyed with."

"I haven't done that. He knows I'm not at the same place as he is in our relationship."

Mom's left eyebrow rose. If you tell him you're not ready and then kiss him, that's toying with his heart, and with Jo's. Lenny told me the other day that Jo is sure her dad is going to marry you because she saw you two kissing."

Grace's chest tightened. A sob pushed through her throat. "I knew it. The first time we kissed was at the farm the other day, and we didn't know Jo was watching us. I saw her grinning from behind the bushes as I drove away That's when I decided I needed to not spend so much time with him."

"I thought *he* broke it off."

"He did. I wanted to continue as friends, but he said he couldn't do that, and that's when we broke up."

Mom heaved a sigh. "Then it's probably best you two take a break from each other until you figure out what's going on with you."

"I don't know how to figure that out. I've always been goal-oriented and not afraid of any challenge. This is so not like me."

"I know it's not. You and I are so much alike. When I was your age, I had dreams of becoming a lawyer and moving to a big city like New York. Then I met your dad and the Great War broke out. There's a Bible verse that says a man can plan his way, but the Lord directs his steps. You need to talk to God first and then your father. He's been concerned about you, and is convinced there's a career out there that involves flying. You haven't even been to the airfield or asked to go flying with him."

Grace stared at her lap. "I know. I don't know why I haven't. I think I'm afraid I'll find out I don't even like it anymore."

"I hardly think that's true, but the only way to find out is to take the Cessna up."

The telephone's sharp ring sounded from the hall and Mom stood. "Who can be calling so early? I'll see who it is. Help yourself to coffee. I'll be right back."

Grace stood and went to the coffeepot on the stove. She was adding her daily allotment of cream into the brew when Mom returned.

"Grace, it's Anne from the Red Cross. It sounded important. You'd better take the call."

Grace went to the phone where it sat on a small table in the hall and picked up the receiver. "Hi Anne. I was planning to come in later today. What's up?"

"If you're busy this can probably wait until you arrive, but as long as we're talking now, I wanted you to know that Mrs. Wilson is leaving at the end of the month, and I'll be stepping down from chairman of Home Service to move into directing the entire Red Cross chapter. I suggested you as a possible replacement for me. I think the decision will be made by day's end, and I wanted you to be forewarned to be prepared for the offer, should it come."

Grace's jaw dropped open. "Oh, my goodness. I don't know what to say."

"You already know the ropes and are familiar with most of what I do. If you are appointed, I can spend next week training on the few things you don't know. It's not like I'm leaving. I'll be right down the hall for any questions you might have. We can talk more after you come in later. By then I might know the final decision."

Grace returned to the kitchen and Mom turned from the stove. "I'm fixing you some quick scrambled eggs from the last batch Mac gave us. It looks like we may not be getting them anymore for a while. You may as well eat up the last of them."

"Only if we split them between us."

Over breakfast, Grace filled Mom in on Anne's news and Mom declared it was not a coincidence this happened. Of course, the Red Cross position wasn't likely to be her life's work, but at least it was a way to contribute to the war effort until the rest of the pieces of her life fell into place.

Before Grace left for the Red Cross office, Mom insisted she pray for her and this new opportunity. As Mom's words filled the room, a sense of peace washed over Grace. Why did that happen when another person did the praying, but not when she prayed herself?

A short time after Grace arrived at the Red Cross, Anne appeared in her office doorway.

"It's been decided. If you want the position, it's yours."

"That was fast," Grace said. "I'm glad you called, because that gave me some time to think about it. Yes, I'd be honored to take the position."

"Oh, Grace, I'm so glad." Anne's smile was dazzling. "I've been praying the Lord would help you to make the right decision. You can start training today."

28

Two Weeks Later

Grace stepped into her home's side entry and kicked off her pumps. Why did she think being the head of Home Service meant she had to dress the part of a business supervisor? Anne had always worn sensible shoes on the job, and she still did as the director of the chapter.

She stretched and pressed her fingertips to the small of her back. Her first week of training had been mostly learning all the ins and outs that Anne found helpful in tracking down military personnel. Although she already knew some of it, her notebook was now full of tips to use.

Today was spent unpacking boxes of new fliers and booklets and getting them placed on shelves in a small storeroom that had no window and little ventilation.

A hot bath sounded wonderful for her sore muscles, but with the outside temperature hovering near ninety, the last thing she needed was to sit in a tub of hot water.

Voices drifted down the hall from the kitchen, and she followed the sound and the enticing aroma of what smelled like apple pie.

Lenny looked up from where he stood next to the kitchen table, turning a food mill over a large pot. "Hi, Grace, we're making applesauce for a school project."

"Good for you, but who is *we*, and where did you learn how to make applesauce? I don't remember Mom ever making it."

"He learned how from me." Jo turned from where she stood on a small stool, stirring something in another large pot on the stove. She looked adorable with Mom's apron tied around her tiny waist. "My grandma taught me. We make it every year."

Grace's breath hitched as unexpected joy bubbled up inside her. "Jo!" She closed the space between them and drew her into a hug. "How have you been? I've missed you so much."

"I've missed you too, Miss Grace. Why did you stop coming to the farm?" Jo let her spoon drop into the pot and embraced Grace.

Loving the feel of the girl's arms around her, Grace blinked at her tears. She couldn't let the child see her crying. "What did your dad tell you?"

"That you weren't going to be spending time together anymore." She leaned back and dropped her arms. "I don't understand. I saw you and Dad kissing and thought ... kissing meant you loved each other."

Grace's heart squeezed and she hugged her again. Why didn't Mac set her straight? "Lenny, can you watch over everything for a few minutes?"

"Um. Sure. Kissing?"

"Never mind." She guided Jo out of the kitchen and into Dad's office, near the side door. They settled on the sofa side by side, and she took the girl's hand. "Jo, I noticed you behind the bushes when I left that day. I'm sorry you saw us kissing, and I hoped what you saw didn't mislead you. But it did."

The girl stared at her. "Why did you kiss my dad if you didn't plan to see him again?"

"Was that what your father told you?" It was the truth, but

she'd hoped Mac had made it more of a "we" decision and less hers for the sake of the child's understanding.

"He didn't say it exactly that way. Ever since I met you, I've been praying you'd be my new mom. You made my dad happy again. Now he's not fun anymore and is grumpy most of the time. Didn't you like being with him?"

"Yes, I did, but sometimes life gets complicated when you become an adult. I would love to have you as a daughter, but sometimes what we want and what is to be aren't the same thing."

"Did you and Dad have a fight?"

"No. If it makes you feel any better, I still have feelings for your father. Sometimes, though, those kinds of feelings don't always mean getting married."

Jo sat back. "I don't understand. If you love each other, why not get married?"

If only it were that simple. "It's not that easy to explain. But it doesn't mean you and I can't still be friends. I'm glad you were here today so we could talk. Maybe sometime soon we can spend time together, just the two of us."

A slight smile replaced the girl's sad expression. "Okay, but I'd prefer it to be with my dad too."

"I know, but two of us is better than nothing." She hugged the child. "Now, you'd better get back to the kitchen before Lenny comes and drags you out of here."

After Jo shut the door behind her, Grace stared up at the ceiling. "Lord, I want to make it better for Jo. Mac says he loves me, but I know if he hears about the awful thing I did, he'll change his mind. I'm sure I did the right thing in not telling him."

Weariness washed over her, and she curled up on the couch, remembering how as a little girl she'd lie on this very sofa and sleep while her father worked. If she could only go back to those days when the most important man in her life was her daddy.

"Grace, wake up." Someone shook her shoulder.

Her eyes popped open.

"Goodness, you were really out." Mom hunched down beside her. "Rough day?

"Yes. Never unpack and reorganize an office when it's ninety degrees in the shade." Grace rubbed sleep out of her eyes. "I was dreaming about Dad. Only I was a child, and he was carrying me around on his shoulders."

"Oh, how you loved it when he did that." The creases around Mom's eyes deepened. "Even back then, you wanted to fly just like your daddy."

"How long was I asleep?"

"I'm not sure. I just got home a short while ago. The kids are cleaning up the kitchen now, so dinner will be a little later than usual. You might want to get out of those clothes and into something more presentable."

After Mom left, Grace stood and stretched then glanced down at her blouse. Of all things to fall asleep in. She'd spent a good bit of time ironing it last night, and now look at it.

The sound of the side door closing wafted in. Jo must have just left. She'd better change her top and get to the kitchen to help Mom. She gathered up her purse, flung the door open, and dashed directly into Mac.

She stumbled back a step and stared at him. "What are you doing here?"

"Waiting for my daughter. What are *you* doing here?"

"I live here."

"That was a stupid question, wasn't it?" He chuckled and ran his gaze over her. His lips twitching like they always did when he was about to tease her.

Hair a tangled mess, blouse half tucked in and wrinkled. Her hand went to her hair, and she tried to fluff it. She had to look a sight. "I fell asleep on Dad's sofa. I'll let Jo know you're here." She took a step toward the kitchen.

"Don't run off." He rested his hand on her arm. "How are you doing, Grace?"

Ignoring the warmth of his touch and the soft tones he used to say her name, she said evenly. "Okay. How about you?"

"All right."

"Jo said you've been grumpy lately."

"She said that?"

"Yes. I hope it's not because of me."

"Whatever would make you think that?"

She shrugged. "I have no idea."

He cast her a wary expression then pulled a business card from his pocket and handed it to her. "I was going to leave this for you while I was here. A crop-dusting service Dad uses was at the farm the other day. I don't know why it didn't occur to me earlier, but is that the kind of thing you could do? The plane Dusty uses is small, but it is a plane, and it involves flying."

"Dusty?"

"His nickname, of course. His real name is Wes Fritz. Like on the card."

"I thought crop dusters were always kind of rough around the edges and flew old biplanes left over from the Great War."

His laugh filled the small hallway. "I suppose that's true about some of them. But the plane Dusty uses is nothing like that. I don't know planes very well, but it's not old. He mentioned he has so much business these days, with farmers trying to grow as much as they can to help feed the troops, he wished he had help."

Wasn't that like Mac to think of her despite the awful way she'd been with him? She didn't deserve half his kindness. "Thank you for thinking of me."

"I've been asking God to show me how I can help you use your flying skills and not be stuck at a desk. You're doing a wonderful service for the Red Cross, but when the war ends, so does the volunteer position, I imagine."

"I'm surprised you still pray for me after the way I've been with you."

"Of course, I still pray for you, Grace.

"Well your prayer is partly answered. I've been promoted to head of Home Service and do get paid a very small stipend. It's not flying related, but it's something."

A grin filled his face. "A promotion? That's great."

"I love the work, but joy in helping people doesn't pay bills, and I can't live with my parents forever." She held up Dusty's card. "Crop dusting intrigues me, but I don't own a plane. Does he have a fleet?"

"I think Dusty's business is a solo operation. But don't depend on me for information. Give him a call."

"Okay. Change of subject. What have you been up to besides tending crops and trees?"

"Repairs, mostly in the barn. The sink needed new plumbing, and one of the tractors needed new sparkplugs. I think tomorrow I may take a break, even though it's a weekday, and spend some time by the lake. It's probably going to be the last good weather day for a while."

"I'll let you know what comes of my conversation with ..." She glanced at the business card. "Mr. Fritz." She stepped toward the back stairs.

"Why don't you join me tomorrow, and we can enjoy the day together?"

She whirled around. "I don't know. My new duties as head of home service just started last week. I'm going in every day so I can get acclimated. Eventually, it'll be three days a week."

"If I take my day off later in the week, could you get away on Friday? I have no idea how the weather will be by then, but we can find something to do, I'm sure. He closed the space between them. "Please don't say no. I've missed you, Grace. I've missed your company and our talks."

I've missed you too. More than you know. She took a step back. She hoped to be caught up by Thursday. "I'll have to check the volunteer schedule before I can say yes."

"I'll call you in a couple of days. Think about it."

"Okay."

He stepped closer. "You look pretty cute with your rumpled blouse and hair."

Pretending to not hear his comment, she rounded the corner and arrived at the back stairs as Jo came from the kitchen. "Your dad is waiting for you in the hall."

The girl's face brightened. "Did you see him?"

"Yes. Don't keep him waiting." Without looking back, Grace went up the stairs.

29

Thursday morning Mac sat at his desk in the tree farm office and stared out at the rolling hills. He loved this place, but not as much as he loved a certain woman who was an enigma. Ever since she told him she couldn't be in a romantic relationship, that was all he wanted. He'd been patient in waiting for her to drop the walls around whatever it was that kept her from allowing him fully into her life. If it weren't for one thing he'd probably still be patient—her kiss

He hadn't kissed a woman since his wife died, and Grace's tender kisses gave him back something he thought he'd lost forever. As he watched her drive down the lane to the road, his head had filled with visions of bringing her here to the farm as his bride.

He'd planned on finishing the second floor of this little house, framed up when Emily became pregnant for the second time. They were very excited for Jo to be a big sister, but at six months Em miscarried, and then later she died.

There was no need for more bedrooms anymore, and the unfinished upstairs was only used by Jo for play space when bad weather forced her inside. Keeping it the same as it was when

Emily was alive was more important for both Jo and Mac than changing the home into something new.

That same afternoon, he'd dug out the plans for the second floor that included three bedrooms and a bathroom, complete with a shower, and went ahead and ordered tile for the bathroom floor. If he and Grace were blessed with a child or two of their own, he wanted to be ready.

It had been several weeks since they had that bittersweet conversation after bowling, when in frustration, he told her it was all or nothing. Last Monday afternoon, he'd jumped at the chance to pick Jo up at the Bauers' in hopes he'd run into Grace, and he wasn't disappointed.

She'd looked so cute and vulnerable with her tousled hair and untucked blouse. He yearned to draw her into his arms and kiss the daylights out of her. But he restrained himself. At least she didn't say no to the suggestion they spend a day together. Was she still open to the idea? It was time to find out.

He picked up the phone and prayed Grace would be home. If he had her on the phone right away, she'd have no choice but to talk with him.

To his surprise, she answered the phone.

"Good morning, Grace."

Silence filled the connection. "Hi, Mac."

"Have you thought about my invitation to spend tomorrow together?"

"Yes. If we can keep it as friends, I'd love to spend the day with you."

He released the breath he'd been holding. "That's swell. Can you be ready at one o'clock? I have some chores to do in the morning. The weather forecast looks good, and I'd like to spend most of the time by the lake, so wear casual clothes."

"It sounds like a fun day. One is fine. See you then."

They said their goodbyes, and he couldn't help grinning. Was it his imagination, or did he hear a lift in her voice? Somehow, by hook or by crook, he was going to win her heart.

GRACE PREPARED HALF a tuna fish sandwich for herself and made one for Lenny. Reenie was due back no later than twelve-thirty, and she hoped her not-always-punctual sister would be there by the time Mac arrived. Having to take her kid brother along was not her idea of a fun time, especially since things between her and Mac were still thawing out. She supposed if Jo were at home, she could suggest they take Lenny to the farm to play with her, if Mac's mom didn't mind.

By the time she finished her sandwich, it was twelve forty-five, and Reenie still wasn't home.

"Why do you keep looking at the clock? Are you expecting someone?" Lenny shoved the rest of his sandwich into his mouth.

"As a matter of fact, I am. Your sister better be here by one. She was due home at twelve-thirty."

"She's your sister too. Where are you going, anyway?"

"None of your business."

"I bet you have a new boyfriend. I don't know why you broke up with Mac. Just think, if you married him, then Jo and I could be brother and sister."

"Step-brother and sister."

"Huh?"

If I married Mac, you two would be ... no, that wouldn't be right. If I married Mac, he would be your brother-in-law, so she would be your niece."

He guffawed. "I'd be her uncle?"

"Yes, I think so. But get that notion out of your head. I'm not going to marry Mac." She stood and rinsed her dish in the sink and set it in the rack to dry. "I'm going to shoot our sister."

"Don't shoot me, I'm here." Reenie exploded into the room. "Sorry for being late. Time got away from me. I saw Mac pull up out at the curb. Looks like I got here in time." She ran her gaze over Grace. "Cute outfit. I love the button yoke on your shorts."

"You don't think the shorts are too short? We're going to be by the lake."

"They're halfway down your thighs, and they're perfect for a day by the water."

Lenny grinned. "You *do* have a date with Mac."

"It's not what you think." Grace glared at him. "There's the doorbell. I'll leave you two to your own devices." On her way to the side door, she grabbed her purse and wide-brimmed hat from the table in the hall and opened the door.

"Am I late?" Mac offered her the heart-stopping smile she'd been missing.

"You're right on time, and I'm happy to escape my little brother's taunting. He's very pleased we're getting together."

"As is my daughter. Why don't we leave the truck here and walk over to the Riv?"

They strolled side by side, Mac with his hands jammed into his trouser pockets and Grace keeping a distance away from him. They arrived at the corner, and he held her elbow as they crossed Main Street. When they reached the other side, he kept his grip.

"Let's sit a bit over there." He directed her to a nearby bench, and they sat. "Much nicer being out here and looking at the water. You look nice. Perfect choice for today."

"Thanks. And yes, it is nice. I'm glad you asked me to go with you today."

"Really?"

"Yes, really. But don't think I've changed my mind about being more than just friends."

He held up his hands surrender fashion. "It never crossed my mind. This is two friends spending an afternoon together."

The tension in her shoulders lessened. "Right."

He stretched his arm across the back of the bench. "So, having my arm loosely over your shoulders is okay?" He cupped her shoulder and tugged her a tiny bit closer.

"Yes." She allowed a slight smile.

"What about holding your hand?"

"Maybe."

He moved his arm off her shoulders and took her hand. "Like this?"

The feel of his skin, roughened by hours of caring for the trees, sparked a familiar tingle of affection for the man. Appealing as he was, she couldn't fall under his spell. She should pull her hand away, but it felt so nice to hold his hand again. The word "no" sat on the tip of her tongue, and she kept it there. "That's okay."

"What about this?" He wove their fingers together.

"I'm not sure."

"Or this." He lifted their clasped hands and kissed the back of her hand.

Shivers shimmied up her arm. "I didn't say kissing was allowed."

"That's not really a kiss."

She stifled a giggle. "You just kissed my hand. How can it not be a kiss?"

"In olden days men often kissed ladies' hands, and they weren't romantically involved. Now, kissing one's cheek might be off limits to your view because that's getting close to the mouth. And I know that must be *verboten*."

She glanced around quickly. "You'd better not let anyone hear you speaking German. But yes, mouth kissing is definitely off limits."

"It's a good thing we're sitting outside or I'd be tempted to try anyway. I've missed you, Grace."

And I missed you too. She was weakening, and as much as she loved being with him, it couldn't happen again. She moved a few inches farther away from him.

"We'd better get a move on. We have a boat to catch." He grabbed her hand and pulled her to her feet. Hang on to your hat. We need to move fast. Do you have your running shoes on?" He glanced at her loafers. "At least you aren't wearing heels. Come on."

His long strides about took her breath away as they scurried down the sidewalk toward the Riviera.

At the Riv, he led her down the walkway that ran alongside the building where they'd danced in the upstairs ballroom just before they broke up. He slowed as they approached the center pier. "There's my man."

A young man who appeared to be college age jumped onto the pier from one of the two wooden speedboats docked in their usual spots. He smiled at Mac. "Paul Gibbons, at your service." He made a slight bow in Grace's direction. "You must be Miss Bauer. May I assist you aboard?"

She smiled and accepted his outstretched hand, despite the fact she'd have no trouble getting on board by herself. Paul helped her settle on the cushioned seat at the back of the boat.

"Do you like your surprise?" Mac dropped onto the cushion next to her.

"Did you hire him for just the two of us?"

"Yes. We're the last ride for today. For the next hour, enjoy." He dropped his arm over her shoulder. "I almost forgot." He reached in his back pocket and pulled out a colorful scarf. "I know you brought a hat, but this scarf of my mom's might be better to wear because you can tie it. The hat might blow off. We'll be going fast, and I know how you women are about your hair."

He'd thought of everything. She tied the scarf over her head. "Good idea about wearing it instead of my hat. The wind will do nothing for my hair. But then, you already saw my hair at its worst Monday afternoon."

"At its worst is your opinion. I thought you were cute with it all tousled."

She answered with a roll of her eyes but let his words marinate and thaw her heart another few degrees.

"Hey, Paul," Mac called out. "Can we put Grace's hat somewhere to keep it from blowing out of the boat?"

"Sure." Paul lifted the lid on a storage box and placed the hat inside then returned to his position behind the wheel.

The boat motor started, and after a deck hand released the craft from the pilings, Paul put the boat in reverse then inched it out into the open water. The familiar aroma of water mixing with gas fumes stirred up a memory of Granddad taking her out on the lake in his new speedboat. She was the only female in the family who loved to go fast, and it was their special time together.

"Thank you." She smiled at Mac, took his hand, and squeezed it.

"You're very welcome."

Even the feel of her hand in his and how well they fit together was stirring up feelings she didn't want. She shouldn't have agreed to this, but it was only one boat ride, and then she could go home.

30

Out on the open water, Grace leaned her head against Mac's outstretched arm and let the warm breeze caress her face.

Paul put the boat in idle then turned and called out to them. "I can go really fast or keep it slow."

"Take it full throttle," Mac called out.

Paul's brows knitted together. "I'm not sure how Miss Bauer will like it."

"I'll love it, Paul." She laughed.

The young man shook his head. "We'll go pretty fast. If it's too much, let me know."

"Grace piloted B-17s for the military. She won't complain."

"Holy mackerel!" Paul stared at her, his eyes wide. "I had no idea there were lady pilots in the service. That takes a lot of moxie."

"I wasn't in the military. He's making too much ado about it. I was part of a group of women pilots called WASP. We flew new planes to air bases in the U.S. I loved it. And yes, let's go faster."

"I'm still impressed. Okay. You might get sprayed, but I guess you don't care."

He faced forward and pushed the throttle forward. The bow

of the boat lifted and bounced over the waves. Each bounce caused Grace to fly higher off the seat. She raised her arms in the air and let out a whoop. Pushing her hair out of her eyes, she grinned at Mac, loving the joy on his face.

An abrupt right turn flung her against Mac, and his arms went around her to stop her from going overboard. They burst out laughing.

"That was close," Mac said. "You'd probably have wanted to go right back home if you went into the water."

She stared at him. "Why? On this hot day a swim would have felt good."

Paul slowed the boat and called out. "Are you okay back there?"

"Yes. Can we do it again?" Grace patted her head. "Mac, I lost your mom's scarf."

"It's no problem." He whispered near her ear. Then facing the bow, he said, "Paul, I don't know why you made the turn like that, but we're fine."

"I wasn't grandstanding." Paul grinned. "There was a loose buoy in the water, and I didn't see it until the last minute."

Grace moved to sit up, but Mac's arms held her against him.

"You don't need to move unless you want to."

She settled into the crook of his arm. In his embrace, she felt as though she'd come home. "Mac, there's Safe Refuge. I didn't realize we were so close."

The old family home sat at the crest of the hill with its distinctive, red-shingled roof and dark shutters. At least from a distance, the place didn't appear as neglected as it had from the shore path. If she squinted, the image blurred enough to make it look as grand as it had before the crash.

Paul glanced at her. "Do you have a connection with that house?"

"Yes, I'm a descendant of the man who built it."

His mouth fell open. "I had no idea."

"Lots of memories for you, right?" Mac nudged her shoulder.

"Yes."

"Tell me about some of the memories," he whispered.

"When my parents were first married, they lived in the cottage that's hidden behind those pines on the north side of the building, and my grandparents lived in the big house. I was born in the cottage's downstairs bedroom, as was my brother Rory. When Reenie was on the way, we moved to the Main Street house we live in now."

Mac and Paul gazed at the house as she talked.

"I don't remember a lot, except for summers that seemed like a whole year. We children would live in our swimsuits and be in the water morning, noon, and night. Mom was a good swimmer, and she taught us all how to swim so she wouldn't worry about us so much. By the end of summer, we all sported tans that weren't as fashionable as they are today." She let go of a sigh. "The house has seen better days. I can't imagine what the inside must look like now."

"Would you like to see it?"

Surprised that Paul had been listening, she brought her focus to him. "I'd love to, but it's owned by a wealthy man who lives in California. He hasn't been seen around the property since the day he acquired it the summer of 1941."

"Well, this is your lucky day." Paul grinned. "That wealthy man is my grandfather."

Grace gaped at him. "Say that again."

He straightened and puffed his chest. "Charles Atwater, the owner of Rose Harbor, what you call Safe Refuge, is my grandfather."

This couldn't be a coincidence. She turned to Mac, her pulse pounding in her ears. "Did you know about this when you arranged for the boat ride?"

"I swear I didn't." He turned his attention to the driver. "Paul, if I can be so blunt, why does your grandfather continue to hang on to the estate if he never comes here?"

"He won the property in a poker game and didn't let my

grandmother know about it for months. Grandma was so upset that he hadn't told her, she refused to even see it. She passed away last year, and he has no interest in keeping the estate. Grandfather was hoping that in time, one of my cousins or I would take an interest, but I'm the only one who has. It's a beautiful place, but what can a guy my age do with such a house?"

Grace opened her mouth then closed it.

"I plan to enlist in the Marines this coming November, when I turn eighteen," Paul said. "My grandfather is paying me to live here until then and make some repairs before he puts it on the market. I only drive these speedboats a few days a week for some extra cash. Would you like to go inside the house? I can let the boat office know I'll be bringing the boat back a little late. There aren't any more rides booked for today, so I'm sure it will be fine."

The offer caught her off guard. "I don't know."

"What's the harm?" Mac nudged her. "I'd like to see it."

"I'm afraid it will be so different I won't recognize it. I'd rather remember it as it was when I was a child."

"I don't think much has changed." Paul started the boat cruising in a wide circle. "The décor appears old-fashioned to me. Of course, there have been some upgrades with the electric and telephone service." He started the boat moving toward shore. "We don't have to stay long."

"I suppose it sounds crazy," Grace whispered. "I know airplanes and how they work, and they're under my control. This is different. And seeing the house now will likely make me sad that I don't have the means of purchasing it back for the family."

Mac took her hand and squeezed it. "If it's His will for your family to get Safe Refuge back, He'll make it happen." He brought his mouth close to her ear and whispered a prayer for God to calm her and give her wisdom to know what to do.

"Thank you." Grace raised her voice. "Yes, Paul. Let's see it."

A few minutes later, Paul cut the boat's speed and let it drift up to the pier. "Can one of you take this rope and hitch it to the piling?"

While the men secured the boat, Grace climbed out and walked to the end of the pier as memories of the swimming parties Rich had mentioned emerged. She ran the toe of her loafer over some painted-over patches where the mounts for the diving board had been and smiled, remembering all the cannonballs she'd done off that board.

She then stared up the incline toward the house. If ever it needed the ivy she remembered growing around the second and third floor balconies, it was now. That was what made it look so different.

Many costly repairs were needed to restore the home to its former glory. If her grandparents moved back in, they'd have to hire a caretaker and a landscaping crew. Then how would they afford the property taxes? The dream of the family retaking the property faded as the expenses mounted in her mind.

"Grace, are you coming?"

"Yes." She snapped out of her contemplation and regarded Mac's outstretched hand. "I guess so." She stared at his hand a second, then took it and he wove their fingers together.

"We'll go in through the side door." Paul started walking toward the shore, the planks creaking under his feet. "The entrance from the front porch is locked."

Grace chuckled. "It sounds funny to call it a front porch. My granny always called it the veranda."

"What's the difference between a porch and a veranda?"

"I'm not sure." She glanced over at a small round structure sitting halfway up the hill. "My parents spent a lot of time in that spring house before Dad left for the war."

"I'm learning all sorts of things from you," Paul said. "What's a spring house?"

"Spring houses are structures placed over a spring for protection," Mac said. "They're a source of water for the property and often served as a place to store food before ice boxes were invented. There are quite a few springs at the west end that feed into the lake, which is why the water is so clear. We have a spring house on our land. The farmer who owned the property before us had a herd of dairy cows, and he stored full milk cans there for pickup each day by a local dairy."

"This is all very interesting to this city boy." Paul pointed to a flagstone path that led to the north side of the house. "That's the way to the side door. Follow me."

They came to the first-floor bedroom wing, added for Grace's father since he couldn't climb stairs when he first returned from the war. Off to the right, thick pine branches completely covered the footpath that led to the cottage.

Paul approached a door and opened it, and they followed him into a small vestibule Grace remembered. Turn left to enter the kitchen, she thought, or go straight behind the door in front of them for the backstairs to the second floor.

"Here's where I spend most of my time." Paul opened the door to the kitchen. "I don't go upstairs at all. I use the downstairs bedroom, the kitchen, and living room. The bedroom has one of those new window air conditioners, but it's very loud. I prefer sleeping on the por ... veranda on hot nights The screens keep the bugs away, and it's peaceful. Hard to imagine there's a war going on sometimes."

Grace glanced around the kitchen, trying to conjure up more memories.

"Does it look familiar, Grace?" Mac asked.

"Not like I thought it would. I was pretty young the last time I was here. I remember the veranda and the cottage—and the pier, of course." She smiled. "My cousins and I would sometimes sleep on the veranda like you do now, Paul." A giggle erupted from her throat. "One night we heard our older boy cousins out on the lawn and got up to peek. In the bright moonlight, we saw a pair of bare behinds racing toward the water as they tossed their pajamas onto the grass. A minute later came loud splashes."

Mac laughed. "Did you join them?"

"No. But we did sneak down to the lawn and hide their pajamas in the bushes. It was all we could do to keep quiet when they came back from the water and couldn't find them."

"I'll be right back. I need to call the boat office." Paul wandered out of the room, and soon his voice was heard as he spoke on the phone.

"I bet a lot of your ancestors skinny-dipped off the pier over the years." Mac nudged her with his elbow. "Don't tell me you never did."

"Girls weren't inclined that way like boys. I probably did as a toddler, but I don't remember."

"You were likely the cutest one in the water." His whispered words warmed her heart.

Her face heated, and she glanced at her feet.

"Sorry, I didn't mean to embarrass you."

The man was making it harder and harder to stop falling madly in love with him.

"Okay." Paul stepped back into the room. "The office is duly notified of our delay."

"After you show us the rest of the first floor, Grace would love to see the cottage where she was born."

There Mac went again. She stepped away from him. *Focus, Grace, focus.*

"You really do have connections." Paul gaped at Grace. "Do you think your family might want to buy the home back?"

An ache filled her chest. "I'm sure if the funds were available they would, but the family's fortune was lost in the crash. Now, if your grandfather wants to give it away ..."

Paul laughed. "I doubt it."

After they inspected the living room and its adjoining parlor and peeked in the downstairs bedroom, they decided not to go upstairs since it was getting late. They stepped outside the same way they came in, and Paul stopped. "I know the path to the cottage is through those pines, but I've never gone over there.

I'd need a tool to cut down some of the weeds and pine branches to get to the door."

"That's okay." Grace waved a hand. "It's been neglected for too long, and there are probably critters in there I don't want to see. I'm ready to leave." She took Mac's hand, and as they descended the hill, she glanced over at the flowerbeds.

Maybe it was just a well they couldn't afford the estate. Even Rory Quinn's roses were suffering from neglect. The property was no longer Safe Refuge. It was time to move on.

31

Back in the boat, Paul got the motor started then glanced over his shoulder. "Since you're a bomber pilot, Miss Bauer, how would you like to try piloting this craft?"

Grace stared at him. "Are you sure it would be okay? With your boss I mean."

"He's in his office at the Riviera, and we'll stay out in the middle of the lake. Just for a few spins in the open water."

She tried to catch Mac's eye for reassurance, but he wouldn't make eye contact. The bad girl side of her had yes on the tip of her tongue, while the good girl side said, "Don't do it." What would a couple of spins matter?

It would be the first time in a long while that she'd have the adrenalin rush that always came after she powered a B-17 into the air. "Sure. I'd love to give it a shot."

"I'll take her out in the open water, and then it's your turn." Paul flashed her a grin.

"Are you sure you want to do this?"

At Mac's question in her ear, she jumped.

"Only for a few minutes."

Paul brought the vessel to a halt in front of Stone Manor, the large Italianate home that ruled the east side of Geneva Bay, and moved over onto the passenger seat. "Miss Bauer, show me your stuff."

Grace squeezed between the front seats and slid onto the driver's seat. The leathery cushion formed to her body like a glove. A lot comfier than the pilot seats she was used to. She gripped the wooden steering wheel then ran her fingertips over the dials on the dashboard, only a few in comparison to the 17. Moving her hand to the throttle, she prepared to take the boat out of idle and propel it forward.

"Quick, trade places. It's the boss."

A distance away a boat sped toward them.

Pulse racing, she slid over to the passenger seat while Paul passed beneath her and got the boat moving toward the approaching boat.

Making every attempt to appear casual, she leaned back and glanced over her shoulder at Mac.

Brows raised, he nodded as if to say, "Good move."

The other boat, a twin of the one they were in, slowed and pulled up alongside them. The man at the wheel pushed his white sea captain's hat back, revealing a bald head. The lines in his tanned face showed his age to be between fifty and sixty.

His steely gaze settled on Paul. "Paul, you were due back almost an hour ago." He glanced at Grace and Mac and nodded. "You folks enjoying your ride?"

"Yes, sir. It's a magnificent vessel." Mac ran his palm over the wood frame. "You must be very proud of your boats. I'm afraid the tardiness was our fault. Grace here is descended from the family who built Rose Harbor, and when we learned Paul's grandfather owns the estate, we couldn't resist asking to have a peek at the old house."

The man frowned and peered at Paul. "Why didn't you let me know you would be late coming back?"

"I called the office and told Rosemarie. Didn't she tell you?"

"No, she didn't. She was gone when I returned to the office. Well, I need you to bring the boat in now. I have a dinner engagement and need to leave early." He waved and turned his boat toward the Riviera.

"Whew. That was close." Paul got the boat up to speed as Mac grabbed Grace's hand and squeezed it.

At the Riviera, Grace thanked Paul again, and after Mac jotted down Paul's phone number at Rose Harbor, they said their goodbyes.

Heading through the arcade on the Riviera's main floor, they passed the ticket window for the boats.

Paul's boss's voice drifted through the open door.

"The woman in the boat is a descendant of the original owner of your property. She wasn't interested in buying, just curious to see the house. No, I don't think they are aware of the hidden cash rumor. Time is running out, Charles. That group from Chicago was out looking over the estate again. All they talked about was how much money they could make by subdividing the property."

Grace froze.

"Come on." Mac tugged on her hand. "Let's get scarce before Paul or his boss sees us still here."

They scurried through the arcade and emerged by the steps that led up to the ballroom, then continued until they were on the sidewalk, heading west. They came to a bench on the grass behind the library and sat.

"Have you heard anything about hidden money at Safe Refuge?" Mac asked. "Or the property being subdivided?"

"No, but subdividing is something that's being done now with some of the original estates." She stared at her lap. "It was foolhardy of me to think about driving that boat. It was a struggle deciding whether to take him up on the offer or not. I'm glad Paul and I switched places when we did. No telling what would have happened if he'd seen me driving the boat."

"You were just anxious to feel the same excitement you felt flying those bombers." He draped his arm over her shoulders. "I think God intervened to stop you from causing problems for Paul."

"I'm sure the Lord has His hands full protecting people from harm at the war front. Why would He be concerned about me or Paul?"

"Don't underestimate the Lord. Do you think your grandfather is seeing patients this afternoon?"

She frowned. "Probably. Why?"

"Maybe the family can't obtain the entire estate, but they could gain a small part of it. It would be better than having nothing at all. He might like to know about the possibility of the estate being subdivided." Mac looked toward the street. "We can probably walk to his office faster than it would take to drive, since my truck is parked a block the other direction."

32

Grace pulled unsuccessfully on Granddad's office door, then glanced at her watch. "It's only three. He's usually here until four."

"Your watch must have stopped. It's four fifteen. Maybe he's still in there." Mac banged on the door. The sound of approaching footfalls on the other side was followed by the turning of the lock.

The door cracked open, and Peggy peeked out. "I'm sorry, but the doctor isn't ... oh, Grace, hello." She swung the door open. "If you're here to see your grandfather, he's about to leave through the backdoor."

"Oh, please catch him. We only need to talk to him a minute or two."

Peggy opened the door wide enough to allow them entrance, and Grace relocked it while Peggy scooted into the hall that led to the exam rooms.

A moment later, Granddad stepped into the room, a smile on his face. "Well, this is a surprise." His gaze toggled from one to the other. "Is everything okay at home?"

"Yes," Grace said. "I have some questions about when Safe Refuge was sold after the crash. Do you have a few minutes?"

He nodded. "Yes, I always have time for you. Grace."

Letting his soothing comment calm her, she took a deep breath. "Do you want to sit?"

"Not unless you plan to be here more than a few minutes."

"Okay. How did the sale come about?"

He crossed his arms and let out a sigh. "We had to do something to bring in ready cash. It was legal for me to sell the property, since I'd been named as administrator of the trust after Rory Quinn passed away. It was fortuitous that I was the overseer and able to handle the transaction in a way that we were able to keep the Main Street house and accrue enough funds to purchase the Dodge Street house for your grandmother and me. Why do you ask?"

"We just took a tour of the big house from the young man who is watching over the property for his grandfather, the current owner. We heard a rumor that money might have been hidden on the property. Have you ever heard anything like that?"

"It's true that money and other treasures are sometimes hidden in the walls of old homes." Granddad's eyes twinkled. "I've heard gold bars were hidden in Stone Manor. But so far as I know, none have been found. I doubt there's anything like that hidden in Safe Refuge. By the time we were forced to sell, none of us had any cash to hide."

"What if money was hidden before Leonard Hartwell passed away?"

Granddad's gray eyebrows knit together. "I do recall Maureen mentioning something like that years ago, but I think they decided it wasn't true because no money was ever found. Are you thinking of searching out there?"

"Maybe not specifically looking for money, but for some kind of clue as to where Leonard might have hidden something of value. It might provide leverage with Paul's grandfather to regain ownership of the property."

"Paul?"

"The grandson of the current owner I mentioned. I've been

thinking the cottage would make a wonderful place of refuge for war widows to live until they can get on their feet again."

"That's certainly an ambitious goal, but to gain entrance to search is problematic." Granddad's eyes misted. "You'll have to ask your father how to legally go about that. Why don't you stop by his office and see if he's there?"

They stepped out on the sidewalk, and Grace glanced at Mac. "Do you think I'm going on a wild duck chase?"

"You mean wild goose." He chuckled.

"I knew I said it wrong." She waved away his remark. "I just can't get the notion out of my mind that the cottage would be a perfect place for a war widow trying to get on her feet."

Mac took her hand. "I love your heart, and the only way to find out if it's doable is to talk to your dad.

Grateful to find her father's law office door open, Grace and Mac stepped inside and Dad's secretary raised her head from her typing.

"Grace, long time no see." She glanced at Mac. "We briefly met when you and your father were here a few days ago. I'm Lorraine Morris."

"I remember." Mac nodded. "Nice to see you again, Lorraine."

"Is my dad in?" Grace asked. "We have time to wait, if he's with a client or on the phone."

"Is that a familiar voice I hear?" Dad stepped into the room and grinned. "My daughter I see most every day, but, Mac, you've been a stranger around our house lately. Good to see you again." He focused on Grace. "And to what do I owe this surprise visit?"

"We have questions regarding the Safe Refuge property."

Dad's eyebrows rose. "My next appointment isn't for half an hour. Come with me."

In Dad's office, he shut the door and sat behind his large oak desk while Grace and Mac took the two chairs across from him. "Okay, the floor is yours."

After giving him the same summary she'd given Granddad,

Grace ended by saying, "It's a long shot, but I'm thinking if Leonard Hartwell hid any money or valuables on the property, he must have left a clue as to where it was hidden. If we could locate the clue, it would help in negotiations to get the property returned to the family."

"That's an ambitious goal, my darling daughter." His brow furrowed. "But there are some high hurdles to leap over to get to that point."

"That's about what Granddad said." She slumped against the back of her chair. "But if we don't at least try to find a possible clue, I'd never forgive myself. So much good could be had from that property, and I'm not talking about hidden treasure."

Dad focused on her. "Are you saying you wouldn't want the money if you found it?"

"Not really. It's the cottage I want most of all."

"Why?" He leaned back in his chair, causing the cushions to squeak. "Because you were conceived and born there?"

"I can't deny there's a bit of sentimentality attached to the cottage, but that's not the reason." She offered a soft smile. "I have a vision of using it as a soft place to land for people who've lost so much during this war. I can't get the thought out of my mind of how many widows and fatherless children are victims already. Not all of them are able to get along with only a small allotment coming in from the military."

Her father rubbed his chin, staring past her as he thought.

Grace moved to the edge of her chair. Her lower lip trembled and she bit down on it. "I only want a shot at searching the property for something Leonard may have left behind to direct us to where he hid any money."

"I don't advocate going in there and smashing into walls." Dad sat forward and rested his elbows on the desk. "But I see no harm in asking the current owner for access to some of the property to search for an item you think might have been left behind by the original owners. I wouldn't say what exactly it is. Better if you make it sound like it's something that would only be of value to the family. Like a photograph or something of the sort."

She grinned. "That's an excellent idea."

"Well, whatever you do, don't go in there without the owner's permission. I don't want to have to come up to Elkhorn to bail you out of jail."

"I'll be careful. I'm first going to start with the papers that came with the family when Safe Refuge was sold. I have a hunch they're in our attic."

33

Mac leaned his head against the truck's seat back and closed his eyes. The warm breeze wafting through the open windows felt good. Grace had gone inside a while ago to make sure they could slip up to the attic without others noticing. She'd been gone almost ten minutes. Searching her attic could be done another day, but if it meant spending a few more minutes with her, he didn't mind. His eyes popped open as she got into the truck.

"Of all times for Lenny and his friends to take over the attic," she said. "He hasn't played up there in ages. If a clue to hidden money is in Hartwell's papers, the attic is likely where it is. We need to get in there."

"My daughter isn't up there too, is she? She wanted to come with me when I told her I was coming here."

"No. It's all boys, and they're playing some kind of war game. I hate how the real war is leaving an impression on kids, as if war is a normal thing when it's not. But that's a discussion for another day."

"Patience." He patted her on her arm. "They'll tire of it and be on to something else soon."

"Not soon enough. I promised Mom I'd get dinner started

since she has to work at the library until six. Being Friday, it stays open later."

"If we can't get in there today. We can do it another day." He opened the glovebox and pulled out a small notebook and pencil. "Let's use the time to plan. If, by the time we finish, they're still up there, you can shoo them out."

"Okay."

"It would appear the only way to get into the big house right now is through Paul." He poised the pencil over the pad. "Do we contact him and ask if we can get into the big house because you're sure something is there the family left behind? Your dad suggested a photo—something that would only hold meaning for the family and have no other monetary value."

"I doubt he'd fall for that." She shrugged. "It's been years since the family has lived there, and another family occupied the home before Paul's grandfather acquired it. Maybe the money isn't hidden in the house at all. It could be in the cottage. The place looks as though it hasn't been used in years."

After he jotted on the pad he glanced at her. "Anything else?"

"Yes. I could say I also want to see the spring house, where my dad proposed to my mom before he went to war. Thing is, if he wants to go with us, how can we search with him being there?"

Mac jotted down the words *cottage* and *spring house*, each with a question mark. "We may have to feel him out and see exactly what he knows about any supposed hidden money. How loyal is he to his grandpa?"

"He's due to join the Marines after he turns eighteen in a couple of months. We don't know much about him."

"Another question. Did Hartwell keep a journal?"

Voices came from the direction of the house. Mac focused over Grace's shoulder as Lenny and three other boys scrambled down the porch steps and onto the sidewalk. Lenny stopped running and stared at the truck. A smile crossed his freckled face, and he ran toward them.

"Mr. Mac! Hi!" He stuck his head in Grace's open window. "Where've you been, Mr. Mac? I've missed you."

"Don't I count?" Grace tweaked his cheek. "I'm sitting here too."

"You're my sister." Lenny rolled his eyes. "I see you all the time."

Stifling a chuckle, Mac said, "I miss seeing you, too, Lenny, and I know Jo has. She's been busy helping me on the tree farm, and her grandmother is teaching her how to cook."

"You two seeing each other again?" Lenny's gaze jumped from Mac to Grace.

Mac wished he could see her face, but her sigh told him it was probably better he didn't.

"As friends, yes. Are you done in the attic?" she asked.

"Yeah, we're headed over to the playground. Tell Jo hi for me." He turned and ran up the street toward the school's playground.

"Did you mean what you said?" Mac nudged her. "We're seeing each other?"

"Notice I said as friends," she answered with a shrug. "Today was fun. I've missed you, Mac."

"I've missed you too." He resisted the urge to hug her. "And the day's not over yet. You ready to search the attic?"

GRACE RESTED her fists on her hips and glanced around the stuffy attic. "I forgot how hot it would be up here. At least they didn't leave too much of a mess." She picked up a shirt that was large enough to have once belonged to Dad from the floor and carried it to an open box full of clothes labeled *Charity* and tossed it in. "Remind me to carry this box downstairs when we leave. I'll take it to the Red Cross for the clothing drive."

"What are we looking for?" Mac picked up the carton and carried it to the head of the stairs. "A trunk, a storage box?"

"Your guess is as good as mine. Could be a trunk, I suppose. My thought is, if he left a clue, it wouldn't be in a legal paper, but hidden inside a book or written in code of some sort in a personal journal. I've been told that when the place was sold, they had only a week to pack up and move."

She stepped over to a small chest of drawers and opened the top drawer. "Lots of old papers in here." She took several out and flipped through them. "These are letters from my dad to Mom when he was overseas in the Great War."

"Didn't you tell me he was a POW?"

"No, thank goodness. After he was shot down over Belgium, he was taken in by an elderly couple, and they hid him in their basement. You should hear some of his war stories."

She opened a folded letter, careful to not tear the thin paper and skimmed her dad's familiar handwriting. "Listen to this. It's written right after he finished flight training for the RAF and was flying bombing runs.

'Dearest Hannah, I'm no longer stationed near London, but I can't disclose my location. Please don't worry. Flying in the air is safer than being a sitting target in the trenches. I have to say, outside of meeting you, my darling Hannah, this has been the best time in my life. I can't explain what it feels like to be flying through the air with the beautiful English countryside below me.'"

She smiled at Mac. "He was flying two-seater biplanes, where the pilot sat in the rear seat." She pressed the letter to her chest. "I can't imagine flying with the wind whipping around you. Cockpits weren't enclosed back then."

Mac came up beside her. "That's what you were imagining when we were in Paul's speedboat weren't you?"

"Yes. I don't want to be flying that kind of plane into a battle, but it would be fun to fly one during peacetime."

"Maybe someday you can." He draped his arm across her shoulders. "Your father must have connections."

"I suppose. I keep thinking God took that joy away from me for a reason, and I shouldn't interfere."

"Do you mean like a punishment?" He frowned.

"I guess so."

"Want to talk about it?"

Would he understand if she told him? Maybe. But if she did, it would be the end of their already precarious friendship. She may have courage to fly a B-17 but not enough to tell him about her past. She refolded the letter and placed it back in the drawer. "Not now. There's nothing but old letters in here. What we came to look for was an old journal or some kind of note written by Hartwell."

Grace pushed the drawer shut and opened the drawer beneath it. Nothing but old photos, many she'd seen over the years of people stiff and staring like they did in the days when cameras had long exposure times. She shut the drawer and spotted a small trunk across the room and headed for it.

Inhaling deeply, she blew at a film of dust on the trunk and coughed. "Whew, this hasn't been opened in a while. Maybe we'll find something in here." After trying to open the latch without success, she looked up. "It's locked and there's no key around that I can see."

"Should I go downstairs and ask if the key is down there?"

"If you don't mind. Meanwhile, I'll keep looking up here."

By the time Mac returned saying no one was home to ask about such a key, Grace was holding a long dress with mutton sleeves up to herself. "I can't imagine wearing dresses like this." She held the garment away from her and gave it a shake. "All this extra fabric in the back must have been for the bustle."

"The what?" Mac chuckled.

"A contraption that attached to their waist. It made their behinds appear twice the size as normal. How they sat with one of those on, I have no idea."

"Would that dress have been worn at the time Hartwell was alive? Is there anything else in the wardrobe besides clothing?"

"Good idea, Watson." She gave him a thumbs-up then tucked her head inside the wardrobe and felt around the bottom. Her hand landed on what felt like a shoe, and she lifted it out. She turned the pump over in her hand, admiring its pretty bow, then reached in the wardrobe and pulled out the matching left shoe. "What cute shoes. I wonder if ..."

"If what?"

"These are the shoes Granny wore when she was recovering from smallpox and she and Granddad began courting. I've heard the story a dozen times. She conveniently stepped on a rock and fell, spraining her ankle."

Mac laughed. "Ah, the wiles of women never change." He came close and hugged her from the side. "You wouldn't do anything like fake a sprained ankle, would you?"

"I'll never tell. It worked, though. Granddad had to carry her back to Safe Refuge, and that's when they shared their first kiss." She gazed into the wardrobe. "These dresses are in great condition. I wonder if we could sell them and put the proceeds in the Safe Refuge fund."

"You didn't tell me about such a fund."

"I just made it up." She gathered her hair and lifted it to the top of her head, then clipped it in place with a large barrette. "That feels better. Long hair and heat don't mix well."

"Did you just happen to have something to clip to your hair?

"No. I found it on the bottom of the wardrobe with the shoes. It probably belonged to Granny when she was young. I think I'll keep it."

"It's very pretty in your hair." Mac turned her until they faced each other, his focus on her mouth, and leaned in.

Anticipating his kiss, she stepped back. "Look around at all this. No one ever comes up here to look at any of it. I'm going to talk to my parents and grandparents about seeing what we might get for these things." She placed the dress and shoes back in the wardrobe. "Let's look around and see if we can find a key that would work in that little trunk."

"Good idea." He sighed and walked to a worktable on the other side of the space. "Here's a hammer. Is it okay if we break the lock with this?"

"Do whatever is needed." She didn't care about the lock being broken but she did care about the look of disappointment she saw on his face when she spurned his intended kiss. If she wasn't careful, he'd tire of having his heart broken because of her fear. She'd have to throw caution to the wind soon and tell him the truth. But not yet.

Hammer in hand, Mac knelt next to the trunk. "Here goes nothing." He raised his arm and brought the hammer head against the lock. "Partial success." He swung again and the lock fell to the floor.

Grace let out a whoop, dropped to her knees beside him, and lifted the lid. "What are these? Old ledgers?" She picked one up and flipped it open. "It looks like records for the landscaping and florist business my great-grandfather Rory ran. Look at the prices. The monthly cost of mowing an estate's large lawn was cheaper than what Lenny makes mowing our neighbors' lawns now."

"Don't forget the cost of living was a lot less back then. Even during the Depression, it wasn't as low. No telling how prices will be when the war ever ends."

"I thought I heard voices up here." Mom emerged from the stairwell, and Grace jumped to her feet. "I'm sorry, I lost track of the time. I was supposed to start peeling potatoes for supper."

"I'm home earlier than I expected." Mom waved a hand. "It's only five-thirty. What are you two up to?"

"Looking for a clue Leonard Hartwell might have left," Grace said, "but all we've found were some nifty old dresses and Dad's love letters to you. I'll wash up and be down to help with dinner."

"Should I be embarrassed by anything in those letters?" Mom came closer.

"Not at all. Lenny would call them mushy, but I think they're sweet."

"They were what kept me going those months he was missing in action. I still come up here and read them once in a while. Every time I do, I fall in love with him all over again." Mom smiled at Mac. "Mac, it's good to see you. Would you like to join us for dinner? Nothing fancy. Just left-over meatloaf and mashed potatoes."

"That sounds good, Mrs. Bauer, but I've been away all afternoon. I'd best get home and make sure my daughter isn't making a pest of herself with my parents."

"I doubt she's being a pest. She's a delightful child whenever she's here."

"Good to know she minds her manners when she's visiting others." He turned to Grace. "I'll call you tomorrow, and we can figure out next steps." He stepped over to the charity box. "Where do you want this?"

"Just leave it by the back door. I'll have to use Mom's car to get it to the Red Cross later."

"Is there a spot there for people to leave donations? I can take it in my truck right now."

"Yes, there is an area by the back door."

"Then consider the job done." He hefted the box and started down the stairs. "No need to see me out. I know the way." His footfalls faded when he reached the second floor, and Mom faced Grace. "Is this what I think it is?"

She lifted her shoulders and let them drop. "What do you think it is?"

"That you two are dating again."

"We've renewed our friendship. It's nothing more than that."

"Okay. But I saw the way you looked at each other, it's apparent the spark between you hasn't died. He's a nice man, and I think he's good for you. That's all I'm going to say. I'll see you in the kitchen." She headed down the stairs, and Grace walked over to the small trunk and closed its lid.

"Friends. That's all we are," she said to no one.

Later that evening she said goodnight to the family and retreated to her room. She'd said she was tired and wanted to go to bed early, but she couldn't shake off Mom's words about Mac. Yes, he was a good man, but was Mom right that he would be good for Grace?

After getting into her nightgown, she climbed into bed and took out the book by Amy Carmichael. She'd leafed through it several times, but the writings brought tears to her eyes, and she'd always tossed it back in the drawer. This time, her eyes fell on an entry from Amy's journal that referenced Psalm 56.

Taking her Bible out of the drawer, she flipped to the psalm and a line jumped out at her.

Thou tellest my wanderings: put thou my tears into thy bottle.

Did that mean God wasn't hiding from her? That He knew of her wanderings away from Him, and He has been aware of her tears? As if on cue, tears erupted and she let the book drop to her side. "Oh, God, help me. If You really are there and have never left me. I've not been fair to Mac, and like Mom said, he is a good man. Too good for me. I need to let him go. He needs someone far better than me."

Grace picked up her Bible to close it, and the last line of the psalm jumped out at her.

For thou hast delivered my soul from death: wilt not thou deliver my feet from falling, that I may walk before God in the light of the living?

She closed the book, turned out the light, and lay down. "Thank you, Lord. I want more than ever to walk before You in the light of the living. I know what I need to do and ask for strength to do it.

34

Mac pulled his truck up to Rose Harbor's entrance and stopped. "I don't remember a locked gate being here. How did I miss it?"

"There never was a gate until now. How is one supposed to call on the residents with a locked gate?" Grace moaned. "We can't even park out here and walk in. I wish Paul would have answered when I called earlier."

"Does that iron fence on either side of the gate go all the way around the property except at the lake front?"

"Yes. It's been there as long as I can remember. I always wondered how much good it did when there was no barrier along the shore on the other side."

"Let's take the truck back to your house and walk over on the shore path. They can't block the path, and we should be able to enter from there."

"I keep remembering what Dad said about being arrested for trespassing. Is it trespassing if we're only trying to get to the door to ring the bell? And what do we say about why we want access to the cottage?"

He put the truck in reverse and used the cement apron in

front of the locked gate to turn around. "We can be honest without divulging all the details."

Mac drove to Main Street and made a right turn. "You know the old saying, honesty is the best policy. I think it's better if we say we're looking for some family photos that weren't with the ones that were brought out with the others."

"That's farfetched to me. Who hides a photo?"

"Perhaps a photo that connects Hartwell to some nefarious situation he didn't want to be connected to."

After parking the truck at Grace's house, they strode through Library Park to the shore path. As they walked, Mac tried to tamp down the nagging warning Grace's dad gave her about trespassing. It wasn't like they didn't try to contact Paul. He sent a mental prayer heavenward asking that, if they were making a mistake, God would cause something to happen that would stop them.

They passed Lake Geneva Manor, where he'd brought Grace several weeks ago, barely giving it a glance. They next came to what used to be called Snug Harbor, now serving as a church camp called Covenant Harbor.

"Grace, maybe we should rethink—"

"I don't believe it. Why didn't anyone stop them?"

"What?" He stared at her.

"See for yourself." She pointed down the path.

He gaped at the chain link fence that stood at least six feet high, blocking anyone from walking past Rose Harbor.

"There's a sign on the part that blocks the path. Let's see what it says, and then I'm going straight to the police." Grace marched down the path, and he had to hurry to catch up.

The largest letters on the sign came into view.

PRIVATE PROPERTY.
ALL TRESPASSERS WILL BE ARRESTED.

"How can he have the gall to put up this metal fence while

others are giving this kind of thing to the war effort?" Grace kicked at the fence, and it wobbled. "And how can he get away with it?" She raised her leg to kick it again but stopped when Mac rested his hand on her shoulder.

"Let's try to figure out what this means."

"What do you think it means?" She faced him. "They don't like us nosing around. Something is rotten in the state of Safe Refuge, and I intend to get to the bottom of it."

"Hamlet, Act 1, Scene 4."

She quirked her head. "What are you talking about?"

"That quote is from Hamlet. I teach from it in Senior English every year. Of course, the line from the play says Denmark, not Safe Refuge." He walked over to the fence and stuck his fingers between the openings and wiggled the barrier.

"As I suspected, it's not secure. A fence like this requires posts sunk into cement." He turned and peered at the steps leading down to the dock. "They even put a locked gate in front of the pier so no one can enter from there. It does seem imposing until you test the fence and see how unstable it is."

"I have half a mind to knock this gate down, march up the hill, and give him a piece of my mind."

"Give who a piece of your mind, Grace? Paul is still a teenager about to go to war." He cautiously draped his arm over her shoulders. The woman had spunk, which didn't surprise him. "I doubt he's the enemy."

"There's someone over there." She pointed to a blond-haired man wearing baggy khaki trousers and a matching shirt with P W and what looked like a number printed on its back. Seemingly oblivious to them, he worked the earth around a small tree with a spade.

"Hey!"

At Mac's shout, he turned in their direction, a wary expression on his face. He focused on Mac.

"Good afternoon. We're looking for Paul Gibbons. Is he home?"

The man frowned. *"Ich spreche kein Englisch."*

"He's speaking German," Grace whispered. "I only know a few words I picked up while ferrying planes. I think he said he doesn't speak English." She stepped closer. *"Wir wollen Paul Gibbons sehen."*

The man's face brightened "Ah, *Herr* Gibbons." He pointed toward the big house.

Farther up the incline, a tall broad-shouldered man with darker hair stepped around the spring house and approached. He said something in German, and the other man waved his hand and returned to his work.

Mac relaxed. Of course. Why didn't he make the connection before?

The new man focused on them. "He, ah, not speak much English. You looking for Herr Gibbons?"

"Yes. Maybe we could speak to him or your guard."

The man nodded. "Yes. Wait here." He strode up the hill to the big house.

"Why did you say guard?" Grace frowned. "Is he from the county jail?"

"They're likely from the POW camp at Mitchell Field in Milwaukee. Our farm was notified a couple of weeks ago that the ones on good behavior are available to perform labor for farmers and others with large property that needs care. It looks like Paul's unpredictable grandfather took them up on the offer, and he's making sure none escape while they're here."

Grace frowned and gazed through the fence at the worker. "I heard there are POW camps all around our state, and a lot of the prisoners are being used to assist on farms, much like what my mother did with the WLA."

He shook his head. "I still can't imagine your mother working on a farm."

"I know. To look at her now, you'd not think she could, but she did."

"There's Paul now."

"Hi, folks." Paul approached them. "Sorry for the fortress. Woke up the other morning to the sounds of the fencing going up. I had no idea what was happening. Grandfather never warned me, but he's very impulsive and used to calling his own shots. I called my grandfather immediately, and he said he had the fencing taken out of storage from one of his warehouses because he'd asked for a few POWs from the camp in Milwaukee to help tend the grounds."

"I figured as much," Mac said.

"I checked into it," Paul continued. "They said they never suggest to anyone assigned a POW that they need to lock them in, but Grandfather doesn't want to be held responsible if one escapes. It's only until they leave."

Grace crossed her arms. "Warehouse where? In California?"

"He has one in Chicago. It came from there."

"I'm surprised he hasn't donated it to one of the scrap drives going on. Our country needs all the metal it can get."

"I know, but you don't know my grandfather."

She glanced at the fence blocking the path. "Are you aware that the shore path is public like a sidewalk, and no one is to obstruct it? The way the fencing is set up, there's no way one can get past the property to continue down the path."

"I told Grandfather it would have to be taken down where it blocks the path, but he's not used to being told he can't do something."

"What if the police tell him he can't do this?" Grace asked. "These men look harmless to me. I imagine they're glad to be out from under those Nazis, even if it's only for a little while."

"If you want to report it to the police, go ahead. I'd feel funny doing it against my own grandfather. I'm sure you didn't come here just to see all this." He swept his arm in a half circle toward the lawn.

"No. We were coming to ask permission to go into the cottage. We think some old photos are missing from what my family took with them, and I want to see if they were left in the cottage, where their belongings were stored until they could be moved."

Paul frowned. "I guess that would be okay. Would you want to look in the main house too?"

"Possibly."

He visibly tensed. "When are you wanting to do this?"

"As soon as possible."

"Okay, but you'll have to check with me first. Since the house is going on the market, I don't want you snooping around while prospective buyers are looking at the property."

"Is it okay if I call you tomorrow to set a time?" She stepped closer to the fence.

"Sure. But don't call before nine."

They agreed to Grace's calling him the next day, and after Paul began to walk back up the hill, she faced Mac. "Do you think he was on the up-and-up?"

Should he tell her that the whole thing smelled fishy to him? He decided to soften his response. No use upsetting her more than she already was. "Partly yes and partly no."

She stared at the house and blinked at the moisture in her eyes.

He pulled a clean handkerchief from his pocket and handed it to her.

Grace dabbed at her eyes. "I never thought I'd see Safe Refuge looking like this, Mac. We ... I need to get it back somehow."

Did she mean we as she and the family, or the two of them? If it were anyone else, he'd not like being presumed on like that, but with Grace, he liked the idea of being a couple. Was it for keeps or just for now?

They returned to the truck, and Mac drove four blocks down Main Street and parked in front of the police station. Grace already had her hand on the door handle.

"Wait, not so fast. Do you know what you want to say?"

"It's pretty obvious." She stiffened. "The owner of Rose Harbor is breaking the law and needs to be arrested."

"Okay, but may I suggest that you soften the tone and make it sound less like an angry order?"

"Well, I am angry."

"I'm just saying that the biblical proverb makes sense; '*A soft answer turneth away wrath: but grievous words stir up anger.*'"

Grace released the door handle and stared at her lap. Was she going to take her anger out on him instead?

Blinking away tears, she lifted her gaze to him. "When did you get so smart about the Bible?"

The tension in his shoulders eased. "Right after my wife's and Jo's accident, I carried a chip around on my shoulder until someone called me out, reminding me of that proverb."

"Who was that?"

"A very wise woman I call Mom. I memorized it, and whenever I feel like I'm going to tell someone off, I repeat those words to myself. The arrogance of Paul's grandfather upsets me too, but let's remember he's not from here and has no interest in the property other than to make money from it. He's protecting what he thinks is his as the legal owner. And he's probably concerned about Paul going into the Marines in a couple of months. Maybe if he's treated with kindness, he'll be kind in return." He leaned over and kissed her cheek. "Now are you ready to file your report?"

"After I make some repairs." She dug into her purse and pulled out a compact and tube of lipstick. After inspecting her image in the tiny mirror, she uncapped the lipstick and applied that ruby red color that about drove him crazy. She dropped the items into the handbag and smiled. "Okay, I'm ready."

Inside the police station's small front office, a uniformed officer at a desk held a microphone to his mouth. He lifted an index finger to signal them to wait, then pressed a button on the microphone. "Dispatch to Car 2. We just received another report about the owner of Rose Harbor blocking the shore path. Can you go out there and check it out?"

The speaker squawked, and a man's voice came through. "Roger. We already tried the front gate, but it's locked up tight. It appears we'll have to hoof it down the path to get in that way."

"Okay. Keep me posted. 10-4." He set the microphone on the desk and faced them. "Happens every time a new resident moves onto the lakeshore. They don't like the public walking through their yard, so they block it off. They'd never do that in town to the sidewalk in front of their house, but out there, it's another story. What can I do for you folks?"

"I think you already did it." Grace smiled. "We were here about the same complaint. The problem is that there is a cyclone fence around the entire property. The owner has a couple of German POWs working for him, and he's afraid they'll try to escape if he doesn't lock them in."

"I don't know how we can get that fence off the path without speaking to someone," the officer said. "I understand the owner is in California. There must be someone on the property we can talk to."

Mac pulled out his wallet and found the note containing Paul's phone number. "Here's the private number to reach the grandson who is staying on the property. I think if you can reach him, he'll be able to take down the fence, at least the part blocking the path."

The officer jotted down the number. "I don't think the central operator had this number. Interesting."

"Officer Langtree," Grace said, "if the fence over the path doesn't come down after you reach the grandson, what comes next?"

"A court order will be prepared that states the fence across the path has to be gone by midnight Friday." He handed Mac the note. "Thank you for this."

"You're welcome. I hope the owner learns he must abide by

the rules." He took Grace by the hand. "It sounds like they've got this under control." When they had settled back in his truck, he gazed at her. "You handled yourself so well in there. How did you know his last name?"

She chuckled. "It was embroidered on his shirt just above his badge."

"I never noticed."

"Women notice details like that. Men don't."

"It sounds like together we make a good team." He grinned. "I need to take you home and then make some calls from my office at the farm. If you're free tomorrow, we should be able to get into the cottage to search without a problem. Are you game?"

She stared at him. "I can't believe you're doing this."

"I guess I should have asked before if it's okay to be involved. After all, it is your family's former property, not mine."

A wide grin split her face. "Not at all. I am loving what you're doing when you have no stake in any of this."

"That's where you're wrong, Miss Bauer." He took her hand. "If we can get this property back in your family's hands, that will make you one happy woman, and that's all I want."

THE NEXT AFTERNOON, Grace sat in Mac's office at the tree farm. They'd decided to call Paul to see if anything had changed since yesterday.

She'd spent a good deal of time that morning reading from Psalms and Proverbs and confessing to God that she'd messed up by not telling Mac what needed to be said. She had the perfect opportunity yesterday, when he asked if she still wanted him to be involved with her quest. But it was harder than she'd thought it would be. She had to do it today, and she was trying to leave it in God's hand as to when to say it.

"Paul, good afternoon. This is Mac McAlister. Grace and I

would like access to the property today to search the cottage for the family photos. We thought it would be less imposing if we did it on a Sunday afternoon rather than a weekday."

Grace watched Mac's face intently.

"I see," he said. "A court order is serious business. So, the shore path is to be reopened soon, but the front gate and access to the house are still under lock and key. When will you know if your grandfather will allow visitors on the property? ... Yes, I realize that if your grandfather wants a fence around the entire property that is his right. What if we agree we come on the property at our own risk and cut the pines back to open access to the cottage ourselves?"

Grace ached to hear what Paul was saying, but the receiver was pressed so hard to Mac's ear no sound escaped, nor could she tell by his expression. If anyone had a good poker face, it was Mac.

"How long will it take to get clearance from your attorney to allow us on the property? Is there a reason she can't at least search in the cottage?" He made a gesture that indicated Paul was talking again. After a minute he said, "I can understand his not wanting to be held responsible if the POWs escape while working for him. But so far, I haven't heard of any doing that in Wisconsin."

Paul was talking again. Then Mac said, "Today would be fine, as I said, or would it be better to come tomorrow? Okay, then tomorrow is okay with us too."

He hung up and grinned. "We're to be there at one thirty tomorrow afternoon, and we're to bring tools to cut back the pines, which I happen to have. Let's head over to my parents' house and check on Jo. I bet Mom's Sunday dinner is ready right about now."

35

Monday afternoon, Grace settled on the seat in Mac's truck and leaned her head against the cushion. Something had happened the past couple of days since she and Mac had reconciled. Yesterday afternoon, having Sunday dinner at his parents' cozy home was wonderful. The stories they shared about Mac and his brothers when they were boys had her giggling. Especially the one about the time they tied their bedsheets together and climbed out the window to go swimming in the creek.

Mac pointed out there was nothing else to do on a hot summer night when you couldn't sleep. He reminded Grace about her cousins skinny-dipping in the lake. His mom said it seemed skinny-dipping was a young boy's rite of passage, and she'd suspected what they'd done when she saw the condition of their sheets the next day.

They finished up the day playing Go Fish with Jo, then Mac took Grace home. She fell asleep pushing away her regret that she'd not said what needed to be said and replacing it with the sweet memories of the day.

Now they were partnering up as amateur sleuths of a sort. She smoothed her palms over her lap, grateful the WASP jumpsuit laundered so well and only needed a bit of ironing. First she'd worn it to help on the tree farm, and now for a bit of detective work.

He glanced over. "Is that a flashlight in your hand?"

"Yes. I'm not sure if there's electricity in the cottage. I thought I'd better bring it."

"Good thinking. I tossed one in too, along with some batteries."

Within a few minutes they were turning onto Snake Road, and shortly after that they came up on the entrance to Rose Harbor.

"Well, look at that. They're unlocking the gate." As Mac stopped the truck, the caretaker for the estate released the lock. He raised a hand as if to say, "Wait a moment," then pushed the gate open and waved them through.

Mac leaned out his window. "Looks like the owner changed his mind."

"I don't know anything about that." The man shrugged. "I was just told to unlock the gates. I've got the fellas from the camp doing the same with the lock on the pier and the cyclone fence. In all my days working here, I've never known the place to be locked up like a fortress. Mr. Gibbons is expecting you."

As they drove down the winding driveway to the circle in front of the big house, memories of riding in the backseat of Dad's car when they visited her grandparents erupted in Grace's head. They came to a stop at the main entrance, and Paul stepped outside and stood on the steps.

Not waiting for Mac to come around to her side, Grace opened her door and jumped to the ground.

"Not too anxious, are you?" Mac came around the back of the truck with a slight smile on his face.

Grateful his whisper was low enough Paul didn't hear, she returned his smile and let it do the talking.

Paul came down the steps, and the men shook hands.

"Where do you want to start? Paul asked. "On the first floor or the second?"

"I thought we agreed not to come in the big house," Mac said. "All we want to do is look in the cottage."

"Okay." Paul's brows rose. "I doubt it's been used in years. I've no idea what condition it's in."

"That's exactly why I want to start there." Grace stepped closer. "Is it open, or do you have the key?"

Paul ran his gaze over her. "I see you're dressed for the task. I need to check the cabinet where all the keys are kept. Wait here." He turned toward the door.

"I'm going with you."

He gaped at her. "What do you think I'm going to do?"

"Nothing unscrupulous, but humor me."

"Okay. The cabinet is in a small office off the kitchen."

She glanced over her shoulder at Mac. "You coming too?"

"Yes, of course."

In the kitchen, Paul led them to a small room she remembered her grandparents had used as a pantry. Now it contained a small secretary desk covered with papers bearing a real estate company's logo.

Paul opened a wooden cabinet. Dozens of keys dangled from rows of tiny hooks. "The keys toward the bottom are the ones that are rarely used." He selected one, studied the attached label, then returned it and took another key. "This one says *Cottage*. Good luck with your search." He handed it to her.

"Thanks. Don't you want to come with us?" She dropped the key into her pocket.

"Nah. I'm not fond of dusty places. Makes me sneeze."

"I'm more concerned about what varmints might have made themselves at home in there. Mac, are you ready to brave the dust and possible critters?"

"You're asking a farmer those questions? I have barns full of those things. Give me the key. I'll go in first and let you know what frightening creatures have taken over."

While Mac went to the truck for his tools, Grace waited at the beginning of the flagstone path that led to the cottage. In the past, the door used to be clearly visible from where she stood. Now, all she saw was pine branches.

Carrying his machete and a gas-powered saw, his flashlight dangling from his belt, Mac approached.

She stared at the large knife. "Won't pruning shears be enough?"

"Not with those thick branches. I'll show you how to weaken them with a whack or two, and I'll come right behind you with my saw to trim them back. There's only a little gas left in the saw, but it should be enough. This is how you do it." He raised the knife and brought it down on a branch. A spray of dead needles flew into her face.

She spit out the needles. "Um. Maybe I should have brought the goggles I have for flying."

"Grace, I'm sorry." He set the knife down and helped her brush the needles off her face and shoulders, his expression full of concern. "Are you okay?"

"I'll live." She spit out another needle. "I'm more surprised than hurt. I shouldn't have stood where I did."

"Do you need another demonstration?"

"No. I get the idea." She tucked her flashlight in her pocket then covered her mouth with a bandanna she'd brought. Never had she been so grateful for the survival training she'd received in the WASP. She picked up the knife and whacked at a branch. Dried needles sprinkled to the ground, exposing the bare branch.

"Good job."

Encouraged by Mac's remark, she moved forward and whacked at the next branch while the motorized saw whirred behind her.

Not more than five minutes later, they emerged at the cottage's front door, and she pulled the bandanna away from her mouth. "That wasn't so bad."

"Good thing we didn't need to go farther. The saw just ran out of gas." He set the saw on the ground, and she placed the knife next to it. Before she could turn to face the door, he leaned in and wrapped her in a hug. "Thanks for being so forgiving earlier."

The embrace was so sudden and fast she didn't have time to turn away, nor did she really want to. She smiled. "No problem. We're both a little distracted."

"You want me to case the place before you come in?" He slid the key into the lock and paused.

"As long as there aren't bats in there, I'm fine. I think."

"They're probably more afraid of you than you are of them."

"You're right. I'm just being silly." She squared her shoulders. "Let's go in." Lit flashlight in hand, she pulled the door open and took the first step. Something clacked against the hardwood floor as it skittered past her. She jumped back and let out a squeal. "What was that?" She aimed the flashlight in the direction of the noise but nothing was there.

Mac spoke from behind her. "It was probably a chipmunk."

"Or a rat. It sounded larger than a chipmunk. Can I just stay here while you look?"

"I don't mind, but I wouldn't know where to look first. I'm right here. I won't let anything hurt you."

"My knight in shining armor."

He laughed. "That's a pretty high calling, but I'll accept the appointment. Do you remember if there's a light switch in here?"

"Yes, to the left of the door. But I expect the power is cut off."

"We'll see." Mac let go of her, and she heard him patting the wall. "Here's a switch. I'm pressing the button." The yellowish lightbulb overhead came to life.

"That's encouraging." Grace aimed her flashlight down the dark hall to her right. "There he is."

"Who and where?"

“He’s staring at me.” She kept her beam aimed at the critter. “Don’t you see him?”

He lowered his head to her level. “I see him now. It’s a squirrel. He won’t bother us.”

Squirrels weren’t on her list of dangerous animals, more on the annoying list. She walked toward what she vaguely remembered was the living room. “There are windows in here. If we open the blinds, we should be able to see with natural light.”

Mac moved to the window facing the lake and opened the blinds. Faded sunlight spilled into the room. “I imagine with the foliage pruned back it’s a nice view from here.”

She came up next to him. “It is nice. If I ever get my hands on the property I’ll have to hire a yard crew to clear all this out.

He laughed. “Are you forgetting what I do for a living when I’m not teaching?”

“I guess I did. But when would you have time to work here with your own work on the farm and teaching?”

“If it’s during summer I’ll have the time.”

“Mac we need to—"

“Who all did you say lived in this cottage?”

She bottled a sigh and answered. “It was originally built by Leonard for his daughter, Anna, and her new husband, Rory Quinn. A true Cinderella story.”

“So, tell me.”

“The short version is that the Hartwells were very rich and high society. Anna was to marry a nasty man through an arranged marriage agreement made when she was an infant. It was intended to merge their wealth with another family’s. The Great Fire disrupted the marriage plans, which was fine with Anna, because she was in love with Rory, an Irish immigrant who was a janitor at the mission school where she volunteered.”

Mac listened intently.

“Anna and Rory became separated by the fire, and after her family moved up here, they reunited. Having lost his parents and sister in the fire, Rory was living with his uncle in an area called

Irish Woods. Of course, her parents were still insisting she marry the nasty man—until the truth about Leonard came out."

"What did he do?"

"This is one of the skeletons in my family's closet that I learned from Granny a month or so ago. Turns out before Leonard married Anna's mother, he'd already married a maid in Chicago on the sly and had two children. When Anna's fiancé's family found out, they cancelled the arranged marriage, and Anna's father agreed to let her marry Rory."

"Wow. The family must have had to live down the fact that Leonard was a bigamist."

"I'm sure that's true. But he later became a believer in Christ, legally married Anna's mother, and became a huge philanthropist. Over the years he earned back most of the money he'd lost in the fire. After Anna and Rory lived here in the cottage, each generation's daughter has lived here, either before they married or as newlyweds."

"Including your mom."

"Yeah, my parents were the last couple to start their married life here. I was born across the hall in the master bedroom. We moved to the Main Street house when Mom became pregnant with Reenie. A few years after that, the crash came, and Safe Refuge was lost."

"No wonder you want to get this house back in your family's possession. Where do you want to start looking?"

She tipped her head from side to side, then let out an impatient huff. "I suppose upstairs. If all the original furniture is up there and no one has used the cottage since my family left, we might be able to find something that points to where Leonard could have hidden a stash."

"Wouldn't that be a good way to end the family saga?" He pulled her close in a side hug. "I'm here for the long haul. What do you say? Shall we get started?"

Her tears welled up, and his face blurred. "You're such a good friend to me. What I was going to say before—"

"Only a friend?" He leaned in.

Her stomach fluttered. She should break the trance that had fallen over them but the pleasant memory of his kisses kept her feet fully planted.

"Let me see if I can help you figure it out." He lowered his lips to hers in a soft kiss.

"You're okay with me kissing you?"

She stepped back. "I always enjoy your kisses, but to say it's okay would be misleading. I'm not ready to go down that road."

His shoulders sagged as he heaved a sigh. "Show me the way to the stairs."

The ache filling Grace's chest matched the disappointment on Mac's face. They needed to have that talk, sooner rather than later. But in the middle of the cottage when Paul could walk in anytime wasn't the right place or time. "The stairs are this way." She led him to the staircase behind a closed door.

On the top landing, Grace paused in front of two closed doors. "I don't remember which room was mine and which was my brother's." She opened one of the doors and grinned. "My old wallpaper is still here. I can't believe it."

She headed over to the wall and ran her fingertips over the faded pink flowers. "I was only five when we moved to the Main Street house. I'm surprised I remember it." She moved to the dresser and pulled open the top drawer then the others below it. "All empty, and that's the only piece of furniture in here. Let's look in Rory's room."

They went to the other bedroom, and her heart fell. "Not a stick of furniture in here. But my parents' bedroom was downstairs. Maybe something was forgotten there."

Downstairs, she opened the door to the master bedroom. No furniture, but the room's built-in bookcase along one wall was still filled with books.

"This was their bedroom?" Mac stepped inside and flicked on the overhead light. He surveyed the room. "It looks more like a study."

"I think it *was* a study at one time. When Granny came down with smallpox, she quarantined over here and stayed in this room so her nurse and doctor didn't have to go up and down the stairs, and the bathroom was down here too. The doctor, by the way, is the man you know as Dr. Murphy."

"I love how the women in your family, as wealthy as they were, married ordinary men and not upper crust." He stepped over to the shelves, selected a book, and flipped through the pages. "This is a history of Wisconsin, up to the copyright date of 1862." He looked up and grinned. "You know, Hartwell could easily have slipped something like a note between the pages of a book. Cash, too, for that matter."

They shared a grin.

"What are we waiting for?" Grace asked. "Let's start looking."

"Why don't you check the lower shelves, and I'll do the upper ones." Mac moved to the end of the far bookcase and reached for the top shelf.

An hour later, as Grace flipped through the last book on the lower shelves, Mac stretched. "I'm convinced that nothing remarkable was left in any of these books. Although I did set aside a few that interested me, if you think it's okay for me to borrow them."

"I don't see why it wouldn't be. They *are* my family's books."

"Books that were sold to someone when they bought the property."

"It feels weird having to ask, but I guess you're right." She sighed. "Maybe you should ask Paul."

They gathered up the books they'd gone through and placed them all back on the shelves in no particular order. When they stepped outside, she faced him. "While you're taking the key back and asking Paul about the books, I'm going to check out the spring house. I just want to be in there a few minutes. It's where Dad proposed to Mom before he went to war."

Thankful the POWs weren't around, Grace quickly made her

way down the hill and approached the spring house. She barely remembered what it was like when she was small, but it surely must have been nicer than it was now.

The spring bubbling under its protective roof was familiar, but not the carved wooden settee sitting off to the side and buried under boxes and old pots and the like. Who would leave a beautiful piece of furniture like that out here to rot?

She removed a box and sat. This couldn't have been what her parents sat on the night Dad proposed and promised to be true to Mom while he was gone. She'd always pictured some kind of cushioned, outdoor settee. She'd have to ask Mom later.

Running her hand over the side of the small bench, she felt something at the end of the seat move beneath her fingertips. She jumped up, prepared to run at first sight of whatever it was. Not seeing anything alive and moving, and not caring if the jumpsuit became soiled beyond the ability of Mom's favorite soap powder to clean it, she knelt on the dirt floor.

She glanced around for her flashlight and realized she'd left it in the cottage. At least her fingertips fit into the gap. Feeling a small strip of metal, she pushed it. It slid over, and the small opening widened. Granddad had mentioned woodworkers sometimes created secret hiding places in their furniture. Could this be one of those?

She poked her index finger in and maneuvered it around, then increased her exploration to two fingers and pushed them in farther until something blocked the movement. It felt like a thin book. Using her fingers like a pair of tweezers, she grabbed the item and tugged it out.

Heart racing, she stepped outside into the light and flipped through the small book's pages. It seemed to be mostly love poems and notes written in the flowery style she'd seen when looking through the old documents at the courthouse. She flipped to the first page and read the inscription.

"For my darling Anna, with all my love, your Rory."

Using her thumb, Grace gently fanned the pages, and a

yellowed paper flew out. She dropped to her knees and picked it up by its edges. The fancy handwriting again, but not quite the same—likely written by someone other than Rory.

For my darling Louise, and our precious daughters, Anna and Callie.

By the time you read this, I will be dead or in jail. Either would be an appropriate punishment for what I've done to you, my dear family. Before the government takes everything that is mine in restitution, I've managed to set aside a sum to help. Louise, you know where to look, in the cottage study under the squeaky floorboard.

You won't be able to live in the style you have enjoyed, but it's all I have left. May the Lord bless you in my absence. I love you all.

Your loving father and husband,
Leonard Hartwell

"Paul said it was okay to take whatever was in the cottage."

Grace jumped, and the paper flew out of her hand.

"Sorry. Didn't mean to startle you." Mac stepped closer and looked at the volume in her hand. "Are you ready to ... What have you got there?"

Grace stooped to retrieve the letter and looked up at him. "We need to go back to the cottage now."

36

Grace handed Mac the note and waited while he read it.

"Good sleuthing. Looks like I need to get the key back from Paul without letting on what we're looking for."

"I left my flashlight in the study." She brushed off the knees of her jumpsuit. "Just tell him we need to go back for it."

"Good idea. I'll meet you at the cottage door." He started up the incline, his long legs moving at a fast clip.

Grace drew in a breath and stared up at the ceiling. "Please, God, if we find money, let it be enough to buy back at least part of the property." She started up the slope, then stopped. "And if keeping the money is wrong, then help me to be willing to turn it over to the rightful owner. Paul's grandfather, I'm guessing. I'll leave it to—" She bit on her lower lip.

When did she start praying to God for herself again? Lately her prayers had seemed to come naturally and not forced when others were around and she thought she had to give the appearance of praying.

Despite the prayers, she still had no assurance God had forgiven her. But maybe the more she turned to Him in prayer, the closer she'd be to forgiveness. She closed her eyes. "I leave this search to You, Lord. If it be Your will that we find something, give us wisdom on what to do with it." She hesitated, then added, "I also need courage to tell Mac what I've been hiding from him. It's not fair to him to spend time with him like I'm doing when he wants our relationship to be more than I can give him."

Mac met her at the cottage and held up a crowbar along with the key. "I figured we'll need a tool to pry up those floorboards so I brought this from the truck and got the key back without a problem. Paul was on a call he found more interesting than our going back in the cottage."

"Who was he talking to? His grandfather?"

"I'm not sure. I think so." He stuck the key into the lock and pulled the door open. "I only heard snatches of conversation. It sounded like he needs to get the place into shape before a showing day after tomorrow."

"That doesn't give us much time to find something—if something is there to be found. You go first."

Inside, they walked together to the master bedroom. He opened the door and hit the light switch. "There's your flashlight, on the floor where you were sitting. And I see a board that appears to be loose." He crossed the room and stuck the crow bar alongside the board and pried it up. He aimed his flashlight beam into the space.

"What do you see?" Grace took tentative steps toward him.

"If Leonard left cash under this board, someone has already removed it."

Her heart sank. "That doesn't mean it was someone who shouldn't have. Maybe his wife or the daughters took it."

"The other floorboards look to be nailed down."

"Leonard said the squeaky floorboard." Grace stepped on a plank and, hearing no squeak, stepped on another. After several tries, one squeaked. Mac stuck the crow bar into the crack and forced it up. He peered inside, using his flashlight. "Nothing." He let the loosened board down and stomped on it. "It probably needs to be better secured. I can let Paul know I'll be back within the week with nails to fix the loose boards."

"Good idea, Mac, and thank you for being so caring."

He smiled at her. "You're welcome. But no thanks necessary. It's the right thing to do."

They did the same with every floorboard that squeaked until they'd lifted them all.

"It's no use, Mac. I only hope whatever money was found, it was taken by one of the Hartwell women."

"Would your grandparents know about it?"

"Maybe. Let's get out of here. I need to talk to my Dad and then my Granddad."

"Is your dad at his office?"

"He should be unless he's doing his air raid warden duties. I think this is his week."

Before Mac had the motor turned off in front of Dad's office, Grace was out of the truck and scurrying to the door.

"Girl, when you are on a mission you let nothing get in your way." Mac came up beside her laughing. "I'm a bit confused though. Shouldn't we be talking to your grandmother to see if she remembers anything about the note from Hartwell?"

"Yes, but I want to clear something up with Dad first."

They stepped into the office, and Lorraine turned from a filing cabinet. "Hi, Grace." Her gaze went to Mac, and she smiled. "Good to see you again, Mac."

He nodded. "Likewise."

"Is my dad here?"

"Yes, but he's with a client. I don't think it will be too long before he's available. You're welcome to wait."

Not wanting to sit, Grace stood in front of the empty chair next to Mac and faced the large window that looked out over Main Street. "There goes Judith Watkins, pushing a baby carriage. My goodness, that must make three children she has now. I think I read in the *Regional News* her husband was called up by the army. Poor thing, having to take care of those kids by herself."

"Was she in your class?" Mac looked up from where he sat.

"No, the year behind me. That would make her twenty-three. She married the boy she'd dated all through high school. He works, or did work, at the post office. What in the world is she doing for money? He can't be paid enough by the army to feed those children and pay the rent."

"Maybe she's moved in with her parents," Mac said.

"I feel guilty that she has such a burden on her, and I have so little in comparison." Grace turned and sat. "Remember what I said before? It's for women like Judith that I want to get at least the cottage back. Women struggling to raise their children alone while their husbands are at war. If not to live in long-term, perhaps as a retreat for them. A little vacation spot away from things."

"I love your compassion, but you can't make a direct comparison." He took her hand and gave it a squeeze. "One thing I've learned. God calls all of us to different paths."

"I know, but there must be some way I can help people like her."

"You *are* helping people with your Red Cross work. Just like you helped my family get ahold of my brothers when we needed to. And your own family too, tracking down your brother, who will soon be home. That's what God has called you to do during this time."

"I know." She let out a sigh. "Maybe if it doesn't work out to help war wives and widows, the cottage would be a perfect place for Rory to recoup, just like Dad did after he came home."

"Yes, it would." He squeezed her hand. "But don't get ahead of yourself. I hear voices. It sounds like your dad is free."

The office door opened. Dad and a tall, thin man stepped into the room. He bid the client goodbye, then turned to Lorraine. "Any calls?"

She spoke in a low tone.

He spun around and grinned. "Well, hello, you two. What did you find today?"

"This." She stood and approached him, holding up the note. "Go ahead and read it."

He unfolded the note and scanned the writing. "Well what do you know. Come back to my office. I have fifteen minutes before my next appointment."

They quickly settled in Dad's office, and she handed him the book. He leaned back in his chair and opened to the inscription.

"Well, I'll be. Old Leonard really did change. Good to see that." He set the book on the desk and picked up the paper. "So, did you find the floorboard and the money?"

"No. There was a loose floorboard that squeaked, and we started there and found nothing. Then we checked the other squeaky boards. Nothing under any of them. We decided to ask Granny if she remembers any of this, since it was her mother and aunt the note refers to. I'm guessing by today's standards the amount of cash he hid wasn't very large. I just hope the other owners didn't find it. As long as it helped our family, that's all that matters."

"I'm glad to hear you say that. You two have better things to put your energies toward." He looked at Mac. "When do you have to be back in the classroom?"

"The Thursday after Labor Day, same as the schools in Lake Geneva. I've still got a little over a month of summer left."

Grace shot him a smile. "I keep telling him how grateful I am for his help and that he has the free time now. Meanwhile, I'm still trying to figure out what to do with the rest of my life. Mac gave me a business card belonging to the man who does crop dusting for their farm. I'm going to call him to see if he can advise me on how to break into the business. Of course, I'll need a plane before I can do anything."

A grin split Dad's face. "And you need to start flying again. I've been waiting to hear you say something like this. The military is using Piper Cub planes a lot, and plenty will be up for sale whenever the conflict ends. I'll help you look into it, and maybe our family can all pitch in some seed money to help you out." Dad rose and came around his desk. "Are you two sleuths heading over to Granny's now?"

"I might." Grace glanced at Mac. "Mac doesn't need to go with me, although if he wants to come, I don't mind."

Dad glanced at her jumpsuit and the smudged knees. "I suggest you clean up a bit before you go over there."

"I didn't even think of that. Thanks, Dad. I think I'll visit her tomorrow instead. See you at home later?"

"After my air warden duties, you will."

A short time later, Grace slumped on the truck seat and waited until Mac got the vehicle started. "Thanks again for helping me today."

"I've enjoyed sleuthing with you. I'm free tomorrow morning if you want me to go with you to see your grandmother."

"You must have other things you need to do on the farm. I can go alone."

"Yes, work awaits me, but nothing that's urgent. If you change your mind, let me know."

She twisted on the seat and faced him. She couldn't put off what she should have said earlier. "Mac, you've done above and beyond most others would do. I've been thinking, I'm not being fair to you. I know you want more in our relationship than just someone to pal around with. Right now, I can't give you that kind of relationship. It's obvious you need a partner in life who can love you deeply and be a mom for Jo. I don't want to stand in your way."

He stared at her and shook his head. "That's the nicest thing anyone has ever said to me."

"What do you mean?"

"You are more concerned for my welfare than taking advantage of my ability to help you. I know you don't feel able to be more to me than a friend right now. Believe me, if I wanted to date someone other than you, I would." He reached over and brushed a curl from her face then took her hand. "I tried to go back to not having you in my life at all and found it a lonely existence. Would you prefer to talk to your grandmother without me there?"

"I think I need to sort out all that we discovered today before I do talk to her. After you drop me off, I'm going over to the park and sit by the lake and pray about it."

"Good idea."

They arrived at her house, and he parked then reached over and took her hand. "I'll be praying for you."

Her heart warmed to his words. For once she didn't answer them with a comment that God didn't care. His assurance that he wanted her in his life even if it was never more than in friendship soothed her. But it didn't mean she had the right to string him along like she had been. She reached for the door handle with her free hand. "Thanks. I'll let you know in the morning about visiting my granny."

"Sound good." He let go of her hand. "Now go on and get to the park."

37

The next morning, Mac decided to use the dark red 1937 Chevy coupe that had been Emily's car when she was alive. Until now he couldn't bear to drive it because of the memories connected to the vehicle. It mostly sat at his parent's house for them to use.

Today it seemed a more appropriate car to use to visit Grace's grandmother than his old truck. He pulled up in front of the house on Dodge Street. Figuring she'd call after her time in the park yesterday and say she wanted to visit her granny alone, he'd gone ahead and planned to work this morning. But instead, she'd called and asked him to meet her here, and he flipped his schedule without a thought.

Last night, he'd lain in bed asking himself if he was helping Grace for the right reasons or for the selfish one of wanting to be with her as much as possible. She'd stopped holding him at arm's length, and it seemed each day they'd been together she'd let him in a bit more. It just didn't seem the right time to pull back, and when he called this morning to tell her to look for this car she sounded genuinely glad he hadn't changed his mind about coming here.

A rapping sound on the passenger window broke into his

thoughts. He waved at Grace, then leaned over and rolled down the window.

"Am I late?" She flashed him the smile he adored.

"No. I got here a little early. Are you ready to go inside?"

"In a minute. I'm a little early too." She stuck her head inside the window and looked around the interior. "This is a nice car. It doesn't appear that you've used it very much."

"I haven't. Mom's been using it since Emily died, but not much of late. I thought it needed to be run a bit." He reached over and opened the door. "Come sit in here until it's time."

She settled on the seat. "Is there any reason you were looking over at the cemetery when I walked up?"

"Nothing in particular. I've driven past it dozens of times but never gave it much attention."

"That's where my ancestors whose journals we've been reading are buried. Mom keeps urging me to visit their graves, but I never have. Now that I feel more of a connection to all of them, I think I'll soon go over there and find their graves. Are your ancestors buried there too?"

"No. We have a nice spot on the farm where we bury family members."

She stared at him. "Isn't it strange to have the cemetery right there?"

"No different than for your grandparents to look across the street and see where they'll be buried someday. Ours isn't in view of my parents' house or mine. But if it were, it wouldn't bother me. I know they're with the Lord, and it's only their remains that are out there."

Grace nodded. "Good point." She faced him, her expression serious. "Mac, I need to warn you that Granny can be a bit outspoken at times. She's asked me several times what's holding us up with making future plans because we never know what life is going to throw us in the future."

He laughed. "You're not alone. My mom has grilled me a few times with similar questions."

Her eyes widened. "What did you tell her?"

"That it's all in God's timing and we're just getting to know each other. What did you tell your grandmother?"

"Something similar. That we're not in any hurry and want to enjoy each other's company this summer." She glanced at the house and waved. "There's Granny at the window. Time to go in."

They walked up onto the porch side by side, and Grace rang the bell. A moment later, the door opened and Mrs. Murphy grinned at them.

"Good morning, Grace. This is a pleasant surprise to have you and your ..." She regarded Mac. "Sorry, I don't know what to call you. Back in my day I would have said beau. Is boyfriend the correct word?"

Mac scrambled to give the answer he thought Grace would like and was about to say friend when she said, "Special friend."

Good to know he'd received a promotion of sorts. Special friend sounded better than just friend. "Mrs. Murphy, it's my pleasure to see you again." He accepted her hand, its skin so thin it reminded him of tissue paper. Fearing if he squeezed too tightly she'd break, he shook her hand lightly.

Her eyes twinkled. "Oh, Grace, you've got yourself a fine young man."

"That I do, Granny." Grace offered a nervous sounding chuckle. "We won't stay long. We have some questions about your mother and grandmother."

"Your mother said you were looking into our family tree or something like that." The older woman's eyebrows arched. "I'm not sure I'll be of much help. The years fade more and more."

GRACE WENT with Granny into her small kitchen to help prepare tea. While Grace poured hot water into a silver teapot, she studied the decorative spout, realizing for the first time that it resembled a bird with its mouth open. "Granny, where did this teapot come from? The design is unusual, but I like it. Was it a wedding gift to you and Granddad?"

"Oh no." Granny turned from placing shortbread cookies on a flowered plate. "Your great-grandmama told me it was one of the few pieces of silver that she was able to rescue from the Chicago house when they fled the Great Fire. My grandmother was determined to bring all of the silver, but they couldn't fit it all in the carriage. They ended up with the teapot and a few place settings of silver, which my grandfather had to sell later."

Grace ran her fingertip over the engraving. "I had no idea we had any artifacts from the fire."

"I wish we had more. When I go, your mother will get it, then it will go to you since you're the firstborn daughter, and then to your firstborn someday. Treasure it, Gracie. It's one of the few links we have to our family's past."

"I'll treasure it with all my heart." Her heart squeezed at Granny's presumption that she'd have a firstborn child someday. She hoped to, but only God knew for sure if it would ever happen. "I'll set up the serving tray, Granny, while you get the tea steeping in the pot."

Grace went for a butler's tray where she remembered Granny kept it, then took three flowered cups and matching saucers from a cupboard and put them on the tray along with a plate of cookies. "I'll carry the teapot if you can take the tray."

She followed Granny into the living room, where Mac sat waiting on the sofa. Granny set the tray on the coffee table, and Grace put the teapot on the space she'd kept empty on the tray for it, then sat next to Mac.

When Grace passed the plate of cookies to Mac, he took one then offered them to Granny, who sat nearby in her favorite chair.

"No, thank you." Granny waved the plate away. "I ate breakfast just before you came. Eat and enjoy. It does me pleasure to be able to serve you."

Grace loved her granny's refined mannerisms that, with the Depression and wars, had been lost to current generations.

Mac bit into his cookie. "This is delicious, Mrs. Murphy. Is it a secret recipe, or dare I ask for a copy to give my Mom?"

"It's no secret." Granny waved a hand. "In fact, I think Grace's mother, has a copy."

"Good, I'll be sure to get it from her." He caught Grace's eye. "Do you want to tell her why we're here?"

She nodded. "As Mom told you, I've been looking into family history. Yesterday, Mac and I had an opportunity to get into the cottage and the spring house at Rose Harbor to look for anything the family may have left behind."

"Oh my," Granny said.

"I found this in a secret compartment in an old piece of furniture that's now in the spring house." Grace reached into her handbag, took out the book, and handed it to Granny. "If you open it, you'll find a folded paper that your grandfather Leonard wrote. He mentions hiding money for your grandmother and mother to find, to keep them going if something happened to him."

Granny opened the book to the title page and let out a small gasp. "There's my father's handwriting." The room grew still as she read the inscription Rory had written. "She touched the page with her fingertips, much the same way Grace had done. "He loved my mother so much, and she loved him. They overcame many obstacles to be together."

"Their love is legendary." Grace dropped to her knees next to her grandmother's chair. "I've heard it spoken of many times."

"Now, what is this?" Granny picked up the folded paper.

"A note from Leonard Hartwell. Read it for yourself."

Granny read the note then looked up. "I remember my mother talking about the money he mentions. I told you not long ago how Grandfather Leonard was not always a man of faith, and did unsavory things before God got ahold of him and radically changed him."

"I remember," Grace said. "I only learned of his bigamy a short time ago. Mom didn't want to tell me and would always gloss over that part of Rory's and Anna's story."

Granny grimaced. "I told her not to do that. As soon as our children were old enough, your grandfather and I told them the truth. There were so many rumors about town, it took a long while for them to go away and for people to accept that Leonard Hartwell was a changed man, thanks to the Lord. Little ones have big ears, and we didn't want our children to be mocked because of their family's past."

She shook her head. "Then she went and named Lenny after him. I encouraged your parents to let him use Nathan, his middle name, instead of his first name, but they didn't. I hope when he's old enough to understand, they don't object if he chooses to do that."

That sounded reasonable to Grace.

"When Leonard Hartwell's bigamy first came to light, he lived in fear he'd be arrested and thrown in prison. If my grandmother hadn't been willing to forgive him and not press charges, that's exactly what would have happened." She looked off then back at Grace. "I actually forgot about that money in the floorboard."

Grace stroked her hand. "I was wondering why Granddad didn't seem to remember it."

"Oh, he knew about it. But that was many years ago. He might have gotten it confused with the money my mother gave us when Nate and I married. It was money Anna found in Leonard's study when they were escaping the fire. She kept it a while in case she needed it to get away from that terrible man she was to marry. She never needed it and gave it to me on my wedding day. It wasn't the same money as that under the floorboard.

"It turned out, he didn't lose any more than what he'd already lost in the fire," Granny went on, "and his holdings increased. Not to the high amount he once had, but substantial, all the same. Years later, when my parents were starting out and Da was building up his landscaping business, my mother reminded him of the cash in the floor, and they invested it in his landscaping and florist business."

Grace glanced over her shoulder at Mac, and they exchanged knowing looks. She refocused on her grandmother. "I'm curious. Do you know how much money he hid?"

"I think it was around three or four thousand dollars. Back then, that amount was worth a lot more than it would be today." She put the paper back in the book and handed the book to Grace. "You'd better keep this. I'd be sure to lose it. These days I can't remember where I put something only a few hours earlier."

"Are you sure? Rory wrote some poems to your mother in there."

"Oh?" Granny's eyes widened. She flipped the book open and read one of the poems to herself. "I would like to read the poems. You'll have to remind me that I have the book."

"I will. Why don't you keep it in your nightstand? That's where I put things I don't want to lose."

"That's a wonderful idea." Granny's face brightened.

"I love you, Granny Maureen." Grace rose on her knees and drew Granny into a hug. "Thank you for clearing up one of the mysteries we uncovered." She stood and moved to her seat beside Mac.

"So, when are you two going to start the next generation of our family?" Granny regarded both of them, her eyes twinkling.

Grace's breath hitched.

"If God wills it," Mac said, "it will happen, Mrs. Murphy. Right now, we're just enjoying each other's companionship."

Granny harrumphed. "That's what Grace's mother told me when I asked. I thought I'd go straight to the source." She gaped at Grace. "Just keep in mind I want to see you as a bride before the Lord takes me home, and I'm not getting any younger."

Heat filled Grace's cheeks. "God hasn't shown me yet what He wants for me."

"Good answer. And now I know how to pray." Grinning, Granny pushed to her feet, using the chair arms for support. "I have some chores, and I'm sure you two have other things to do rather than pass the day with an old lady."

They soon said their goodbyes. Since Grace had walked over, Mac offered to take her home. "And by the way, thanks for forewarning me about your granny's candid remarks. You gave a good answer. Where do you want me to drop you off? I need to get some work done on the farm this afternoon."

"I'm going to the Red Cross," she said. "It's only a couple of blocks down. I can walk. I've been ignoring my duties there because of all this. That will help me take my mind off all that Granny told us."

38

"Grace, I'm glad you're home. How did it go with Granny this morning?" Dad shrugged out of his suit coat and tossed it over the back of an easy chair.

"Very enlightening." She dropped the novel she was attempting to read onto the floor. "Granny was touched to see the book with the love poems her dad wrote to her mother. And she explained Rory and Anna used the money hidden in the cottage floor to fund his landscaping and florist business. She said it was only a few thousand dollars."

He pushed her feet over on the ottoman and sat on it. "I figured something like that happened. I'm surprised your granddad didn't know about it, though."

"She thinks he might have confused it with some other cash Anna found in her father's study the night of the fire and took it for emergency purposes. She ended up giving that money to Granny the day of her wedding."

He smiled. "I love how all the pieces of the past fall together into a cohesive story." He looked her in the eye. "On another topic, I have a question. Have you contacted the crop duster Mac told you about?"

"No, I haven't." Grace pulled Dusty's card from her skirt

pocket and turned it over in her hand a few times. "I carry his card around, thinking every day I'll give him a call, but I don't."

"Why not? It could be the solution to making flying your life's work."

"I wish I knew why. All I know is, every time I've picked up the phone to call the man, I chicken out. One time I even gave the phone number to the central operator. But as soon as a man answered, I hung up."

"Are you afraid of getting sick when you wouldn't have a copilot to take over like last time?"

"Maybe. I think it's more that I'm afraid I'll find out I don't enjoy flying like I used to, or I'm not meant to be a pilot at all."

"Once flying gets in your blood it's hard to let go."

"How would you know? You're still flying."

"I never told your mother, but after getting my kicks out of flying those bombers, I entertained the idea of not finishing law school and finding work as a pilot. Although that dream went away the day I lost my leg, by owning that little plane out there at the airfield, I'm able to get the yen for piloting out of my system."

She looked off and then back at him. "I don't know if I'll ever fly again."

"Your dream of piloting commercial aircraft after the war is gone, but there's no reason you need to punish yourself by giving up on your dreams altogether."

"Do you think I'm punishing myself by not piloting any plane?"

"That, my darling daughter, is for you to decide." He patted her leg. "The best way to find out if you're still meant to fly is to take a plane up and see how it feels to you. If you ever change your mind, let me know, and we can take *Amazing Grace* up for a spin."

"I didn't know you named the plane."

"That's because you haven't seen it since you've been home. The song 'Amazing Grace' has always been my favorite, and it is by God's amazing grace I made it back to the U.S. and your wonderful mother. I owe it to Him. Not to mention you, Grace. Your being born to us was my inspiration to keep at the hard work of getting through law school and rehabbing at the same time."

She smiled through her tears. "God is the amazing one, not me."

"Agreed. But you're remarkable in your tenacity and strength, something you've inherited from the women in the Hartwell line." He leaned closer and lowered his voice. "I'm very impressed with Mac. I came away from our conversation at my office yesterday feeling good that he's invested in your dreams and wanting to help you. That you're not doing this alone. It's clear by the way he looks at you that he's crazy about you."

"That's what people tell me." She dropped her gaze to her lap.

"I saw a similar expression on your face. I'm sure it won't be long before he'll be asking for your hand."

"It seems my whole family is ganging up on me." She rolled her eyes. "Granny decided to be blunt this morning and right in front of Mac asked when we would be adding to the next generation then said she wanted to be at my wedding and she wasn't getting any younger.

Dad's hearty laugh filled the room. "That's Granny. What did you say?"

She shrugged. "Nothing. I tried to find the right words but failed miserably.

"What about Mac?"

"He told her it was up to God and for now we were just enjoying each other's companionship."

"The thing is, you can say you are friends only, but the way you two look at each other says it's more than that."

"What you saw on my face is only infatuation." She removed her feet from the ottoman and stood. "I'm going to my room. As far as I'm concerned, this day is done."

Climbing the stairs, she prayed for enough courage to tell Mac everything. She wasn't nearly as strong as Dad thought she was.

SEVERAL DAYS LATER, Grace settled into Helen's chair at her salon and stared at her reflection in the mirror. Horrified at the dark circles beneath her eyes, she wanted to pull up the cape Helen had draped over her until it covered her face.

Her intention several days ago of talking to Mac as soon as possible never had a chance to happen. His family farm had an emergency the day after they'd last been together at Granny's. One of the farmhands had a bad accident, and Mac had to shift his schedule around to fill in for him until he could hire a new man.

The stretch of long evenings with only a few short phone calls from Mac had made her anxious. Last night when he called, he sounded exhausted yet insisted they talk a while. His words still rang in her ears this morning. "I keep thinking if we were married, you'd be right here when I got home."

Grace snapped out of her thoughts and used part of the salon cape to dab her eyes. They needed to have that conversation sooner rather than later. Once he heard what she'd done, he'd stop having those thoughts of marriage. They hoped to have some of the POWs from the camp in Milwaukee come, starting today. After a day or two of training them, Mac would have time to get together again.

Helen approached the chair and stood behind Grace, fluffing her curls with her fingers. She caught Grace's eye in the mirror. "What will it be today? Want to keep the victory rolls, or a new style?"

Grace lifted her chin. "I'm wearing V-rolls until this war is over. Right now, my hair style is all I have energy for. Good thing

I'm not still flying those planes. Those helmets do nothing for hair."

"You don't look well. Summer colds can be miserable."

"It's not a cold. No worries about catching it."

"What's going around these days that isn't contagious?" Helen scrunched her nose.

"You don't want to know."

Helen spun the chair around until they were face-to-face. "Is this about Mac?"

"Yes."

Her eyes widened. "What happened now?"

"It's too long a story."

"Okay, but if ever you need a shoulder to cry on, I'm here." Helen patted her own shoulder. "Come on, let's get your hair shampooed."

At the wash basin, Grace leaned her head back as Helen sprayed warm water over her head, added shampoo, and began scrubbing. She didn't mind that Helen's nails sometimes dug into her scalp a bit too hard. Maybe the pressure would release the thoughts that refused to leave. Her eyes stung, and she blinked.

"Grace, you're crying." Helen dabbed at her cheeks with a towel. She shut off the water and dropped a dry towel over Grace's wet head, working it through the hair with a vigorous motion. After fluffing the wet curls, she helped Grace stand. "I'm hanging a closed sign on the door, and we're going talk. Sit over there on the settee, while I get us some tea."

Thankful for time to collect herself, Grace nodded. She dropped onto the small couch Helen used as a waiting area and rested her elbows on her knees.

"Lord," she whispered. "I know my sadness is more from missing Mac than anything. We've been together a lot lately and I'm kind of surprised at how much I've missed him. Not having been able to talk to him like I planned is really eating at me."

"Here we are." Helen returned holding a tray with a teapot and a pair of cups. We have to share a tea bag. I only had one left. Tomorrow I'll be getting more ration stamps and will buy more. If it steeps long enough, I think we'll be fine. Can you please move those magazines from the table next to you? Just drop them on the floor for now."

Grace jumped up and gathered a stack of magazines from a side table and placed them on the floor under the table.

Helen set the tray on the table and sat beside Grace. She poured the steeping liquid from the teapot into the cups, then handed Grace one. "Now, why don't you tell Auntie Helen what's going on?"

Grace bit down on her trembling lip. Maybe telling her part of it would at least release some of the pressure in her chest "I'm scared. Mac said the other day that he loves me, and last night on the phone he said it again. I'm afraid his patience in waiting for me to be ready for the next step is running out, and he's going to propose."

"Oh, that's wonderful." Helen hugged her.

"No, it's not."

"Why?"

"Because I can't marry him without telling him about my past."

"The same thing you've mentioned before?"

"Yes."

"Do you love him, Grace?"

"Yes, very much."

"Then tell him whatever it is you did. Let him decide if he can't marry you."

Grace hauled in a breath. "I'm praying for the courage to do that. I had it the other day, but before I could talk to him, that accident happened and he's been working twelve-hour days on the farm. I want to tell him everything. But before I do, I need to be sure I can still fly a plane. Then if he rejects me, I'll at least have something that makes me employable."

Grace fished Dusty's card from her skirt pocket. "Mac gave me this card for a crop dusting service they use on the farm. It's not the same as flying a commercial plane, but it's flying. If I need to move away, I can find work doing this. There's only one problem."

"What's that?"

"I haven't flown since I got sick, and I'm scared to even fly my Dad's little plane."

"Oh, honey. That can't be. I'll pray God helps you with that. Just acknowledging your fear is a good start."

"Thank you. You're a dear friend." Grace managed a smile. "I'm reading all the Scripture that has to do with not being afraid." She glanced at her watch. "We'd better get my hair done. You're losing customers while I'm sitting here blubbering."

"My next appointment isn't for another hour." Helen stood. "Let's get your hair fixed up real cute, so you'll look your best when you talk to Mac."

AN HOUR LATER, Grace entered her house and was relieved not to find anyone else at home. She went directly to her room and shut the door then grabbed her Bible and turned to the Psalms.

Kicking off her loafers, she fluffed her pillows and leaned against them with her legs stretched out across the comforter.

She closed her eyes. "Lord, I'm back again. I keep thinking this delay in getting to talk to Mac is happening for a reason. If it hadn't been the accident to block us from being together, it would have been something else."

She drew her legs up under her. "I am very grateful the McAlisters' farmhand will be okay in a few weeks, but the delay has caused me see how much I do love Mac. I'm scared he's going to propose soon, and he needs to know my past before he does. Sometimes I feel complete peace knowing You have truly forgiven me, but then suddenly the weight of guilt returns."

She flipped through the Psalms until the thin pages fell open at Psalm 51 and read. Tears fell onto the words as she began to pray, using the psalm as a guide.

"Yes, Lord, have mercy on me and blot out my transgressions. My sin is ever before me, Lord. I've tried to leave it with You, but it never leaves. Please, create a clean heart within me and don't cast me away from Your presence."

She sobbed and blew her nose in her handkerchief.

"I'm sorry that for a while I lost all faith in Your promises. Please restore the joy of salvation to me. I ask that Your will be done with Mac and me. If my past is too much for him to bear, I'll accept it as Your will. At least once he knows about my past, it will be easier for him to stop loving me."

That night, Mac sounded more himself when he called. Three POWs had arrived that afternoon. All were farmers before the war, and his workload would lighten. He never mentioned his wish to married as he did before, but he ended the conversation with, "Bye, Grace. I love you," but hung up before she could respond.

Tomorrow, she'd tell him. and by this time tomorrow night, it would all be over.

39

The next day, Grace called her father's office. When he came on the line, she smiled. "I'd like to make an appointment with my lawyer today, if there's an opening."

"Am I to assume I'm your lawyer?" He chuckled.

"The only one I have."

"Well, it just so happens I have the next hour free, if you can come right away."

"I'll be there. See you soon."

Dad was standing next to Lorraine's desk when she stepped into the office ten minutes later. He checked his watch. "Good heavens, did you run the whole way?"

"No. I used Mom's car."

"Go on back to my office. I'll be there after I explain something to Lorraine."

In his office, Grace settled into one of the chairs near his desk. Behind his chair stood a wall of bookcases filled to the brim with law books, where he often searched for precedents that had been set by earlier decisions.

Funny how her mom once aspired to be an attorney and actually attended a year of law school, until the Great War interrupted. She never returned to school, but worked to support Dad through his remaining years at the school, working as a telephone operator and caring for Grace, who arrived ten months after they were married. Juggling it all, including the arrivals of her siblings, Mom was the hero in the family, not her.

Dad stepped into the office and shut the door. "Let's sit over there on the sofa."

A comfortable silence fell between them, as they settled on the couch.

"Well, Grace, you called this meeting. You have the floor."

"I've been thinking about what you said about flying." She stared at her lap. "You were right. All I ever dreamed about was flying a big plane, and I was living my dream. I've been fearful I'll get sick again and not have a copilot to take over like last time. But there's another reason. If God took flying away from me, maybe He did it for good reason."

"What was that?"

"When I was flying for my country, I felt like I was doing my part for the war effort and taking up where you left off after you were shot down. It's not the same war, but Germany is still the enemy."

"Is that why you applied to WASP?" His eyes misted. "To make up for my not being able to continue serving?"

"At first it was, but after I went through training and started flying the 17s, I realized it wasn't just that. It was what God called me to do. When WASP discharged me, it felt as though a part of me died. A passage I read in the Bible this morning showed me I'd made flying an idol. I think that's why I lost my job with WASP. I've asked God to forgive me, but I don't know if He will allow me to fly again. I need to fly again, Dad."

He scooted over and pulled her into a hug. "I don't know what to say, Gracie, except God has always been my copilot and I've never taken flying for granted. It's easy to make the things we love into idols. I struggled with it all the while the old couple hid me in their cellar. They were strong believers, and they took great risk hiding me. German officers routinely slept in their extra bedroom during their two-day leaves, but God protected us. Observing how they lived their lives with faith in the Almighty and never took any of their blessings for granted helped me a lot."

Grace's throat ached.

"I didn't think I was good enough for your mother, coming home with a messed up leg that needed to be amputated, but she set me straight. My work for the U.S. as a pilot was over the day I was shot down. What you did for our country as a pilot was done the day you took ill."

She nodded, knowing it was true.

"Psalm 139 says every day of our lives is already in God's book before it comes to be," Dad said. "Good and bad, it's all in there. I find comfort in that." He looked her in the eyes. "It so happens I have nothing on my schedule tomorrow afternoon, and there's enough fuel in the Cessna for about an hour's worth of air time. Be at the airfield at one. The weather report says sunny, with no rain in sight."

"Are you sure we can't go today, while I have the nerve?"

He chuckled. "I wish we could, but my schedule is packed all the way until 5 p.m. Get a good night's sleep, and tomorrow will be here before you know it."

WEARING a pair of khaki pants and a light blue, button-down shirt, Grace arrived at the airfield fifteen minutes before one. She recognized Dad's plane from a photo he'd shown her, and she walked over to the beauty. It had been a long time since she'd flown his other plane, which he'd sold after acquiring this four-seater. She ran her hand over the words *Amazing Grace,* painted in red and blue on the plane's side.

Ever since she was small, her parents had told her they named her Grace because God had shown them His amazing grace through their rough times being separated by the war, when Mom didn't know for sure if he was dead or alive.

On her eighteenth birthday, Dad told her it was time to solo. She hadn't forgotten the thrill. Holding her head high, she'd hoped he wouldn't see how nervous she was, despite her lessons being completed except for the solo flight.

After that, whenever she was home on school breaks or during the summer, she flew the plane—sometimes alone and sometimes with Dad. The talks with Helen and her parents, along with prayer, had convinced her to let Mac make up his own mind. But first she had to fly again.

Dad's Buick rolled into the field parking lot. He climbed out of the car, wearing the khaki pants and one of the shirts he called his flying uniform and approached her. "You're here early."

"Mom dropped me off because she needed the car. You'll need to drive me home."

"Or I could just push you out of the plane over our house, and you can parachute down."

She laughed. "Sorry. I haven't parachuted since the one time I did during training. No thanks."

"Knowing how driven you are, that's a surprise." He winked and patted the plane. "Isn't she a little beauty?"

"Oh, yes. What a blessing that you were able to purchase her."

He opened the cockpit door and tossed the leather case he always took on flights into the back seat. "You go ahead and get in the other side."

"But that's the pilot's seat."

"I know. You're the pilot today."

Her breath caught. "I thought I'd take over after we reached altitude."

"You need to start with takeoff. I know you can do it, Grace. How many planes much bigger than this have you flown in the past several years? You won't make a mistake. But if you do, I'm right there."

"Okay." She nodded. "But you had better be ready to grab the controls."

"I'm not worried."

After checking off all the boxes on their pre-flight inspection, she climbed in, shut the cockpit door, and gripped the steering column's handles while Dad jumped into the passenger seat.

Suddenly, everything came back as if she'd flown only yesterday, and she soon was taxiing to the grass runway. She grinned at Dad. "Am I cleared for takeoff?"

Looking to the left and right, then up, he craned his neck. "All clear. Permission granted."

She sequenced the dials where they needed to be, then sped the plane up as it raced down the runway. At the right point shown on the dials, she pulled back, and the plane lifted. Within a couple of minutes, off to the southwest Geneva Lake appeared, stretched out in its familiar, boot-like shape.

The lake glistened in the sun like a large jewel, and she couldn't resist taking the plane over town and the Riviera beach, then up the north shore until Safe Refuge came into view. Below, a man in a suit walked the grounds with another man. "It looks like the property is being shown by a Realtor."

Dad pressed his face against the window for a better view. "That's John Wilson. He specializes in listings on the lakeshore. Did you know it was listed?"

A lump that felt as big as the spring house down below formed in her throat. "No, but I'm not surprised." She turned the plane and headed south until they were near the Illinois state line, then headed northeast. The plane did her bidding at every turn and every increase or decrease in speed. She was home.

"I really love this place, Dad—Geneva Lake, the town, the green hills … . She headed the plane back over town, this time over their house. "I don't want to leave, even if the family can never own Safe Refuge again."

"Does that mean you're ready to give Dusty a call?"

"Yes. But there's a problem. I need a plane to work for him."

"I have an idea."

"What?"

"I'll tell you when we land."

They were almost to Mac's Christmas tree farm, and she angled in that direction and brought the aircraft lower as she approached. Below, wearing denim work pants and a plaid button-down shirt, Mac walked between the rows of trees he'd soon harvest for the Christmas season.

"There's Mac." She swooped lower, tipping the wings up and down, then circled around, laughing at him standing there, fists planted on his hips. Then an expression of recognition crossed his face and he waved.

"Grace, he has no idea who's in the plane."

"Sure he did. Didn't you see him wave?"

"I'm not so sure. Sometimes people do that as a friendly gesture, like boaters waving at other boaters they don't know," Dad said. "You'd better be careful. He's likely to report you to his air raid warden."

"Who happens to be you, Dad."

"Nope. Not my jurisdiction. I know how excited you are to be flying, but during wartime we need to behave. Let's take her in. My mission here is done."

After a smooth landing, she sat motionless. Now that they were back on the ground, guilt over her thoughtless behavior fell over her. She sat staring out the windshield.

"Do you want to hear my idea?" Dad's voice snapped her back to reality.

"Yes, of course. But not until I apologize for my recklessness with your plane."

He reached over and gave her shoulder a squeeze. "I know you meant no harm, and if you tell Mac right away it was you, I doubt he'll report you."

"I hope you're right."

"Now, about crop dusting. I agree such a business is the way to go for you. Right now, farmers are pressured to grow as many crops as possible. The crop dusters are being stretched thin. I have a feeling that after the war the business will grow even more. Get a head start by working for someone like Dusty, and at the right time you might even want to break off and start your own company."

She stared at him as a wave of excitement flowed over her. "If I only could."

"You can." Dad continued. "A lot of pilots will be looking for work when they come home. Many are already flying Piper Cubs in the war, and when the conflict ends, those planes will be for sale cheap. They're perfect for crop dusting. A few of the ones used earlier in the war are already for sale. That's the kind of plane you need."

"Crop dusting is a seasonal thing. What would I do in winter for income?"

"Same as people in town with restaurants and stores, who make most of their money during tourist season. They earn enough during summer to carry them through the winter."

"But I don't have money to buy a plane. I barely have two quarters to rub together."

"I think the family can help by chipping in, and you can pay us all back out of your profits."

"And if the business fails, then what?"

"We all cry together. That's what family is, Grace. We hold each other up, rejoicing at our victories and crying together when trouble hits. We'll talk later and put a plan together for you. Right now, I promised Lenny I'd attend a father-and-son Boy Scout supper, so I need to get home and clean up. Do you want to come home with me?"

"Can you drop me off at Mac's? It's not too far from here, and I owe him an apology."

"For buzzing him and scaring the daylights out of him?"

"Yes, and to discuss a few other things."

40

At the entrance to the McAlister farm, Grace waved goodbye to Dad. He wanted to wait to be sure Mac was there, but she said she'd take her chances. His Buick disappeared around a bend, and she started down the lane, hoping that when she passed by Mac's parents' house no one would see her. If he wasn't at home, she'd wait for him on his porch. She'd almost made it past the main house when Jo burst out the back door and scampered down the steps.

Rats. Since she was in the only part of the yard without trees, her only option was to say hello.

She waved and Jo ran toward her, a hopeful expression on her face.

"Hi, Miss Grace. Are you looking for my dad?"

"I am looking for him. Do you know if he's at your house?"

The girl shook her head. "I don't think so. "He's out in the fields training the men from the POW camp."

Oh, I thought I saw him by the tree farm earlier."

The girl quirked her head. "How did you see him? You weren't here before, were you?"

"No. I saw him from the airplane I was flying. I think I scared him."

Jo's eyes widened. "That was you? I didn't know you had a plane."

"The plane belongs to my dad. Today was my first day flying since I was sick."

Her face lit up. "Oh, it must be fun to be up in the air like that. Maybe sometime you can take me up with you." Jo's eyes glistened. "I want to be like you when I grow up."

Her heart squeezed. "You want to be a pilot?"

"I'm not interested in that. I want to be like you are. Unafraid of anything, and willing to serve your country the way you did. You did all that and were a good Christian at the same time."

Grace turned away to hide her grimace. Now she really needed to talk to Mac. Not tomorrow, today. He'd straighten Jo out and help her understand Grace was not a good role model for a young girl. "Do you know when he'll be done training those men? I'll wait for him at your house."

"He'll come here first for me, and knowing Grandma, she'll convince him to stay for supper. I hope so, anyway. Dad's an okay cook, but nothing like my grandma."

"Your grandma has had more experience with cooking. Your Dad will get better in time."

"I hope so. Why don't you wait here? You can help us with canning. We're making applesauce, like I made with Lenny at your house."

"Okay." Grace knew when to admit defeat. "But I have no idea how to make applesauce."

"I couldn't believe it when Lenny said your family never made applesauce from scratch. I offered to help him when he was assigned to make it for a project at school. Now I'll show you." Jo took her hand and pulled her toward the back door.

A couple of minutes later, they stepped into the warm, cozy kitchen, and Jo announced, "Look who I found in our yard."

Ella turned from the stove, and a wide grin filled her round face. "Well, isn't this a surprise? Grace, you are a sight for sore eyes, if I don't say so. Mac didn't tell us you were coming by."

"He doesn't know. I decided to drop in and say hello on impulse. Jo told me he'll be coming here when he's done working with the POWs."

"Did Jo tell you what happened earlier?" Ella asked. "A plane flew low over Mac and those men, and the POWs about lost their lunches, they were so scared."

Grace's face heated, and she worked to stop her chin from quivering. "I'm so sorry I scared them."

"It was *you*?" Ella's eyes rounded.

"Mac waved, so I thought he knew it was me."

Ella smiled. "We wave at everyone out here, whether we know them or not."

"You might not remember, I was a pilot before I took ill, and I flew bombers for WASP."

"How could I forget something like that?" Ella replied. "I knew about you long before we met, thanks to the articles in the paper. I thought at the time how brave you were to do such a thing."

Those articles again.

"You flatter me too much. It's the men flying those planes into battle who are the brave ones. I haven't piloted a plane since I came home sick, but my dad let me fly his Cessna today. It was fun being back in the air, and when I saw Mac inspecting the trees, I swooped in and rocked my wings at him. I didn't realize he had the POWs with him. He's never seen my dad's plane, and I didn't tell him we were going to take it up this afternoon. I'm very sorry for scaring everyone. Ella, please forgive me."

Ella tossed the spoon she was holding into the sink, and her arms came around her. Grace soaked in the loving gesture. Over the past weeks, Ella had become almost like a second mother to her. Not only was she going to miss Mac, but his whole family.

"You did cause quite a scare." Ella said, all the while patting Grace's back. "If we knew you were in the plane ... Everyone is jittery these days, with all the admonitions to keep our eyes to the sky and, if you see anything unusual, report it."

A sinking feeling fell over Grace. "Mac didn't report it, did he?"

Ella released her from the hug. "I don't think so. They've been too busy working. Come on. You can help Jo and me with the canning until Mac gets back."

"I don't know anything about canning. My mom wasn't into that kind of thing and I never learned."

"There's no time like the present to learn. These apples I've been stirring are about ready to be put through the food mill. All you need to do is turn the handle while Jo scoops in the cooked apples."

"I remember seeing Jo and my brother do that when they made applesauce at my house."

"Good. And there is one thing more. I hope you can stay for supper after you and Mac talk. You don't have to answer, but there's plenty to go around."

By the time Mac called to Jo through the open window that he was back and she should gather her things, they had a dozen jars of applesauce lined up on the kitchen table and ready for storage in the cellar.

Still in her flying clothes with a borrowed apron tied around her waist and her hair tied back with a scarf, Grace knew she had to look a mess. She patted her hair, quickly trying to reconstruct the victory roll on top of her head, to no avail.

Mac stepped into the room, and his gaze went to her. The grin she loved filled his face. "Grace! This is a surprise. I'd have quit sooner if I knew you were here. Where did you park?"

"Dad dropped me off. We were at the airfield, and I took a chance you'd be able to give me a ride home."

"She came to see you, Dad." Jo scooted up to him and wrapped her arms around his waist. "To apologize for scaring you."

"Scaring me?" He stared at Grace.

"It was her in the plane that came low, Dad. She was the pilot."

Understanding filled his features. "That's why you were at the airfield."

"Yes. Dad convinced me I needed to get back in the air. We were near the farm, so I flew over it. And when I saw you, without thinking, I came in low and rocked my wings. Of course, you had no idea it was me." She studied her scuffed boots. Maybe she should have gone home to change before coming. "I'm very sorry. I guess I scared the POWs. I never saw them. I only saw you. I hope you didn't report me to the air raid warden."

He stepped over and gave her a side hug. "You'd have to do a lot worse than what you did for me to do that. I knew you weren't the enemy. Didn't you see me wave?"

"Yes."

He squeezed her shoulder and removed his arm. "Well, you sure did make this afternoon exciting." He threw his head back and laughed. "But you didn't need to stop by just to apologize."

She looked away then back at him, expecting judgment, but only saw love in his eyes. "There's something else I want to talk about. But not here."

"Okay. Jo can stay here a bit longer. If that's okay with Mom."

"Of course it is," Ella said. "Take all the time you two need. Then plan on coming back here for supper."

"It was good to see you again, sweetie." Grace removed her borrowed apron and handed it to Jo, then bent and hugged the girl. "Maybe I'll see you when you next visit Lenny."

"Okay, but won't you be coming back here to eat?" Jo's face still wore that hopeful expression.

"I don't know." She smiled at Ella. "Thanks for everything."

Outside, Mac started walking toward the lane. "We can talk at my house."

"Okay. Any place that's private."

His brow furrowed. "Now you've got me curious."

They walked in silence. Not to be tempted to reach for his hand, she kept her distance, Right then, she could use a reassuring squeeze. But this had to be done solo.

"How did it feel to be flying again?"

"Wonderful. Dad's plane flies like a dream. We flew over town and the lake. A Realtor was showing Rose Harbor to someone. I hope whoever buys it takes better care of it than Paul's grandfather has."

"Maybe it was the people before Atwater who let it run down."

"Or a little bit of both."

"Sounds like a fun plane ride," Mac said. "I'd love it if you'd take me up sometime."

"Your daughter already made a reservation for a ride."

He chuckled. "Then you can take us both up at the same time. I know fuel is scarce. We're happy to wait." They arrived at his house, and he stopped walking. "Do you want to sit on the porch swing or inside?"

"The porch is good."

They sat side by side. She folded her hands in her lap to still the shaking, while he kept his resting on his thighs.

"You go first." He faced her, his eyes questioning.

She swallowed, wishing she'd asked for water, but didn't want to put this off any longer. "I can't deny my growing feelings for you any longer, Mac. You deserve to know what I've been scared to tell you and why I've insisted we only be friends. I've reached the point where it's impossible to be only friends with you because ... I'm in love with you." She inhaled, held her breath a moment, and let it out.

"I'm in love with you too." He took her hand and kissed it. "But I sense that's not all you wanted to say." He squeezed her hand. "Go ahead. I'm right here listening."

"I already told you about the man I was engaged to marry."

"Yeah. Frank. He wasn't a nice guy."

"No, he wasn't. The last night before he was to ship out, we decided not to be apart those final hours, and to sit up all night and talk. We couldn't do that on the base, so we got a cheap hotel room. Our intentions were in the right place. At least mine were, but it was a very emotional time, and before long we were making love."

Mac didn't say anything.

She took a deep breath. "It was my first time. I'd wanted to wait for my wedding night, but I rationalized he was leaving for war and it might be the one and only time we'd be together that way. I was right about one thing. It was the one and only time. I'm not a virgin, Mac."

He drew her into a hug. "Oh, Grace, if that's what you've been afraid to tell me, I still love you. You weren't the first couple to do that before the guy went off to war, and you won't be the last." He kissed her, but she refrained from kissing him back and tried unsuccessfully to put space between them.

"It's more than that, Mac. A month went by without my hearing from him. I worried that he'd already been a casualty and sent several letters to the general address I was given when he left, asking him to write back."

"And that's when you got the letter, right?" Mac stretched his arm across her shoulders and snuggled her into the crook of his arm. "That guy was a real cad. I'm so sorry he did that to you."

"That's not all. At the same time that I received the letter, I found out I was two months pregnant."

Silence hung over them, but if he had an adverse reaction, he wasn't showing it by loosening his hold on her.

After several seconds, he said softly, "Go on, sweetie, I'm right here listening."

Hearing him call her a pet name for the first time about broke her heart. "I was in line to be moved up for training on the B-29, which would be my ticket to possibly flying for a commercial airline after the war. I was an emotional wreck. Once WASP knew I was pregnant, I would be dismissed from the program. I couldn't come back to Lake Geneva single and pregnant."

She started to pull away, but Mac held her fast, and she went on. "People talk around here about unmarried girls getting pregnant and having to get married. In my case, there wasn't anyone to make me an honest woman. I may as well have hung a large letter *A* around my neck if I came home in that condition. It wasn't just my reputation, but my family's as well."

Mac let out a quiet sigh, but he still wasn't talking.

"My only choice would be to stay in Texas until the baby was born," she said, "and give the child up for adoption. Then come home with some kind of fib as to why I quit the job I loved so much. I considered going to a home for unwed mothers, but the closest one was in San Antonio, far from the only friends I had in Texas."

"I'm confused," Mac said. "You were still flying for WASP when you got sick. How did you manage that?"

If only they could end the conversation right there, but he needed to know everything. Her pulse raced, but she forced herself to go on. "One of the local women who worked in the mess hall found me hiding in a pantry when I couldn't hold back my tears. I confided in her, and she told me about a doctor in Juarez, Mexico, who did surgeries for much less money than doctors in the U.S. who did back alley abortions. She was willing to take me there."

Tears burst from her eyes and a sob escaped.

He handed her a handkerchief. "It's clean."

"Thanks. This is so hard."

"I know it is, baby." He hugged her closer. "Remember I love you, and I'm right here and not going anywhere. Take your time. You were talking about the lady who worked in the mess hall."

"I knew abortion was wrong, but I felt I had no choice. I prayed that whole night, begging God for a solution, but none came. In the morning, I told the woman I'd do it and requested a two-day leave for the same two days she already had scheduled off two weeks later."

The enormity of it struck her afresh, and she felt sick.

"As if God was already heaping punishment on me, I had terrible morning sickness during the wait, a grim reminder of my sin and the sin I was about to do. Long story short, we took an all-night bus to San Juan, Texas, walked across the border into Mexico, and found the doctor."

They sat in silence for a moment. Mac rubbed her shoulders as if trying to release the tension.

"After the procedure, I bled a lot. The doctor told me, with my friend translating, that he must have nicked something, and I might never be able to have children. I was in too much pain to take it all in. I just wanted out of there. We took another all-night bus back to the base. I slept most of the way and was still bleeding when we arrived. I told the others it was my time of the month, and within a few days the bleeding stopped."

She searched his face for any sign of judgment but only saw compassion. "That's why I can't marry you, Mac. You don't want anyone who would do such a thing to her child or not have saved herself for marriage."

His somber expression showed her the truth was finally sinking in.

"I've been thinking for months that even God had deserted me," she said. "But I've started praying a lot about this and asked Him to show me in the Scriptures what I needed to know. He took me to Psalm 51, and I prayed my way through that beautiful psalm. I'm assured now that God has forgiven me and hasn't ever left me. But that doesn't mean you have to feel the same." She moved to stand, but he tightened his hold and kept her tucked under his arm.

"Why did you think God had deserted you?"

She sniffed. "When I was small, I turned my life over to Him and promised to be obedient to Him. I failed Him."

Mac hugged her closer. "I wish you'd told me all this sooner, but I understand why you didn't. I'm grateful to hear you have been praying about this and that the Lord led you to that psalm. Do you remember what the angel said to Joseph about the baby Mary was carrying?"

"That what was happening to her was being done by God and she would have a son."

"Yes, and there's something else the angel said, "Thou shalt call his name Jesus: for he shall save his people from their sins. Jesus came because we can't be saved from our sins by anything we do. He's already paid the price for your sin, Grace. You are forgiven, and He sees you as blameless. How can I see you any other way?"

"But I still don't understand why He was silent with me for all those months."

"You've recovered from your illness, and you're home under the loving care of your family. He's given you a new purpose of working for the Red Cross and blessing others while you figure out what He is calling you to do next, and today you regained your joy of flying. And you've been a blessing to me and Jo in countless ways."

Her mind whirled. "You may see me as good, but is it okay that Jo told me she wants to be like me when she grows up? Do you want her turning out like me?"

"Yes, I'd love it if she did."

"You can't mean that." She gaped at him. "I killed my own child, and to top it off, I can't give you more children because of what I did. I'm a terrible role model. You think I've been attending the late service. The Sunday I came to the early service and sat with you is the last time I've been to church—the only time since I came home."

"I've suspected as much. I saw the tears in your eyes that Sunday, but felt I needed to give you time to work through whatever burden you've been carrying around."

He couldn't have understood what she was saying.

"If I'd not done that terrible thing, my baby would be over a year old now, Mac. That day I said I was sick and couldn't bowl would have been his first birthday. Or hers."

"My darling Grace." He ran his free hand across her face and brushed a lock of hair away. "Do you think I've never sinned? Only Jesus lived that perfect of a life. If you and I marry, neither of us will come to each other sinless. If you confessed your sins to God and asked forgiveness, He's forgiven you the same as He forgives me when I confess my sins to Him. We are all sinners, saved by grace."

Unsure if she should weep or laugh, she stared at him. Mac loved her in spite of her terrible past. "It doesn't matter I can't give you more children?"

"Not in the way you think. I'd love to have children with you, but if it never happens, I still want to spend the rest of my life married to you. Have you asked any other doctor for an opinion?"

"The only doctor I've seen since it happened is my grandfather, and I'm not about to ask him."

"I guess that wouldn't be a good idea. We can have you examined by a doctor in Milwaukee or Chicago and find out that way. If you can't, we can always adopt. But we already have Jo, and I think you know she loves you almost as much as I do."

"And I love her too. I'd love to be a mom to her. Not to replace her real mother, of course."

"Well then, there is nothing else left to do. I'll be right back." He stood and went into the house.

Grace sat staring up at the porch ceiling. "God, You have blessed me more than I could ever imagine. Thank You."

"I don't know what to show you first." Mac sat next to her and handed her a book. "Let's start with this."

"What is it?"

"Open it and you'll see." He kissed her on the temple.

She turned the cover and read the inscription in Mac's handwriting.

For my precious, Grace, whom I love with all my heart, Mac.

"Did you do this since yesterday?"

"I started it a couple of months ago. I'd write in it after coming back from seeing you and feeling frustrated at your refusal to let me into your heart. I'd write to you and pour out my feelings, then put it aside until the next time. I found it interesting that your great-grandfather wrote in a book to Anna, in the same way I was writing in this book to you."

The pages blurred as she turned back several pages and read what he wrote back in the spring, then flipped a few more toward the back and read what he wrote in June. She looked at him. "I'm surprised you stuck with me."

"I had a sense that you loved me as much as I love you. I just kept praying that God would help you trust me enough to be honest with me, and you'd be set free to love me."

She flipped to the last entry. "This was written last night."

"Go ahead and read it out loud."

"Okay. It looks like a prayer. 'Dear God, I've always felt You were encouraging me to keep on loving Grace despite her rejections of my love. I'm reminded of how Hosea got the same message from you when Gomer kept leaving him. I'm certainly not comparing Grace to Gomer, but I am convinced she is struggling with some terrible sin in her past that makes her think she's unworthy to have a loving relationship with me or any other man.

'I admit my patience is growing thin, and after today, I'm thinking maybe I've been misreading Your intentions. That I love Grace so much and can't bear to go through life without her, so I'm imagining Your will for us, when it's not what You want. I'm willing to walk away from her and give her what she seems to want. I'm leaving it in Your hands.'"

She looked up at him. "Oh, Mac. I'm so sorry for putting you through all this. I guess God did make His will for us known, didn't He? Otherwise I wouldn't be sitting here with your arm around me."

He brought his lips to hers, and she snuggled closer to him as the kiss lingered.

Delicious flutters filled her stomach. Never had she felt so loved. They parted, and she leaned back. "Mac McAlister, I am totally and completely in love with you."

"Finally, the words I've longed to hear." He grinned and slid off the swing and onto one knee, then dug into his pocket and held out a diamond solitaire. "Grace Bauer, will you do me the honor of becoming my wife? I love you more than anything and want to be your husband and love the daylights out of you for the rest of your life." He slipped the ring on her finger.

The diamond glittered in the afternoon sun that shown through a crack in the porch roof. She shifted her gaze back to him, her eyes so full of tears she could barely see him. "Yes, Mac, of course, I'll marry you."

"Oh, Grace, my darling Grace." He rose to sit next to her and drew her into his arms. "I love you so much."

Their lips connected, and tingles trailed down her neck. She'd never tire of feeling his lips on hers the way they were at that moment.

He sat back. "I have something else to show you." He took a folded paper from the back of the book and handed it to her. "This is a document signifying someone put earnest money down on the property you know as Safe Refuge. The man you saw there with the Realtor is a real estate attorney. He was there today to evaluate the estate. He reported to us earlier, and everyone agrees an investment in the property would be a sound venture."

"You're buying the property?" She gave her head a mental shake. "How can you have that kind of money?"

"It's not all my money. Your dad helped us put our property here in a trust held by a foundation made up of me and my parents and brothers. It's an investment for all of us, you included once we're married. I presented your situation with Rose Harbor to them a few weeks ago, and they all agreed."

"But you can't live there. This is your home. Your business is here."

"I could live there and drive out here every day, or we could live here in this house, which I plan to finish enlarging, and you can go back and forth to Safe Refuge as you wish. Remember what you said about using the cottage to provide a place for women whose husbands are at war? If we own it, you can do exactly that."

"Oh, Mac." She stared at him as her disbelief splintered.

"Or a thought came to mind as you were telling me about your ordeal," he said. "The house would make a good home for unwed mothers as they wait for their children to be born. We could have a tie-in with an adoption agency, to arrange for the babies who aren't going to be raised by their natural mothers to be adopted."

"That was the first thought I had when we first talked about how the property could be used. I felt suggesting it wasn't a good idea, since I didn't want the family to know what I'd done."

"Does that mean you're going to tell them?"

"I don't think so. You needed to know. The rest of them don't."

Mac nodded.

"But I'm finally going to call Dusty and talk to him about crop dusting. Either working for him or starting my own business. Dad told me that he and the family would help me buy a little Piper, which is what crop dusters use these days.

"You can add the Foundation to the list of possible contributors."

"We'll see. Just buying Safe Refuge is more than enough. I think I'd rather live here. Maybe one of the other family members would like to live in the cottage."

"We can talk about all that later. Right now, let's let our parents and our daughter know we're getting married."

"You mean your daughter."

"She'll be ours after we're married. May as well start calling her ours now." He stood. "I need to change before we announce. I've been working in the field all day."

"And do I look any better? I've been flying a plane, canning applesauce in a steamy kitchen, and sobbing my heart out. My hair's a mess, and I probably smell like cooked apples.

"I love your curly mess." He tousled her hair. "And I love that you smell like apple pie, but I do need to get out of these dirty workpants. I'll only be a couple of minutes. I know you ladies like big weddings with bridesmaids and all that, so we'd better start planning soon."

"I'm not like other women." She laughed and stood on tiptoes to kiss him. "I'd love to get married soon. What about two weeks from today?"

"What about three weeks? That's Labor Day weekend. If we get married on Friday afternoon, we'll have three days to honeymoon before I have to prepare for the first day of school on Thursday. Not a long time for a getaway, but maybe we can take a longer trip after Christmas, when the tree lot is closed for the year.

THE FOLLOWING SUNDAY, Grace woke up and stretched, then held up her left hand and grinned at the diamond twinkling in the morning light. Mac told her he'd bought it a month ago, after he talked to Dad and asked for her hand. She smiled at how Dad had suggested Mac would probably want to have that conversation soon. What a couple of sneaks they were.

In less than three weeks, Mac would slip a matching wedding band onto that finger and she would be Grace McAlister—Mrs. Robert McAlister. No. He'd always be Mac to her. Mrs. Mac McAlister. She couldn't wait to move out to the tree farm.

Plans for their wedding were quickly falling into place. The church was reserved for that Friday afternoon. They'd toyed with the idea of getting married outside at the farm, but Granny wouldn't do well walking across the lumpy ground to the setting Mac had suggested next to a creek.

Reenie would be her maid of honor, and Jo would be a junior bridesmaid. Mac's dad would be his best man, since his brothers wouldn't be able to come home, and Lenny a junior groomsman. They would keep the guest list to only about thirty people, given it was wartime, and her parents would host a wedding supper buffet at their home for family and very close friends.

A knock came at the door and she called out, "Come in."

"Good morning." Mom stepped into the room wrapped in her peach-colored robe. "Mac just called and said to tell you he'll be here in an hour. I took the liberty of asking him to come earlier and have breakfast here, since we're having the wonderful eggs he brought us yesterday. I envy you being able to have fresh eggs every day after you move out there. I didn't think you'd mind."

"I think I'll be able to bring you eggs once in a while." She giggled. "I guess I'd better start getting ready."

By the time the doorbell rang, Grace was in the kitchen, helping Mom get the scrambled eggs onto plates.

"Hello!" Mac's voice called out, "I'm here!"

She loved how he was already like a member of the family, not having to wait for someone to admit him.

"Good morning, Mrs. McAlister-to-be." He came up behind her and hugged her, then punctuated the greeting with a kiss to her ear that sent a shiver down her neck.

"Good morning, Mr. McAlister." Sensing they were momentarily alone, she pivoted and kissed him. "I think you'd better save those ear kisses for after we're married. Now I'm too flustered to think what I need to do next."

He laughed and stepped back, then picked up two of the prepared plates. "This looks great. Should I carry these to the dining room?"

"Yes, after adding a strip of bacon to each plate." She paused, taking in how handsome he was in his suit and tie. "The bacon is on the stove. I wish we could have more than one piece each, but that's all we have. Jo isn't with you?"

"No. She attended first service with my parents. She wanted to get home early to do her chores. I think she's saving the money she's earning by doing extra farm chores for a wedding gift for us. I have no idea what she has in mind."

"That's so sweet." Grace smiled. "What kind of chores is she doing?"

"Feeding the chickens and gathering eggs every day and helping Mom around the house. I might add doing some of the work on the new addition."

"She knows carpentry?"

"A little, but there's no reason she can't learn a few things like laying tile and painting what will be her new bedroom in the color of her choosing. I know I'm taking a risk she won't pick out something garish."

"If she does, it can always be painted over when she leaves for college."

"Don't even talk about that. To me, she's still the three-year-old who refused to stop wearing a diaper."

A few minutes later, the family settled around the table with Grace and Mac seated next to each other on one side Reenie and Lenny across from them, and Mom and Dad at either end.

Dad glanced around the table. "Soon I hope we'll have to add another leaf to this table."

"What do you mean by that?" Grace stared at her father.

"Don't start on them that way, Ted." Mom narrowed her eyes. "It's all in God's timing."

"I was thinking about Rory coming home, but a grandchild would be nice." He winked, and Grace felt heat rise to her face.

Beneath the table, Mac took her hand and gave it a slight squeeze.

After breakfast, he suggested they walk the few blocks up Madison Street to the church. Grace agreed and grabbed her cardigan from the hook by the side door as they made a fast exit.

"I'm surprised no one else wanted to join us." He took her hand and wove their fingers together.

She laughed. "Lenny wanted to, but I heard Mom tell him we needed time together alone."

"And Lenny didn't protest?"

"Oh, yes. He said, 'What's the difference? They're gonna get married in a few weeks and have all the time in the world to be together.' I think when Rory gets back, some of Lenny's desire to spend time with you will lessen. He really misses his big brother a lot. As have we all."

"I'm happy to be a surrogate big brother in the meantime. I can't wait to meet Rory. Too bad he can't be home in time for our wedding."

She let go of a sigh. "I thought of postponing the ceremony, but then we don't know for sure when he'll get home. He's doing well at the hospital in San Diego. His voice was strong the last time he called. He said he's put on most of the weight he lost in captivity. But I don't want to wait any longer. I don't know how couples do it when they get engaged and take months to plan the wedding."

"That's how it was when Emily and I got engaged. Of course, we were barely twenty, and our parents encouraged us not to be so quick with things."

"How long was your engagement?"

"About ten months."

"Maybe it's because of my time with WASP that's influencing me, but once something is set with me I want to move forward. As I've said before, I'm not like other women."

He leaned down and kissed her cheek. "I love you just the way you are, Grace Bauer."

"You may not say that after a week of my cooking."

"Sure, I will. If you burn dinner, we can just hoof it over to my folks' house for some of my mom's cooking."

"I wouldn't mind that. She's a wonderful cook. I intend to ask for some of her recipes."

"Good idea, but don't ask for her liver and onions. That meal is not one of my favorites."

"Don't worry, I won't. I hate liver and onions too."

They arrived at the church and had just stepped into the foyer when Helen rushed up, wearing her trademark grin. "Okay, let me see it."

"See what?" Grace teased.

Helen grabbed Grace's left hand. "Oh, it's beautiful. You have great taste, McAlister."

"I know," Mac said. "Look at the woman I fell in love with."

"I suppose this means you won't be bowling this season." Helen hugged Grace.

"Says who? We both plan to be there. Mac isn't giving up helping out on league nights, and I'd miss spending time with you girls. At least that's the plan."

Organ music sounded from the sanctuary. "There's our cue. Shall we get seated?" Mac offered Grace his arm.

They sat several rows down the aisle, shoulder to shoulder. Was it only a few weeks ago they'd sat this way the first time she'd attended church with him? Little did she know that the next time they sat together during church they'd be engaged.

On the first hymn, she sang all the verses of "Amazing Grace" with passion, a new emotion for her, and a pleasant one. After the hymn, Mac took her hand and squeezed it. A warm feeling rushed over her. If it were possible, she'd have asked the pastor to perform the ceremony right then. She couldn't wait to be this man's wife.

41

Three weeks later

Grace stood in front of the full-length mirror in her bedroom and studied her image. She loved how well Mom's wedding dress fit with only a few alterations, and she loved that the dress was first worn by Granny, and then by Mom, and now her.

It made sense to have this wedding quickly and without a fuss. And because it was wartime, she didn't receive many objections from her mother or grandmother to have such a simple wedding. After all, Mom and Dad got married in a hospital chapel with two days' planning. Grace had the luxury of three weeks to prepare.

A knock came at the open door and Reenie stepped in, wearing the moss-green, tea-length dress Mom had made for her.

"You look beautiful, Reenie." Grace smiled at her sister. "That color suits you perfectly."

Reenie hugged her, careful not to crush Grace's dress. "Thanks, but you're the star today, and a beautiful bride."

"Everyone says that about the bride. But I have to admit, I look in the mirror and keep asking, 'Who is that?' With Helen doing my hair, Mom helping me with my makeup, and the glow I feel at this being my wedding day, how could I not look beautiful?" She grinned at Reenie. "Is Jo dressed?"

"Yes, Mom's helping her. She was just having the flowers pinned into her hair. It was a good idea for her to sleep here last night so we could dress together." She stepped over to the mirror. "Do my flowers look okay the way Mom pinned them in?"

"They look perfect, and so natural." Grace brushed her fingertips over the tea roses and baby's breath. Her own bouquet of peonies and roses from the garden at the farm was made by Ella and would arrive at the church with the McAlisters.

A few minutes later, Grace stood at the door to the bedroom and gave it one last glance. It had been her bedroom since she was five years old, and she'd never sleep here again, at least not as a single woman.

She headed for the stairs, loving the rustle her skirts made as she walked. She was to wait in the living room until everyone gathered to caravan the short distance to the church. Voices wafted up from downstairs. After making sure the short train on her dress lay flat on the floor behind her, she descended the stairs.

In the foyer, she found Granddad, wearing his good black suit, and Granny, who had on a beautiful pale-yellow, tea-length dress with three-quarter sleeves and a net skirt overlay.

Granny's eyes glistened as she gazed at Grace. "Well, look at you in my wedding dress. It looks much better on you than it did on me."

"Maureen, my dear, you were a vision in that dress, as was Hannah and now Grace." Granddad leaned over and kissed his wife on her cheek. "I think you'd better give her the gift. Time is short."

"What gift?" Grace stepped closer. "You already gave us that beautiful quilt as a wedding gift."

Granddad stepped aside and revealed a wrapped box behind him.

"This is a special gift from me to you." Granny picked it up. "Let's take it over to the table so you can open it." She walked to a long folding table that held their wedding gifts.

"I can't imagine what this could be." Grace came up beside her grandmother, removed the ribbon and paper, then lifted the lid and reached inside. Her hand landed on what felt like a teapot spout. "Is this what I think it is?"

"Take it out and see for yourself." Granny grinned.

Grasping the handle, Grace lifted out the silver teapot and gasped. "It *is*. Oh Granny, are you sure? Isn't it supposed to go to Mom next?"

Mom walked up. It was the first time Grace had seen her in her mother-of-the-bride dress, a dusty mauve color with cap sleeves and a sweetheart neckline. The skirt fell in tiny pleats. It, too, was tea length, as wartime dictated saving on fabric.

"Mama told me how much you admired the teapot the other day, and she wanted to give it to you now. I want you to have it, too, Gracie."

"Yes." Granny said. "I wanted to be alive when you received it, not six feet under."

The foyer erupted in laughter, and Grace turned and laughed with them. She hugged Granny. "Mac and I will treasure it and I'll be sure it stays in the family. I love it. Thank you."

"Okay, folks, it's time we head over to the church." Dad clapped his hands and looked around the room. "I'll be driving Hannah, Grace, and Jo. Granddad and Granny will take Reenie and Lenny. I think that's everyone."

A few minutes later, Grace settled into Dad's front seat after Mom made sure her skirts were arranged properly. It was the last time she'd leave that home as Grace Bauer and never live there again. She swallowed down a lump and looked at the house as Dad pulled away from the curb. Across the street, the neighbors had come out on their lawn to wave, and she waved back.

Once at the church, Grace and Dad stood behind a pillar in the foyer while Jo walked first down the aisle, looking darling and very grown-up, followed by Reenie.

Dad lifted Grace's veil and kissed her on the cheek, then let the fabric drop and peeked around the pillar. "Everyone is in their places now. It's our turn." He held out his arm and she gripped it as they approached the open double doors.

The guests all stood, but the only person Grace saw was Mac at the end of the aisle, wearing a joyous grin. She was sure the smile she returned was equally full of joy as she and Dad made their way down the aisle. Her family and friends filled the front rows on the left, with Mac's family and friends on the right. They came to the first row, and she looked to her left to share a smile with Mom. Her mouth fell open.

Rory rose to his feet, wearing his navy dress uniform and a wide grin. "You didn't think I'd miss my big sister's wedding, did you?" he whispered.

"When did you get here?"

"I came from Chicago on the morning train. Mac picked me up and took me to his house to get ready."

Not caring about disturbing her dress, she hugged him. Behind her, applause broke out and she turned and grinned at the guests.

"This is our son, Rory," Dad announced. "He was released from a POW camp in Burma a short time ago. He just arrived home this morning, and Grace didn't know until just now that he was here."

She set her gaze on Mac, standing a few feet away. He winked, and Dad led her to a spot in front of her groom.

Mac grinned. "You're stunning in that dress, my beautiful bride."

"And you're looking very attractive in your new suit, my handsome bridegroom."

The rest of the ceremony was a blur: the beautiful solo, the pastor's short charge to them, the exchange of their vows, and the giving of the rings.

Suddenly, the pastor was announcing, "May I introduce for the first time, Mr. and Mrs. Robert Mac McAlister."

The crowd applauded, but Grace hardly noticed because she was busy kissing her new husband.

EPILOGUE

Eleven Months Later

A sharp pain about took Grace's breath away as she cradled her large stomach. Granddad stood from examining her. "There is no way you'll make it to the hospital in time. "You're almost fully dilated."

"Every other baby in the family has come fast and in the middle of the night." She huffed a laugh. "Why should my child be any different?

"This is going to be a big baby." He scratched his head. "I'd prefer to have you in the hospital and not at home. Prepare yourself. I may have to cut."

"Do whatever you have to." Grace bit her lower lip and reached for Mac's hand. "I just want this child born healthy."

"This is where I ask the father to step into the waiting room." Granddad looked at Mac.

"No!"

They stared at Grace.

"I want Mac here. It's his baby as well as mine."

Granddad frowned. "Let's let Mac decide."

"We already talked about it and we decided on having the

baby at home if possible," Mac said. "I grew up on a farm helping deliver calves that were breech. I'll be fine. I want to be here with Grace and our baby."

A couple of minutes later, another pain struck, and she let out a yowl and squeezed Mac's hand as tight as she could.

"You're doing good, Gracie." Mom laid a cool washcloth on her forehead. "Breathe easy and rest between contractions."

Another contraction came, stronger than the previous one, and she screamed.

"You're strong, Grace," Mac whispered. "It won't be long. I'm right here, honey."

"Okay, Grace," Granddad said. "It's time to push."

She took a deep breath and pushed, amazed at how she'd been able to gather such strength.

"Here comes the head," Granddad said. "Look at that beautiful red hair. Another Quinn baby. Give it one more push, Gracie. Come on little one. Come to your great-granddad."

She pushed.

"It's a girl! Granddaughter, you just delivered a girl."

"Annie is here." Mac leaned over and kissed her, then raised his head. "Her name is Anna Maureen McAlister."

"I want to see her." Grace tried to raise her head.

"You will." Mac patted her shoulder. "Nate just cut the cord, and your mom is cleaning her up."

A slightly wrinkled infant, looking startled at her surprise entrance into the world, was laid across Grace's chest. She smiled at her daughter. God's miracle baby. "She's so beautiful. Welcome to our family, Annie. I love you so much."

"We both love you, Annie." Mac leaned in and caressed their daughter's head.

"My Aunt Annie will be pleased she has a namesake," Grace said. "I haven't seen her in a long while, with her living in Ireland. Leave it to her to go over there to meet our Irish cousins and fall in love with an Irishman. Then Aunt Margie to do the same."

"Well I'll be," Granddad said.

"What's wrong, Pop?" Mom asked.

Granddad pushed gently on Grace's abdomen, and she grimaced at him.

"Hold on." He put his stethoscope's earpieces into his ears and pressed the other end to her stomach. "I believe there's one more infant hiding in there."

"Twins?" Grace's voice came out like a squeak. "Mac, we're having twins."

Mom carried Annie to a bathinette, which was set up in the adjoining bathroom. "I'll get this little one swaddled."

"Okay, Gracie, push one more time."

At Granddad's command, she gave a push and felt the infant begin to leave its warm nest.

"This one's got brown hair, and is coming fast. ... It's a boy!"

"Can you believe it, honey?" Mac squeezed Grace's hand, grinning. "We have one of each. Robert Quinn McAlister is here." He kissed her forehead then announced, "His name is Robby."

"I've heard of instances happening like this." Granddad scratched his head. "But I've never seen it in my practice."

"You think you're surprised?" Grace stared at him. "I had no idea I was carrying around two babies. No wonder I was so large."

Granddad stood from his stool. "Okay, both placentas are out and the cords are cut. Hannah, can you help Grace get washed?" He removed his rubber gloves and tossed them in a wastebasket then looked at Mac. "Congratulations, son. You're now the father of three, just like that."

After she'd sponge-bathed Grace, Mom carried Annie over to Mac while Granddad laid Robby on Grace's chest. The same emotions she'd felt for her daughter washed over Grace as she gazed at her boy. "He looks like you, Mac."

Mac leaned in. "I don't see the resemblance, but I'll take your word for it."

"Now we'll need another bassinette and crib." She pressed her lips against Robby's fuzzy head.

"I'm sure you can borrow from some of the ladies at church," Mom said. "But for now, both babies are small. Your bassinette is large. You can put them both in it together. That might be comforting for them. They've been together in your tummy for months." She turned to leave the room. "I need to call the farmhouse and tell Jo and Mac's parents the news, then call home. Ted will be beside himself."

Granddad helped clean up then left, leaving Grace with instructions on how to nurse, even though she assured him that with the two grandmas nearby she'd have plenty of help. Mom assisted her into a clean nightgown then back into bed.

"You and Mac need some alone time with your babies. I'll tell him it's okay to come in and join his little family. I'll be in the other room."

Mac lifted Annie out of the bassinette the babies were sharing and laid her in Grace's arms. He then gently lifted Robby and held him as he sat on the bed next to Grace.

"That grin of yours hasn't left your face since Annie was born." She laughed.

"Nor has your smile left your beautiful face." He kissed her on the cheek.

"Can you believe I was carrying around two babies?" She rested her head on his shoulder. "No wonder I looked so huge. It appears the crop-dusting business will be put on hold for a while."

"We'll figure out how to make it work." Mac kissed her. "God willing, it will happen."

AUTHOR'S NOTE & ACKNOWLEDGMENTS

I began writing this book in January of 2020, and the draft was about one-third complete when the U.S. was put on lockdown because of Covid. Unlike some authors who were able to take advantage of the extra free time to write, I had the opposite reaction. I tried to keep writing, but my brain refused to function.

As spring turned into summer and summer inched toward fall, I realized I had a January deadline for *Rose Harbor,* and I'd better start writing. God blessed me, and by His grace, the words flowed.

Rose Harbor is bittersweet for me because it is the last book in the *Newport of the West Series,* and I must bid my characters goodbye. I've fallen in love with every one of them, from Anna and Rory Quinn, to Maureen and Nate Murphy, to Hannah and Ted Bauer. And now, the final pair, Grace and Mac McAlister in *Rose Harbor*. I always think my favorites are the ones I'm writing about at the time, but I really do think Grace and Mac are my favorites.

It was easy for me to write about the stores and landmarks in this book because nothing much had changed in Lake Geneva between 1943 and the 1950s and 60s, when I was growing up.

I spent a lot of time at the Clair Lanes, rolling my own gutter balls (Where was Mac when I needed him to teach me how to avoid the dreaded gutter ball?), and I remember the Lazzaroni family, its owners, very well. I also remember going to the Gargoyle Restaurant's Rathskeller in the lower level with my parents. It was there that I said my first full sentence from my high chair pushed up to the table. I don't remember that, but I do remember dining there in later times.

And, as a teen, I frequented Frediani's Confectionary and Soda Fountain after the movies. Eventually the building was sold, and the movie theater next door took over that space.

The home the Bauers live in on Main Street is the house my family doctor lived in, and where he practiced medicine, in a small suite of rooms you entered from the side door.

Mac's Christmas tree farm and the tree lot are strictly from my imagination, but the hill on the north side of town where Mac takes Grace to talk is real. It really was a favorite parking spot for teens back in the day, as I've been told (wink, wink). Nowadays, private homes are up there, all with wide windows to take in the gorgeous view of the downtown and lake.

I'm very grateful for the Internet, which has proved invaluable while researching for this story during the Covid lockdown. There are countless articles online about the Women Airforce Service Pilots (WASP). When I first came across mention of these brave women pilots who ferried bombers and other types of aircraft from their point of manufacture to bases on the coasts, I knew that was what Grace Bauer had to be.

A couple of years ago, before this story had even been formulated in my mind, a local regional airport held a fly-in of vintage planes. One of the planes on display was a B-17. I climbed on board and couldn't believe how tight the interior was. The cockpit was roped off, but I could at least see it. I was able to traverse to the back of the fuselage, past the bomb bays and turrets, and into the rear, where I exited. Between that tour and YouTube videos of how to fly the B-17, I was able to craft the opening scene.

I've read conflicting reports as to when WASP first began. I used a form of poetic license under the assumption it was functioning during the date of my story. But there were other similar organizations that offered the same ferrying service during 1942-43, and no matter what organization the women flew for, all the female pilots of WWII were courageous women who served our country well.

I was blessed that all the microfilms of past copies of the *Lake Geneva Regional News* were digitized just prior to Covid. For my previous books in the series, I made countless trips to the Lake Geneva Library to scroll through reels of microfilm of the local paper that covered the specific time period of my book.

Now, I can go online from home and call up the *Regional News* editions for the time period I'm working in. When I wanted to know what movie was playing at the time Grace and Mac went to the movies, I referred to that paper, and the Cary Grant movie described was actually at that theater around that time.

By reading the 1942-43 articles in the *Regional News,* I learned about the Home Service Department of the Red Cross and how they helped countless families connect with their enlisted loved ones. In some cases, I used the real names of real people, including Anne Senft, as recognition for the woman who worked tirelessly as chairman of the Home Service Department during those war years.

Where do I begin to say thank you to my friends who have critiqued this story, especially Yvonne Anderson, who offered her critique of the entire book from start to finish on short notice? Y, you are the best!

I always depend on prayer to get to the end of a book—both my prayers and the prayers of others. I value so much the prayers of the women in my life group, my church family, my readers, and author friends. Thank you all!

This past year, the other authors who wrote for Mantle Rock Press and I were very blessed that when the MRP was sold, the new owners did not take the company in a new direction. I'm very pleased to write for Scrivenings Press under the guidance of Linda Fulkerson and Shannon Taylor Vannatter, who was my content editor. My line editor, Susan Page Davis, also deserves a load of thanks for stepping in at the last minute to do my edit. We've known each other for years as authors and fellow members of a large writing organization, and I'm grateful for how easy she made it for me while having to adjust to a new editor.

Although this is the last book in my current series, it isn't the last book for the setting of Lake Geneva, Wisconsin, my beautiful hometown. I'll be taking a little writing break, but even while I'm involved in other things, the muse is churning away, and I hope, Lord willing, to write a timeslip novel set in Lake Geneva in the near future.

Of course, last, but never least, I thank my Lord Jesus Christ for blessing me with the desire to write novels and the ability to do so. Without Him, none of this would ever have happened, and it's my prayer that all my works bring Him glory.

Many blessings, and I hope to see you soon!
Pam

ABOUT THE AUTHOR

Raised in Lake Geneva, Wisconsin, Pamela has published articles various magazines. In her non-writing life, she has served as a sign language interpreter for her church, and is currently a leader of a women's Bible study group.

Her author tag line, "Take a Sentimental Journey," describes her stories, both contemporary and historical, as most are centered in small Wisconsin towns.

Pam resides in Illinois with her two rescue cats. She's not too far from her native Wisconsin, where you will often see her nosing around for more story ideas.

ALSO BY PAMELA S. MEYERS

Safe Refuge

Newport of the West—Book One

In two days, wealthy Chicagoan, Anna Hartwell, will wed a man she loathes. She would refuse this arranged marriage to Lyman Millard, but the Bible clearly says she is to honor her parents, and Anna would do most anything to please her father–even leaving her teaching job at a mission school and marrying a man she doesn't love.

The Great Chicago Fire erupts, and Anna and her family escape with only the clothes on their backs and the wedding postponed. Father moves the family to Lake Geneva, Wisconsin, where Anna reconnects with Rory Quinn, a handsome immigrant who worked at the mission school. Realizing she is in love with Rory, Anna prepares to break the marriage arrangement with Lyman until she learns a dark family secret that changes her life forever.

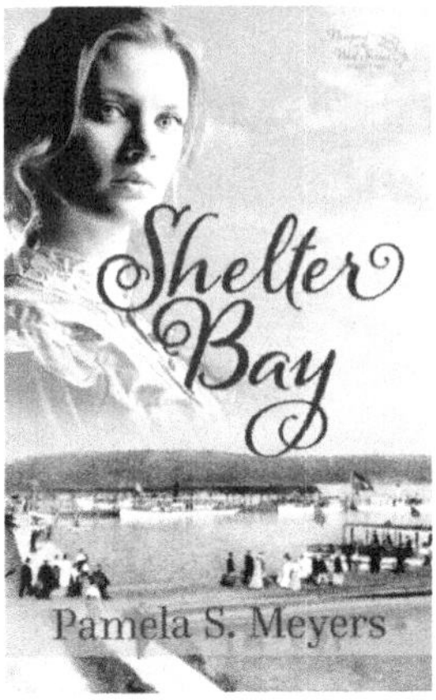

Shelter Bay

Newport of the West—Book Two

Adventure girl, Maureen Quinn, isn't yet sure of her life's direction, but she knows she isn't cut out to be a bookkeeper for the town's undertaker. Wearing her stylish new bloomers, she suffers a bicycle accident in the middle of downtown and her long-time crush and fellow childhood mischief maker, Preston Stevens, comes to her rescue. He's back in the area and he couldn't have shown up at a better time. It isn't long before they become inseparable and she's sure he's the man God has for her.

Unlike his older brothers who are shackled to desk jobs at their father's financial services company, Preston yearns to see the world. What better person to do that with than Maureen? But after being expelled from Yale, because of a prank that brought embarrassment to the family, his dad has issued an ultimatum: Enlist in the military or join his brothers in the family business. He signs up with the U.S. Life Saving Service, a division of the Coast Guard, reasoning the time spent on the shores of Lake Michigan, keeping people safe, is far better than being stuck in a landlocked encampment. After his two-year stint, he intends to live out his dream of world travel before settling in Lake Geneva. But it isn't long before life-altering events occur affecting both his and Maureen's lives forever.

Returning to historic Lake Geneva for Book Two in the *Newport of the West* series, the Hartwell family saga continues through the life of Maureen Quinn, the daughter of Rory and Anna Quinn from *Safe Refuge*. Set mainly in beautiful Lake Geneva, *Shelter Bay* also carries the reader to the northern shore of Michigan and to the 1893 World's Fair in Chicago, also known as the Columbian Exposition.

Tranquility Point

Newport of the West—Book Three

Hannah Murphy is determined to make the summer of 1916, the best it can be before she heads off to law school in the fall. Like her mother and grandmother before her, she is inclined to "break the mold" when it comes to societal expectations of a young woman of means. Her mother was the first woman in town to wear bloomers, and Hannah becomes the first to ditch swim dresses in favor of a practical swimsuit that allows freedom to move through the water.

At the first gathering of the summer, she reacquaints with tall, handsome Ted Bauer, also an aspiring attorney. Ted, who is of German descent, had a huge crush on Hannah when he was in eighth grade, and she was in sixth. He's no longer the gangly boy she remembers and is quite appealing. With Geneva Lake as their backdrop, their summer romance escalates, until the dark cloud of the Great War can no longer be ignored. Although the U.S. has not yet joined the fray, people of German descent are seen with mistrust, and Ted enlists with the British Army to take the heat of discrimination off his family. With the future on hold, Hannah bids her fiancé farewell as he goes to war. Only God knows if she will ever see him again or if they will ever be able to recapture what they had those few short summer months.

MORE HISTORICAL ROMANCE FROM SCRIVENINGS PRESS

Love's Kindling

by Award-winning Author Elaine Marie Cooper

Book One of the Dawn of America Series

This title includes *War's Respite*, prequel to the Dawn of America series.

During the American Revolution, Aurinda Whitney lives with her cold and calloused father, an embittered veteran of the previous war. Aurinda's life changed forever when her father returned for her after that war, taking her away from the only place she'd ever experienced affection. Since her father blamed Aurinda for the death of his wife in childbirth, Aurinda is convinced she is unworthy of love.

Zadok Wooding believes he is a failure as he tends the smithy at home while others go to battle against the British. Just when he has an opportunity to become a hero, he is blinded in an accident. Now he fears he will never live up to the Biblical "mighty man of valor" for whom he was named.

When the couple meet, they are both challenged to overcome adversity as well as their inadequacies. Unexpected secrets of their past emerge that can change their lives forever. But can they look past their present circumstances to heal—and find love?

The Rancher's Legacy

Homeward Trails

Book One

Matthew Anderson and his father try to help neighbor Bill Maxwell when his ranch is attacked. On the day his daughter Rachel is to return from school back East, outlaws target the Maxwell ranch. After Rachel's world is shattered, she won't even consider the plan her father and Matt's cooked up—to see their two children marry and combine the ranches.

Meanwhile in Maine, sea captain's widow Edith Rose hires a private investigator to locate her three missing grandchildren. The children were abandoned by their father nearly twenty years ago. They've been adopted into very different families, and they're scattered across the country. Can investigator Ryland Atkins find them all while the elderly woman still lives? His first attempt is to find the boy now called

Matthew Anderson. Can Ryland survive his trip into the wild Colorado Territory and find Matt before the outlaws finish destroying a legacy?

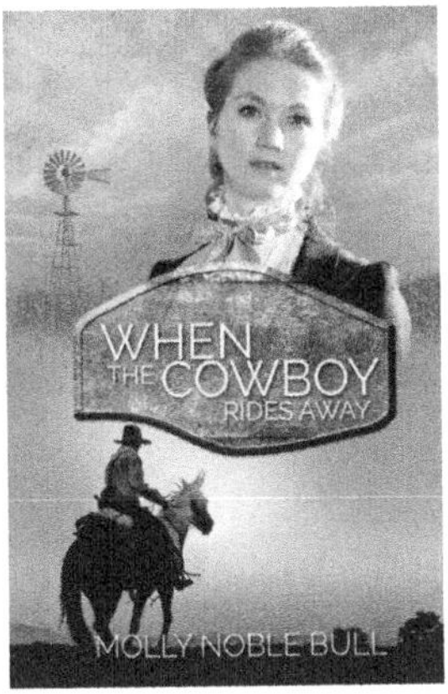

When the Cowboy Rides Away

Western Romance

Maggie Gallagher, twenty-one, runs the Gallagher Ranch in South Texas and has raised her little sister and orphaned nephew since her parents and older sister died. No wonder she can't find time for romance!

When the Cowboy Rides Away opens two years after Maggie loses her family members. Out for a ride with her sister, she discovers Alex Lancaster, a handsome cowboy, shot and seriously wounded, on her land. Kind-hearted and a Christian, Maggie nurses him back to health despite all her other chores.

How could she know that Alex has a secret that could break her heart?

Books Afloat

Columbia River Undercurrents

Book One

Blaming herself for her childhood role in the Oklahoma farm truck accident that cost her grandfather's life, Anne Mettles is determined to make her life count. She wants to do it all–captain her library boat and resist Japanese attacks to keep America safe. But failing her pilot's exam requires her to bring others onboard.

Will she go it alone? Or will she team with the unlikely but (mostly) lovable characters? One is a saboteur, one an unlikely hero, and one, she discovers, is the man of her dreams.

Made in the USA
Monee, IL
08 January 2022

87051907R10188